"Walter Mosley is a gifted writer who captures the lingo and culture of the 1950s Watts with skill. . . ."
—*Chattanooga Times*

"Mr. Mosley knows his characters so intimately. . . . At times, several of the urban people in Mr. Mosley's Watts are not far removed from those living in Catfish Row in *Porgy and Bess.* Mr. Mosley has depicted a special locale and a corner-cutting way of life that most readers will find far more riveting than the crime pages of their newspapers."
—*The New York Times Book Review*

"Mosley proves himself a master at delineating the foibles of his characters. The plotting is equally masterful in this earthy story set in 1950s Watts."
—*Indianapolis Star*

**Books by Walter Mosley**

Devil in a Blue Dress
A Red Death
White Butterfly
Black Betty

Available from POCKET BOOKS

# a red death

## walter mosley

**POCKET BOOKS**

New York   London   Toronto   Sydney   Tokyo   Singapore

POCKET BOOKS, a division of Simon & Schuster Inc.
1230 Avenue of the Americas, New York, NY 10020

Copyright © 1991 by Walter Mosley

Published by arrangement with W. W. Norton & Company, Inc.

ISBN: 0-671-01006-9

First Pocket Books printing August 1992

15  14  13  12  11  10  9

POCKET and colophon are registered trademarks of Simon & Schuster Inc.

Cover art by John Jinks

Printed in the U.S.A.

*Dedicated to the memory of*
Alberta Jackson and Lillian Keller
*with special thanks to*
Daniel and Elizabeth Russell

"If it wasn't for bad luck
I wouldn't have no luck at all . . ."

—*old blues refrain*

# 1

I ALWAYS STARTED SWEEPING ON THE TOP FLOOR OF THE Magnolia Street apartments. It was a three-story pink stucco building between Ninety-first Street and Ninety-first Place, just about a mile outside of Watts proper. Twelve units. All occupied for that month. I had just gathered the dirt into a neat pile when I heard Mofass drive up in his new '53 Pontiac. I knew it was him because there was something wrong with the transmission, you could hear its high singing from a block away. I heard his door slam and his loud hello to Mrs. Trajillo, who always sat at her window on the first floor—best burglar alarm you could have.

I knew that Mofass collected the late rent on the second Thursday of the month; that's why I chose that particular Thursday to clean. I had money and the law on my mind, and Mofass was the only man I knew who might be able to set me straight.

I wasn't the only one to hear the Pontiac.

The doorknob to Apartment J jiggled and the door came open showing Poinsettia Jackson's sallow, sorry face.

1

She was a tall young woman with yellowish eyes and thick, slack lips.

"Hi, Easy," she drawled in the saddest high voice. She was a natural tenor but she screwed her voice higher to make me feel sorry for her.

All I felt was sick. The open door let the stink of incense from her prayer altar flow out across my newly swept hall.

"Poinsettia," I replied, then I turned quickly away as if my sweeping might escape if I didn't move to catch it.

"I heard Mofass down there," she said. "You hear him?"

"I just been workin'. That's all."

She opened the door and draped her emaciated body against the jamb. The nightcoat was stretched taut across her chest. Even though Poinsettia had gotten terribly thin after her accident, she still had a large frame.

"I gotta talk to him, Easy. You know I been so sick that I cain't even walk down there. Maybe you could go on down an tell'im that I need t'talk."

"He collectin' the late rent, Poinsettia. If you ain't paid him all you gotta do is wait. He'll be up here soon enough to talk to you."

"But I don't have it," she cried.

"You better tell'im that," I said. It didn't mean anything, I just wanted to say the last word and get down to work on the second floor.

"Could you talk to him, Easy? Couldn't you tell'im how sick I am?"

"He know how sick you are, Poinsettia. All he gotta do is look at you and he could tell that. But you know Mofass is business. He wants that rent."

"But maybe you could tell him about me, Easy."

She smiled at me. It was the kind of smile that once made men want to go out of their way. But Poinsettia's fine skin had slackened and she smelled like an

2

old woman, even with the incense and perfume. Instead of wanting to help her I just wanted to get away.

"Sure, I'll ask 'im. But you know he don't work for me," I lied. "It's the other way around."

"Go on down there now, Easy," she begged. "Go ask 'im to let me slide a month or two."

She hadn't paid a penny in four months already, but it wouldn't have been smart for me to say that to her.

"Lemme talk to 'im later, Poinsettia. He'd just get mad if I stopped him on the steps."

"Go to 'im now, Easy. I hear him coming." She pulled at her robe with frantic fingers.

I could hear him too. Three loud knocks on a door, probably unit B, and then, in his deep voice, "Rent!"

"I'll go on down," I said to Poinsettia's ashen toes.

I pushed the dirt into my long-handled dustpan and made my way down to the second floor, sweeping off each stair as I went. I had just started gathering the dirt into a pile when Mofass came struggling up the stairs.

He'd lean forward to grab the railing, then pull himself up the stairs, hugging and wheezing like an old bulldog.

Mofass looked like an old bulldog too; a bulldog in a three-piece brown suit. He was fat but powerfully built, with low sloping shoulders and thick arms. He always had a cigar in his mouth or between his broad fingers. His color was dark brown but bright, as if a powerful lamp shone just below his skin.

"Mr. Rawlins," Mofass said to me. He made sure to be respectful when talking to anyone. Even if I actually had been his cleanup man he would have called me mister.

"Mofass," I said back. That was the only name he let anyone call him. "I need to discuss something with you after I finish here. Maybe we could go somewhere and have some lunch."

"Suits me," he said, clamping down on his cigar.

3

He grabbed the rail to the third floor and began to pull himself up there.

I went back to my work and worry.

Each floor of the Magnolia Street building had a short hallway with two apartments on either side. At the far end was a large window that let in the morning sun. That's why I fell in love with the place. The morning sun shone in, warming up the cold concrete floors and brightening the first part of your day. Sometimes I'd go there even when there was no work to be done. Mrs. Trajillo would stop me at the front door and ask, "Something wrong with the plumbing, Mr. Rawlins?" And I'd tell her that Mofass had me checking on the roof or that Lily Brown had seen a mouse a few weeks back and I was checking the traps. It was always best if I said something about a rodent or bugs, because Mrs. Trajillo was a sensitive woman who couldn't stand the idea of anything crawling down around the level of her feet.

Then I'd go upstairs and stand in the window, looking down into the street. Sometimes I'd stand there for an hour and more, watching the cars and clouds making their ways. There was a peaceful feeling about the streets of Los Angeles in those days.

Everybody on the second floor had a job, so I could sit around the halls all morning and nobody would bother me.

But that was all over. Just one letter from the government had ended my good life.

Everybody thought I was the handyman and that Mofass collected the rent for some white lady downtown. I owned three buildings, the Magnolia Street place being the largest, and a small house on 116th Street. All I had to do was the maintenance work, which I liked because whenever you hired somebody to work for you they always took too long and charged too much. And when I wasn't doing that I could do my little private job.

On top of real estate I was in the business of favors. I'd do something for somebody, like find a missing husband or figure out who's been breaking into so-and-so's store, and then maybe they could do me a good turn one day. It was a real country way of doing business. At that time almost everybody in my neighborhood had come from the country around southern Texas and Louisiana.

People would come to me if they had serious trouble but couldn't go to the police. Maybe somebody stole their money or their illegally registered car. Maybe they worried about their daughter's company or a wayward son. I settled disputes that would have otherwise come to bloodshed. I had a reputation for fairness and the strength of my convictions among the poor. Ninety-nine out of a hundred black folk were poor back then, so my reputation went quite a way.

I wasn't on anybody's payroll, and even though the rent was never steady, I still had enough money for food and liquor.

"What you mean, not today?" Mofass' deep voice echoed down the stairs. After that came the strained cries of Poinsettia.

"Cryin' ain't gonna pay the rent, Miss Jackson."

"I ain't got it! You know I ain't got it an' you know why too!"

"I know you ain't got it, that's why I'm here. This ain't my reg'lar collectin' day, ya know. I come to tell you folks that don't pay up, the gravy train is busted."

"I can't pay ya, Mofass. I ain't got it and I'm sick."

"Lissen here." His voice dropped a little. "This is my job. My money comes from the rent I collect fo' Mrs. Davenport. You see, I bring her a stack'a money from her buildin's and then she counts it. And when she finishes countin' she takes out my little piece. Now when I bring her more money I get more, and when I bring in less . . ."

Mofass didn't finish, because Poinsettia started crying.

"Let me loose!" Mofass shouted. "Let go, girl!"

"But you promised!" Poinsettia cried. "You promised!"

"I ain't promised nuthin'! Let go now!"

A few moments later I could hear him coming down the stairs.

"I be back on Saturday, and if you ain't got the money then you better be gone!" he shouted.

"You can go to hell!" Poinsettia cried in a strong tenor voice. "You shitty-assed bastard! I'ma call Willie on yo' black ass. He know all about you! Willie chew yo' shitty ass off!"

Mofass came down the stair holding on to the rail. He was walking slowly amid the curses and screams. I wondered if he even heard them.

"BASTARD!!" shouted Poinsettia.

"Are you ready to leave, Mr. Rawlins?" he asked me.

"I got the first floor yet."

"Mothahfuckin' bastard!"

"I'll be out in the car then. Take your time." Mofass waved his cigar in the air, leaving a peaceful trail of blue smoke.

When the front door on the first floor closed, Poinsettia stopped shouting and slammed her own door. Everything was quiet again. The sun was still warming the concrete floor and everything was as beautiful as always.

But it wasn't going to last long. Soon Poinsettia would be in the street and I'd have the morning sun in my jail cell.

# 2

"YOU GOT YOUR CAR HERE?" MOFASS ASKED WHEN I climbed into the passenger's side of his car.

"Naw, I took the bus." I always took the bus when I went out to clean, because my Ford was a little too flashy for a janitor. "Where you wanna go?"

"You the one wanna talk to me, Mr. Rawlins."

"Yeah," I said. "Let's go to that Mexican place then."

He made a wide U-turn in the middle of the street and drove off in the direction of Rebozo's.

While Mofass frowned and bit down on his long black cigar I stared out the window at the goings-on on Central Avenue. There were liquor stores and small clothes shops and even a television repair shop here and there. At Central and Ninety-ninth Street a group of men sat around talking—they were halfheartedly waiting for work. It was a habit that some southerners brought with them; they'd just sit outside on a crate somewhere and wait for someone who needed manual labor to come by and shout their name. That way they could spend the afternoon with their friends, drinking from brown paper bags and shooting dice. They might even get lucky and pick up a job worth a couple of bucks—and maybe their kids would have meat that night.

Mofass was driving me to his favorite Mexican restaurant. At Rebozo's they put sliced avocado in the chili and peppered potato chunks in the burritos.

We got there without saying any more. Mofass got out of the car and locked his door with the key, then he went around to my side and locked that door too. He always locked both doors himself. He never trusted that someone else could do it by holding the door handle so that the lock held. Mofass didn't trust his own mother; that's what made him such a good real estate agent.

Another thing I liked about Mofass was that he was from New Orleans and, though he talked like me, he wasn't intimate with my friends from around Houston, Galveston, and Lake Charles, Louisiana. I was safe from idle gossip about my secret financial life.

Rebozo's was a dark room with a small bar at the back and three booths on either side. There was a neon-red jukebox next to the bar that was almost always playing music full of brassy horns, accordions, and strumming guitars. But even if the box was silent when we walked in Mofass would always drop a few nickels and push some buttons.

The first time he did that I asked him, "You like that kinda music?"

"I don't care," he answered me. "I just like to have a little noise. Make our talk just ours." Then he winked, like a drowsy Gila monster.

Mofass and I stared at each other across the table. He had both hands out in front of him. Between the fingers of his left hand that cigar stood up like a black Tower of Pisa. On the pinky of his right hand he wore a gold ring that had a square onyx emblem with a tiny diamond embedded in its center.

I was nervous about discussing my private affairs with Mofass. He collected the rent for me. I gave him nine percent and fifteen dollars for each eviction, but we weren't friends. Still, Mofass was the only man I could discuss my business with.

"I got a letter today," I said finally.

"Yeah?"

He looked at me, patiently waiting for what I had to say, but I couldn't go on. I didn't want to talk about it yet. I was afraid that saying the bad news out loud would somehow make it real. So instead I asked, "What you wanna do 'bout Poinsettia?"

"What?"

"Poinsettia. You know, the rent?"

"Kick her ass out if she don't pay."

"You know that gal is really sick up there. Ever since that car crash she done wasted away."

"That don't mean I got to pay her rent."

"It's me gonna be payin' it, Mofass."

"Uh-uh, Mr. Rawlins. I collect it and until I put it in yo' hands it's mine. If that gal go down and tell them other folks that I don't take her money they gonna take advantage."

"She's sick."

"She got a momma, a sister, that boy Willie she always be talkin' 'bout. She got somebody. Let them pay the rent. We in business, Mr. Rawlins. Business is the hardest thing they make. Harder than diamonds."

"What if nobody pays for her?"

"You will done fo'got her name in six months, Mr. Rawlins. You won't even know who she is."

Before I could say anything more a young Mexican girl came up to us. She had thick black hair and dark eyes without very much white around them. She looked at Mofass and I got the feeling that she didn't speak English.

He held up two fat fingers and said, "Beer, chili, burrito," pronouncing each syllable slowly so that you could read his lips.

She gave him a quick smile and went away.

I took the letter from my breast pocket and handed it across the table.

"I want your opinion on this," I said with a confidence I did not feel.

9

While I watched Mofass' hard face I remembered the words he was reading.

Reginald Arnold Lawrence
Investigating Agent
Internal Revenue Service

July 14, 1953

Mr. Ezekiel Rawlins:

It has come my attention, sir, that between August 1948 and September of 1952 you came into the possession of at least three real estate properties.

I have reviewed your tax records back to 1945 and you show no large income, in any year. This would suggest that you could not legally afford such expenditures.

I am, therefore, beginning an investigation into your tax history and request your appearance within seven days of the date of this letter. Please bring all tax forms for the time period indicated and an *accurate* record of all income during that time.

As I remembered the letter I could feel ice water leaking in my bowels again. All the warmth I had soaked up in that hallway was gone.

"They got you by the nuts, Mr. Rawlins," Mofass said, putting the letter back down between us.

I looked down and saw that a beer was there in front of me. The girl must've brought it while I was concentrating on Mofass.

"If they could prove you made some money and didn't tell them about it, yo' ass be in a cast-iron sling," Mofass said.

"Shit! I just pay 'em, that's all."

He shook his head, and I felt my heart wrench.

"Naw, Mr. Rawlins. Government wants you t'tell

10

'em what you make. You don't do that and they put
you in the fed'ral penitentiary. And you know the
judge don't even start thinkin' 'bout no sentence till
he come up with a nice round number—like five or
ten."

"But you know, man, my name ain't even on them
deeds. I set up what they call a dummy corporation,
John McKenzie helped me to do it. Them papers say
that them buildin's 'long to a Jason Weil."

Mofass curled his lip and said, "IRS smell a dummy
corporation in a minute."

"Well then I just tell 'em I didn't know. I didn't."

"Com'on, man." Mofass leaned back and waved his
cigar at me. "They just tell ya that ignorance of the law
ain't no excuse, thas all. They don't care. Say you go
shoot some dude been with your girl, kill 'im. You
gonna tell 'em you didn't know 'bout that killin' was
wrong? Anyway, if you went to all that trouble t'hide
yo' money they could tell that you was tryin' t'cheat
'em."

"It ain't like I killed somebody. It ain't right if they
don't even give me a chance t'pay."

"On'y right is what you get away wit', Mr. Rawlins.
And if they find out about some money, and they
think you didn't declare it . . ." Mofass shook his
head slowly.

The girl returned with two giant white plates. Each
one had a fat, open-ended burrito and a pile of chili
and yellow rice on it. The puffy burritos had stringy
dark red meat coming out of the ends so that they
looked like oozing dead grubs. The chili had
yellowish-green avocado pieces floating in the grease,
along with chunks of pork flesh.

One hundred guitars played from the jukebox. I put
my hand over my mouth to keep from gagging.

"What can I do?" I asked. "You think I need a
lawyer?"

"Less people know 'bout it the better." Mofass
leaned forward, then whispered, "I don't know how

you got the money to pay for those buildin's, Mr. Rawlins, and I don't think nobody should know. What you gotta do is find some family, somebody close."

"What for?" I was also leaning across the table. The smell of the food made me sick.

"This here letter," Mofass said, tapping the envelope. "Don't say, fo'a fact, that he got no proof. He just investigatin', lookin'. You sign it over t' some family, and backdate the papers, and then go to him, prove that it ain't yours. Say that they was tryin' t'hide what they had from the rest of the family."

"How I back-whatever?"

"I know a notary public do it—for some bills."

"So what if I had a sister or somethin'? Ain't the government gonna check her out? 'Cause you know ev'rybody I know is poor."

Mofass took a suck off his cigar with one hand and then shoveled in a mouthful of chili with the other.

"Yeah," he warbled. "You need somebody got sumpin' already. Somebody the tax man gonna believe could buy it."

I was quiet for a while then. Every good thing I'd gotten was gone with just a letter. I had hoped that Mofass would tell me that it was alright, that I'd get a small fine and they'd let me slide. But I knew better.

Five years before, a rich white man had somebody hire me to find a woman he knew. I found her, but she wasn't exactly what she seemed to be, and a lot of people died. I had a friend, Mouse, help me out though, and we came away from it with ten thousand dollars apiece. The money was stolen, but nobody was looking for it and I had convinced myself that I was safe.

I had forgotten that a poor man is never safe.

When I first got the money I'd watched my friend Mouse murder a man. He shot him twice. It was a poor man who could almost taste that stolen loot. It got him killed and now it was going to put me in jail.

"What you gonna do, Mr. Rawlins?" Mofass asked at last.

"Die."

"What's that you say?"

"On'y thing I know, I'ma die."

"What about this here letter?"

"What you think, Mofass? What should I do?"

He sucked down some more smoke and mopped the rest of his chili with a tortilla.

"I don't know, Mr. Rawlins. These people here don't have nothin', far as I can see. And you got me t'lie for ya. But ya know if they come after my books I gotta give 'em up."

"So what you sayin'?"

"Go on in there and lie, Mr. Rawlins. Tell 'em you don't own nuthin'. Tell 'em that you a workin' man and that somebody must have it out for you to lie and say you got that property. Tell 'em that and then see what they gotta say. They don't know your bank or your banker."

"Yeah. I guess I'ma have to feel it out," I said after a while.

Mofass was thinking something as he looked at me. He was probably wondering if the next landlord would use him.

# 3

IT WASN'T FAR TO MY HOUSE. MOFASS OFFERED TO DRIVE, but I liked to use my legs, especially when I had thinking to do.

I went down Central. The sidewalks were pretty empty at midday, because most people were hard at work. Of course, the streets of L.A. were usually deserted; Los Angeles has always been a car-driving city, most people won't even walk to the corner store.

I had solitude but I soon realized that there was nothing for me to consider. When Uncle Sam wanted me to put my life on the line, fighting the Germans, I did it. And I knew that I'd go to prison if he told me to do that. In the forties and fifties we obeyed the law, as far as poor people could, because the law kept us safe from the enemy. Back then we thought we knew who the enemy was. He was a white man with a foreign accent and a hatred for freedom. In the war it was Hitler and his Nazis; after that it was Comrade Stalin and the communists; later on, Mao Tse-tung and the Chinese took on an honorary white status. All of them bad men with evil designs on the free world.

My somber mood lifted when I came to 116th Street. I had a small house, but that made for a large front lawn. In recent years I had taken to gardening. I had daylilies and wild roses against the fence, and strawberries and potatoes in large rectangular plots at the center of the yard. There was a trellis that enclosed

14

my porch, and I always had flowering vines growing there. The year before I had planted wild passion fruit.

But what I loved the most was my avocado tree. It was forty feet high with leaves so thick and dark that it was always cool under its shade. I had a white cast-iron bench set next to the trunk. When things got really hard, I'd sit down there to watch the birds chase insects through the grass.

When I came up to the fence I had almost forgotten the tax man. He didn't know about me. How could he? He was just grabbing at empty air.

Then I saw the boy.

He was doing a crazy dance in my potato patch. He held both hands in the air, with his head thrown back, and cackled deep down in his throat. Every now and then he'd stamp his feet, like little pistons, and reach both hands down into the soil, coming out with long tan roots that had the nubs of future potatoes dangling from them.

When I pushed open the gate it creaked and he swung around to look at me. His eyes got big and he swiveled his head to one side and the other, looking for an escape route. When he saw that there was no escape he put on a smile and held the potato roots out at me. Then he laughed.

It was a ploy I had used when I was small.

I wanted to be stern with him, but when I opened my mouth I couldn't keep from smiling.

"What you doin', boy?"

"Playin'," he said in a thick Texas drawl.

"That's my potatas you stampin' on. Know that?"

"Uh-uh." He shook his head. He was a small, very dark boy with a big head and tiny ears. I figured him for five years old.

"Whose potatas you think you got in your hands?"

"My momma's."

"Yo' momma?"

"Um-huh. This my momma's house."

"Since when?" I asked.

The question was too much for him. He scrunched his eyes and hunched his boy shoulders. "It just is, thas all."

"How long you been here kickin' up my garden?" I looked around to see daylilies and rose petals strewn across the yard. There wasn't a red strawberry in the patch.

"We just come." He gave me a large grin and reached out to me. I picked him up without thinking about it. "Momma losted her key so I had to go in da windah an' open up the door."

"What?"

Before I could put him down I heard a woman humming. The timbre of her voice sent a thrill through me even though I didn't recognize it yet. Then she came around from the side of the house. A sepia-colored woman—large, but shapely, wearing a plain blue cotton dress and a white apron. She carried a flat-bottomed basket that I recognized from my closet, its braided handle looped into the crook of her right arm. There were kumquats and pomegranates from my fruit trees and strawberries from the yard on a white handkerchief that covered the bottom of the basket. She was a beautiful, full-faced woman with serious eyes and a mouth, I knew, that was always ready to laugh. The biceps of her right arm bulged, because EttaMae Harris was a powerful woman who, in her younger years, had done hand laundry nine hours a day, six days a week. She could knock a man into next Tuesday, or she could hold you so tight that you felt like a child again, in your mother's loving embrace.

"Etta," I said, almost to myself.

The boy tittered like a little maniac. He squirmed around in my arms and worked his way down to the ground.

"Easy Rawlins." Her smile came into me, and I smiled back.

"What . . . I mean," I stammered. The boy was running around his mother as fast as he could. "I mean, why are you here?"

"We come t' see you, Easy. Ain't that right, LaMarque?"

"Uh-huh," the boy said. He didn't even look up from his run.

"Stop that racin' now." Etta reached out and grabbed him by the shoulder. She spun him around, and he looked up at me and smiled.

"Hi," he said.

"We met already." I motioned my head toward the lawn.

When Etta saw the damage LaMarque had done her eyes got big and my heart beat a litter faster.

"LaMarque!"

The boy lowered his head and shrugged.

"Huh?" he asked.

"What you do to this yard?"

"Nuthin'."

"Nuthin'?" You call this mess nuthin'?"

She reached out to grab him, but LaMarque let himself fall to the ground, hugging his knees.

"I's just gard'nin' in the yard," he whimpered. "Thas all."

"Gard'nin'?" Etta's dark face darkened even more, and the flesh around her eyes creased into a devil's gaze. I don't know how LaMarque reacted to that stare, but I was so worried that I couldn't find my breath.

She balled her fists so that her upper arms got even larger, a tremor went through her neck and shoulders.

But then, suddenly, her eyes softened, she even laughed. Etta has the kind of laugh that makes other people happy.

"Gard'nin'?" she said again. "Looks like you a reg'lar gard'nin' tornado."

I laughed along with her. LaMarque didn't exactly know why we were so cheery but he grinned too and rolled around on the ground.

"Get up from there now, boy, and go get washed."

"Yes, Momma." LaMarque knew how to be a good boy after he had been bad. He ran toward the house, but before he got past Etta she grabbed him by one arm, hefted him into the air, and gave him a smacking kiss on the cheek. He was grinning and wiping the kiss from his face as he turned to run for the door.

Then Etta held her arms out and I walked into her embrace as if I had never heard of her husband, my best friend, Mouse.

I buried my face in her neck and breathed in her natural, flat scent; like the smell of fresh-ground flour. I put my arms around EttaMae Harris and relaxed for the first time since I had last held her—fifteen years before.

"Easy," she whispered, and I didn't know if I was holding her too tight or if she was calling my name.

I knew that embrace was the same thing as holding a loaded gun to my head, because Raymond Alexander, known to his friends as Mouse, was a killer. If he saw any man holding his wife like that he wouldn't even have blinked before killing him. But I couldn't let her go. The chance to hold her one more time was worth the risk.

"Easy," she said again, and I realized that I was pressing against her with my hips, making it more than obvious how I felt. I wanted to let go but it was like early morning, when you first wake up and just can't let go of sleep yet.

"Let's go inside, honey," she said, putting her cheek to mine. "He wants his food."

The smells of southern cooking filled the house.

Etta had made white rice and pinto beans with fatback. She'd picked lemons from the neighbor's bush for lemonade. There was a mayonnaise jar in the center of the table with pink and red roses in it. That was the first time that there were ever cut flowers in my house.

The house wasn't very big. The room we were in was a living room and dining room in one. The living-room side was just big enough for a couch, a stuffed chair, and a walnut cabinet with a television in it. From there was a large doorless entryway that led to the dinette. The kitchen was in the back. It was a short alley with a counter and a stove. The bedroom was small too. It was a house big enough for one man; and it held me just fine.

"Get up from there, LaMarque," Etta said. "The man always sit at the head of the table."

"But . . ." LaMarque began to say, and then he thought better of it.

He ate three plates of beans and counted to one hundred and sixty-eight for me—twice. When he finished Etta sent him outside.

"Don't be doin' no more gard'nin', though," she warned him.

"'Kay."

We sat across the table from each other. I looked into her eyes and thought about poetry and my father.

I was swinging from a tree on the tire of a Model A Ford. My father came up to me and said, "Ezekiel, you learn to read an' ain't nuthin' you cain't do."

I laughed, because I loved it when my father talked to me. He left that night and I never knew if he had abandoned me or was killed on his way home.

Now I was half the way through Shakespeare's sonnets in my third English course at LACC. The love that poetry espoused and my love for EttaMae and my father knotted in my chest so that I could hardly even breathe. And EttaMae wasn't something slight like a sonnet; behind her eyes was an epic, the whole history of me and mine.

Then I remembered, again, that she belonged to another man; a murderer.

"It's good to see you, Easy."

"Yeah."

She leaned forward with her elbows on the table, placed her chin in the palm of her hand, and said, "Ezekiel Rawlins."

That was my real name. Only my best friends used it.

"What are you doing here, Etta? Where's Mouse?"

"You know we broke up years ago, honey."

"I heard you took him back."

"Just a tryout. I wanted to see if he could be a good husband and a father. But he couldn't, so I threw him out again."

The last moments of Joppy Shag's life flashed through my mind. He was lashed to an oaken chair, sweat and blood streamed from his bald head. When Mouse shot him in the groin he barked and strained like a wild animal. Then Mouse calmly pointed the gun at Joppy's head . . .

"I didn't know," I said. "But why are you up here?"

Instead of answering me Etta got up and started clearing the table. I moved to help her, but she shoved me back into the chair, saying, "You just get in the way, Easy. Sit down and drink your lemonade."

I waited a minute and then followed her out to the kitchen.

"Men sure is a mess." She was shaking her head at the dirty dishes I had piled on the counter and in the sink. "How can you live like this?"

"You come all the way from Texas to show me how to wash dishes?"

And then I was holding her again. It was as if we had taken up where we'd left off in the yard. Etta put her hand against the bare back of my neck, I started running two fingers up and down either side of her spine.

I had spent years dreaming of kissing Etta again. Sometimes I'd be in bed with another woman and, in my sleep, I'd think it was Etta; the kisses would be like food, so satisfying that I'd wake up, only to realize that it was just a dream.

When Etta kissed me in the kitchen I woke up in another way. I staggered back from her mumbling, "I cain't take too much more of this."

"I'm sorry, Easy. I know I shouldn't, but me and LaMarque been in a bus for two days—all the way from Houston. I been thinkin' 'bout you all that time and I guess I got a little worked up."

"Why'd you come?" I felt like I was pleading.

"Mouse done gone crazy."

"What you mean, crazy?"

"Outta his mind," Etta continued. "Just gone."

"Etta," I said as calmly as I could. The desire to hold her had subsided for the moment. "Tell me what he did."

"Come out to the house at two in the mo'nin' just about ev'ry other night. Drunk as he could be and wavin' that long-barreled pistol of his. Stand out in the middle'a the street yellin' 'bout how he bought my house and how he burn it down before he let us treat him like we did."

"Like what?"

"I don't know, Easy. Mouse is crazy."

That had always been true. When we were younger men Mouse carried a gun and a knife. He killed men who crossed him and others who stood in the way of him making some coin. Mouse murdered his own stepfather, daddyReese, but he rarely turned on friends, and I never expected him to go against EttaMae.

"So you sayin' he run you outta Texas?"

"Run?" Etta was surprised. "I ain't runnin' from that little rat-faced man, or no other one'a God's creatures."

"Then why come here?"

"How it gonna look to LaMarque when he grow up if I done killed his father? 'Cause you know I had him in my sight every night he was out there in the street."

I remembered that Etta had a .22-caliber rifle and a .38 for her purse.

"After he done that for ovah a month I made up my mind to kill 'im. But the night I was gonna do it LaMarque woke up an' come in the room. I was waitin' for Raymond to come out. LaMarque asked me what I was doin' with that rifle, and you know I ain't never lied to that boy, Easy. He asked me what I was fixin' t' do with that rifle and I told him that I was gonna pack it and we was goin' to California."

Etta reached out and took both of my hands in hers. She said, "And that was the first thing I said, Easy. I didn't think about goin' to my mother or my sister down in Galveston. I thought'a you. I thought about how sweet you was before Raymond and me got married. So I come to you."

"I just popped into your head after all these years?"

"Well." Etta smiled and looked down at our tangled fingers. "Corinth Lye helped some."

"Corinth?" She was a friend from Houston. If I happened to run into her at Targets Bar I'd buy a bottle of gin and we'd put it away; sit there all night and drink like men. I'd told her many deep feelings and secrets in the early hours. It wasn't the first time that I was betrayed by alcohol.

"Yeah," Etta said. "I wrote her about Mouse when it all started. She wrote me about how much you still cared for me. She said I should come up here, away from all that."

"Then why ain't you wit' her?"

"I wus s'posed t', honey. But you know I got t' thinkin' 'bout you on that ride, an' I tole LaMarque all about you till we decided that we was gonna come straight here."

"You did?"

"Mmm-hm," Etta hummed, nodding her head. "An' you know I was glad we did." Etta's grin was shameless.

She smiled at me and the years fell away.

The one night I had spent with Etta, the best night of my life, she woke up the next morning talking about Mouse. She told me how wonderful he was and how lucky I was to have him for a friend.

LaMarque had never seen a television. He watched everything that came on, even the news. Some poor soul was in the spotlight that night. His name was Charles Winters. He was discovered stealing classified documents at his government job. The reporter said that Winters could get four ninety-nine-year sentences if he was found guilty.

"What's a comanisk, Unca Easy?"

"What, you think that just 'cause this is my TV that I should know everything it says?"

"Uh-huh," he nodded. LaMarque was a treasure.

"There's all kindsa communists, LaMarque."

"That one there," he said, pointing at the television. But the picture of Mr. Winters was gone. Instead there was a picture of Ike in the middle of a golf swing.

"That kind is a man who thinks he can make things better by tearin' down what we got here in America and buildin' up like what they got in Russia."

LaMarque opened his eyes and his mouth as far as he could. "You mean they wanna tear down Momma house and Momma TV up here in America?"

"The kinda world he wants, nobody owns anything. It's like this here TV would be for everybody."

"Uh-uh!"

LaMarque jumped up, balling his little fists.

"LaMarque!" Etta shouted. "What's got into you?"

"Comanisk gonna take our TV!"

"Time for you to go t'bed, boy."

"Nuh-uh!"

"I say yes," Etta said softly. She cocked her head to the side and tilted a little on the couch. LaMarque lowered his head and moved to turn off the set.

"Tell Unca Easy g'night."

"G'night, Unca Easy," LaMarque whispered. He climbed on the couch to kiss me, then he crawled into Etta's lap. She carried him into my bedroom.

We'd decided after the meal that they'd take my bed and I'd take the couch.

# 4

I WAS RESTING ON THE COUCH AT ABOUT MIDNIGHT, WATCHing a bull's-eye pattern on the TV screen. I was smoking Pall Malls, drinking vodka with grapefruit soda, and wondering if Mouse could kill me even if I was in a federal jail. In my imagination, he could.

"Easy?" she called from the bedroom door.

"Yeah, Etta?"

Etta wore a satiny gown. Coral. She sat down in the chair to my right.

"You sleepin', baby?" she asked.

"Uh-uh, no. Just thinkin'."

"Thinkin' what?"

"'Bout when I went down to see you in Galveston. You know, when you an' Mouse was just engaged."

She smiled at me, and I had to make myself stay where I was.

"You remember that night?" I asked.

"Sure do. That was nice."

"Yeah." I nodded. "You see, that's what's wrong, Etta."

"I don't follah." Even her frown made me want to kiss her.

"That was best night of my life. When I woke up in the morning I was truly surprised, because I knew I had to die, good as that felt."

"Ain't nuthin' wrong with that, Easy."

"Ain't nuthin' wrong with it until you tell me that 'it was nice' stuff. You know what you said to me when you got up?"

"That was fifteen years ago, baby. How'm I s'posed to 'member that?"

"I remember."

Etta looked sad. She looked like she'd lost something she cared for. I wanted to stop, to go hold her, but I couldn't. I'd been waiting all those years to tell her how I felt.

I said, "You told me that Mouse was the finest man you ever knew. You said that I was truly lucky to have a man like that for a friend."

"Baby, that was so long ago."

"Not fo' me. Not fo' me." When I sat up I realized that I had an erection. I crossed my legs so that Etta wouldn't see it pressing against my loose pants. "I remember like it was only this mo'nin'. When we got up you started tellin' me how lucky I was to have a man like Mouse fo'a friend. You told me how great he was. I loved you; I still do. An' all you could think of was him. You know I had plenty'a women tell me that they love me when we get up in the mo'nin'. But it only made me sick 'cause they wasn't you sayin' it. Every time I hear them I hear you talkin' 'bout Mouse."

Etta shook her head sadly. "That ain't me, Easy. I loved you, I did, as a friend. An' I think you's a beautiful man too. I mean, yeah, I shouldn'ta had you over like that. But you came t'me, honey. I was mad 'cause Raymond was out ho'in just a couple a days after I said I'd marry him. I used you t'try an' hurt him, but you knew what I was doin'. You knew it, Easy. You knew what I was givin' you was his. That's why you liked it so much.

"But that was a long time ago, an' you should be over it by this time. But, you know, it's just that some men be wantin' sumpin' from women; sumpin' like a woman shouldn't have no mind of her own. It's like when LaMarque want me t'tell'im that he's the strongest man in the world if I let him carry my pocketbook. I tell'im what he wants t'hear 'cause he just a baby. But you's a man, Easy. If I lied t'you it would be an insult."

"I know, I know," I said. "I knew it then. I never said nuthin', but now here you are again. An' here I am wit' my nose open.

"You know somebody saw you get on that bus, Etta. Somebody told somebody else that they heard you went to California. And Mouse could be outside that door at this very minute. Or maybe he be here tomorrah. He's comin', though, you could bet on that. An' if he finds you been in my bed we gonna have it out." I didn't add that I knew Mouse well enough to be afraid. I didn't need to.

"Raymond don't care 'bout if I got boyfriends, Easy. He don't care 'bout that."

"Maybe not. But if Mouse think I done taken his wife an' child fo' my own he see red. And now here you are talkin' 'bout him bein' crazy—how I know what he might do?"

Etta didn't say anything to that.

Mouse was a small, rodent-featured man who believed in himself without question. He only cared about what was his. He'd go against a man bigger than I was with no fear because he knew that nobody was better than him. He might have been right.

"And here I am again," I said. "Tryin' to keep offa you when I got so many problems I shouldn't even think about it."

Etta leaned forward in the chair, resting her elbows on her knees, revealing the dark cleft of her breasts. "So what you wanna do, Easy?"

"I . . ."

"Yeah?" she asked after I stalled.

"I know a man named Mofass."

"Who's he?"

"He manages some units up here and I work fo'im."

When Etta shifted, her gown slid and tremors went down my back.

"Yeah?" she asked.

"I think I could get him to find a place for you and LaMarque. You know, some place fo' you t'live. Without no rent, I mean." I was talking but I didn't want to say it: I wanted her for myself.

Etta sat up and her gown rose over her breasts. Her nipples were hard dimes against the slick material.

"So that's it? I come all this way an' now you gonna put us out." She stuck her lower lip out and shrugged, ever so slightly. "LaMarque an' me be ready by noon."

"You don't have t'rush, Etta . . ."

"No, no," she said, rising and waving her hand at me. "We gotta settle in someplace, and the sooner the better. You know chirren need a home."

"I'll give you money, Etta. I got lotsa money."

"I'll pay you back soon as I find work."

We looked at each other awhile after that.

Etta was the most beautiful woman I'd ever known. I'd wanted her more than life itself, once. And the fact

27

that I had let that go was worse than the fear of the penitentiary.

"'Night, Easy," she whispered.

I made to get up, to kiss her good night, but she held her hand against me.

"Don't kiss me, honey," she said. "'Cause you know I been thinkin' 'bout you long as you been thinkin' 'bout me."

Then she went off to bed.

I didn't sleep that night. I didn't worry or think about taxes either.

# 5

THE GOVERNMENT BUILDING WAS ON SIXTH STREET, downtown. It was small, four stories, and built from red brick. It almost looked friendly from the outside, not like the government at all.

But once you got past the front door all the friendliness was gone. A woman sat at the information desk. Her blond hair was pulled back so tight that it pained my scalp just to look at her. She wore a gray business-like jacket and dark horn-rimmed glasses. She squinted at me, wincing as if her skull might have actually hurt.

"May I assist you, sir?" she asked.

"Lawrence," I said. "Agent Lawrence."

"FBI?"

"Naw. Revenue."

"IRS?"

"I guess that's what you call it. Spells taxes no matter what way you say it."

As government workers went she was polite, but she wasn't going to smile for my joke.

"Go down to the end of this hall." She pointed it out for me. "And take the elevator to the third floor. The receptionist there will assist you."

"Thanks," I said, but she had turned back to something important on her desk. I peeked over the little ledge and saw the magazine, *The Saturday Evening Post*.

Agent Lawrence's office was just down the hall from the reception desk on the third floor, but when the woman called him he told her that I had to wait.

"He's going over your case," the fat brunette told me.

I sat down in the most uncomfortable straight-backed chair ever made. The lower back of the chair stuck out farther than the top so I had the feeling that I was hunched over as I sat there watching the big woman rub pink lotion into her hands. She frowned at her hands, and then she frowned again when she saw me staring through her glistening fingers.

I wondered if she would have been performing her toilet like that in front of a white taxpayer.

"Rawlins?" a military-like voice inquired.

I looked up.

There I saw a tall white man in a crayon-blue suit. He was of a good build with big hands that hung loosely at his sides. He had brown hair, and small brown eyes and was clean-shaven, though there would always be a blue shadow on his jaw. But for all his neat appearance Agent Lawrence seemed to be somehow unkempt, disheveled. I took him in for a few seconds. His bushy eyebrows and the dark circles under his eyes made him seem pitiful and maybe even a little inept.

It was my habit to size up people quickly. I liked to think I had an advantage on them if I had an insight into their private lives. In the tax man's case I figured that there was probably something wrong at home. Maybe his wife was fooling around, or one of his kids had been sick the night before.

I dropped my speculations after a few moments, though. I had never met a government man who admitted to having a private life.

"Agent Lawrence?" I asked.

"Follow me," he said with a gawky nod. He turned around, avoiding eye contact, and went down the hall. Agent Lawrence might have been a whiz at tax calculations but he couldn't walk worth a damn; he listed from side to side as he went.

His office was a small affair. A green metal desk with a matching filing cabinet. There was a big window, though, and the same morning sun that came into the Magnolia Street apartments flowed across his desk.

There was a bookcase with no books or papers in it. There was nothing on his desk except a half-used packet of Sen-Sen. I had the feeling that if I rapped my knuckles on his cabinet it would resound hollow as a drum.

He took his place behind the desk and I sat before him. My chair was of the same uncomfortable make as the one in the hall.

Taped to a wall, far to my left, was a crumpled piece of paper on which was scrawled I LOVE YOU DADDY in bold red letters that took up the whole page. It was as if the child were screaming love, testifying to it. There was a photograph in a pewter frame standing on his windowsill. A small red-haired woman with big frightened eyes and a young boy, who looked to be the same age as LaMarque, both cowered under the large and smiling figure of the man before me.

"Nice-lookin' fam'ly," I said.

"Um, yes, thank you," he mumbled. "I assume that you received my letter and so you know why I wanted to meet with you. I couldn't find your home address in our files, and so I had to hope that the address we found in the phone book was yours."

I was never listed in a phone book from that year on.

"The only address we had for you," Lawrence continued, "was the address of a Fetters Real Estate Office."

"Yeah, well," I said. "I been in that same house for eight years now."

"Be that as it may, I'd like you to write your current address and phone number on this card. Also any business number if I need to get in touch with you during the day."

He produced a three-by-five lined card from a drawer and handed it to me. I took it and put it down on the desk. He didn't say anything at first, just stared until finally he asked, "Do you need a pencil?"

"Um, yeah, I guess. I don't carry one around with me."

He took a short, eraserless pencil from the drawer, handed it to me, and waited until I had written the information he wanted. He read it over two or three times and then returned the pencil and card to the drawer.

I didn't want to start the conversation. I had taken the position of an innocent man, and that's the hardest role to play in the presence of an agent of the government. It's even harder if you really are innocent. Police and government officials always have contempt for innocence; they are, in some way, offended by an innocent man.

But I was guilty, so I just sat there counting the toes of my right foot as I pressed them, one by one, into the sole of my shoe. It took great concentration for the middle toes.

I had reached sixty-four before he said, "You've got a big problem, son."

The way he called me *son* instead of my name returned me to southern Texas in the days before World War Two; days when the slightest error in words could hold dire consequences for a black man.

But I smiled as confidently as I could. "It must be some mistake, Mr. Lawrence. I read your note and I don't own nuthin', 'cept fo' that li'l house I done had since 'forty-six."

"No, that's not right. I have it, from reliable sources, that you purchased apartment buildings on Sixty-fourth Place, McKinley Drive, and Magnolia Street in the last five years. They were all auctioned by the city for back taxes."

He wasn't even reading from notes, just rattling off my life as if he had my whole history submitted to memory.

"What sources you talkin' 'bout?"

"Where the government gets its information is none of your concern," he said. "At least not until this case goes to court."

"Court? You mean like a trial?"

"Tax evasion is a felony," he said, and then he hesitated. "Do you understand the severity of a felony charge?"

"Yeah, but I ain't done nuthin' like that. I'm just a maintenance man for Mofass."

"Who?"

"Mofass, he's the guy I work for."

"How do you spell that?"

I made up something, and he pulled out the card with my information on it and jotted it down.

"Did you bring the documents I asked for in the letter?" he asked.

He could see I didn't have anything.

"No, sir," I said. "I thought that it was all a mistake and that you didn't have to be bothered with it."

"I'm going to need all your financial information for the past five years. A record of all your income, all of it."

"Well," I said, smiling and hating myself for smiling, "that might take a few days. You know I got some shoe boxes in the closet, and then again, some of it might be in the garage if it goes all that far back. Five years is a long time."

"Some people make an awful lot of noise about equality and freedom, but when it comes to paying their debt they sing a different song."

"I ain't singin' nuthin', man," I said. I would have said more but he cut me off.

"Let's get this straight, Rawlins. I'm just a government agent. My job is to find out tax fraud if it exists. I don't have any feeling about you. I've asked you here because I have reason to believe that you cheated the government. If I'm right you're going to trial. It's not personal. I'm just doing my job."

There was nothing for me to say.

He looked at his watch and said, "I have a lot of business to see to today and tomorrow. You've served in the army, haven't you, son?"

"Say what?"

He stroked the lower half of his face and regarded me. I noticed a small, L-shaped scab on the forefinger knuckle of his right hand.

"I'm going to call you this afternoon at three sharp," he said. "Three. And then I'm going to tell you when I can meet with you to go over your income statements. I want all your tax returns, and I want to see bank statements too. Now, it might not be regular office hours, because I'm doing a lot of work this month. There's a lot of bigger fish than you trying to cheat Uncle Sam, and I'm going to catch them all."

If there was something wrong at home for Agent

Lawrence, he was going to make sure that the whole world paid for it.

"So it may not be until tomorrow evening that I can see you." He stood up with that.

"Tomorrow! I can't have all that by tomorrow!"

"I have an appointment at the federal courthouse in half an hour. So if you'll excuse me." He held his open hand toward the door.

"Mr. Lawrence . . ."

"I'll call you at three. An army man will know how to be at that phone."

# 6

THE FIRST THING I DID AFTER LEAVING THE TAX MAN WAS TO go to a phone. I called Mofass and told him to have somebody get the empty apartment at the Sixty-fourth Street building ready for two tenants. Then I called Alfred Bontemps at his mother's house.

She answered sweetly, "Yes?"

"Mrs. Bontemps?"

"Is that you, Easy Rawlins?"

"Uh-huh, yeah. How you been, ma'am?"

"Just fine," she said. There was gratitude in her voice. "You know Alfred's come back home 'cause of you."

"I know that. I went up there an' got 'im. I could see how you missed him."

Mrs. Bontemps' son, Alfred, stole three hundred dollars from Slydell, a neighborhood bookie, and then he ran out to Compton because he was afraid that Slydell wanted him dead—which he did. Alfred stole the money because his mother was sick and needed a doctor. Slydell hired me to find the boy and his money. I went straight to Mrs. Bontemps and told her that if she didn't tell me about Alfred, Slydell would kill him.

She gave me the address after I told her how Slydell had once torn off a man's ear for stealing the hubcaps from his car.

"But you workin' fo' that man," she'd told me. Tears were in her eyes.

"That's just business though, ma'am. If I could get what Slydell wants I could maybe cut a deal with him."

She was so scared that she told me the address. Woman's love has killed many a man that way.

I found Alfred, threw him in the back of my Ford, and drove him to a hotel on Grand Street in L.A. Then I drove over to the bookie shop; that was the back room of a barbershop on Avalon.

I gave Slydell the forty-two dollars Alfred had left and told him, "Alfred's gonna give you fifteen dollars a month until that money is paid, Slydell."

"The hell he is!"

I had no intention of letting that boy get killed after I'd found him, so I brought out my pistol and held it to the bookie's silver-capped tooth.

"I said I'd bring you yo' money, man. You know Alfred cain't pay you if he's dead."

"I cain't let that boy get away wit' stealin' from me. I got a reputation t'think of, Easy."

Slydell was only tough with a man who cowered at threats of violence. And he knew I wasn't the kind of man who bowed down.

"Then it's either you or him, man," I said. "You know I don't look kindly on killin' boys."

We settled it without bloodshed. Alfred got a good job with the Parks Department, paid Slydell, and got his mother on his health insurance.

Mrs. Bontemps kind of took me on as her foster son after that.

"You ever gonna get married, Easy?" she asked.

"If I ever find somebody t'take me."

"Oh, you'd be a good catch, honey," she said. "I know lotsa good women give they eyeteeth fo'you."

But all I was interested in was Alfred at that moment. He was a small boy, barely out of his teens, and skitterish, but he felt he owed me a debt of honor for standing up against Slydell. And I think he might have been happy to get back home to his mother too.

"Could I talk with Alfred, ma'am?"

"Sure, Easy, an' maybe you could come over fo' dinner sometimes."

"Love it," I said.

After a few moments Alfred came on the line.

"Mr. Rawlins?"

"Listen up, Alfred. I gotta move somebody t'day an' I need a helper ain't gonna go runnin' his mouth after it."

"You got it, Mr., um, Easy. When you need the help?"

"You know my house on 116th Street?"

"Not really."

I gave him the address and told him to be there at about one-thirty.

"But first go over to Mofass' office an' tell 'im that you gonna use his truck fo' the move," I said.

All the time I was on the phone the idea of the government taking my money and my freedom was gnawing at me. But I didn't even let that become a thought. I was afraid of what might happen if I did.

So instead I went to Targets Bar after my phone

36

calls. It was still early in the day, but I needed some liquor and some peace.

John McKenzie was the bartender at Targets. He was also the cook and the bouncer, and, though his name wasn't on the deed, John was also the owner. He used to own a speakeasy down around Watts but the police finally closed that down. An honest police captain moved into the precinct, and because of the differences between honest cops and honest Negro entrepreneurs, he put all our best businessmen out of trade.

John couldn't get a liquor license because he had been a bootlegger in his youth, so he took an empty storefront and set out a plank of mahogany and eighteen round maple tables. Then he gave nine thousand dollars to Odell Jones, who in turn made a down payment to the bank. But it was John's bar. He managed it, collected the money, and paid the mortgage. What Odell got was that he could come in there anytime he wanted and drink to his heart's content.

It was John who gave me the idea of how to buy my own buildings through a dummy corporation.

Odell worked at the First African Baptist Day School, which was around the corner from his bar. He was the custodian there.

Odell was at his special table the day I came from the IRS. He was eating his regular egg-and-bacon sandwich for lunch before going back to work. John was standing at the far end of the bar, leaning against it and staring off into the old days when he was an important man.

"Easy."

"Mo'nin', John."

We shook hands.

John's face looked like it was chiseled in ebony. He was tall and hard. There wasn't an ounce of fat on John, but he was a big man, still and all. He was the kind of man who could run a bar or speakeasy, because violence came to him naturally, but he preferred to take it easy.

He put a drink down in front of me and touched my big knuckle. When I looked up into his stark white-and-brown eyes he said, "Mouse been here t'day, Easy."

"Yeah?"

"He askin' fo' EttaMae, an' when that failed he asted 'bout you."

"Like what?"

"Where you been, who you been wit'. Like that. He was wit' Rita Cook. They was goin' t' her house fo'a afternoon nap."

"Yeah?"

"I just thought you wanna know 'bout yo' ole friend bein' up here, Easy."

"Thanks, John," I said, and then, "By the way . . ."

"Yeah?" He looked at me with the same dead-ahead look that he had for a customer ordering whiskey or an armed robber demanding what was in the till.

"Some people been talkin' 'bout them buildin's I bought a while back."

"Uh-huh."

"You tell anybody 'bout them papers we did?"

At first he moved his shoulders, as if he were going to turn away without a word. But then he straightened up and said, "Easy, if I wanted to get you I could put sumpin' in yo' drink. Or I could get one'a these niggahs in here t'cut yo' th'oat. But now you know better than that, don't you?"

"Yeah, I know, John. But you know that I had t'ask."

We shook hands again, still friends, and I moved away from the bar.

I said hello to Odell. We made plans to get together in the next couple of days. It felt like I was back in the war again. Back then I'd see somebody and make plans, just a few hours away, but I wondered if I'd be alive to make the date.

"Hi, Easy," Etta said in a cool voice when I got to the door. The potatoes were replanted and the flower beds were tended. My house smelled cleaner than it ever had, and I was sorry, so sorry that I wanted to cry.

"Hi, Unca Easy," LaMarque yelled. He was jumping up and down on my couch. Up and down, over and over, like a little madman, or a little boy.

"Mouse went to John McKenzie's bar t'day. He was lookin' fo' you an' askin' 'bout me," I told Etta.

"He be here tomorrow then, an' me an' LaMarque be gone."

"How you know he ain't on his way here right now?"

"You say he was in John McKenzie's bar just today?"

"Yeah."

"So he had t' be either wit' a girl or after one."

I didn't say anything to that, so Etta went on, "Raymond always gotta get his thing wet when he get to a new place. So he be here tomorrah, after he get that pussy."

I was ashamed to hear her talk like that and looked around to see where LaMarque was. But something about her bold talk excited me too. I didn't like to feel anything about Mouse's woman, but things were going so poorly in my life that I was feeling a little reckless.

Luckily Alfred drove up then. He was a tiny young man, hardly larger than a punk kid, but he could work. We put Etta's bags and a bed from my garage in the truck. I also gave her a chair and a table from my store of abandoned furniture.

Etta softened a little before she left.

"You gonna come an' see us, Easy?" she asked. "You know LaMarque likes you."

"Just gotta get this tax man offa my butt an' I be by, Etta. Two days, three at top."

"You tell Raymond that I don't wanna see 'im. Tell 'im that I tole you not t'give'im my address."

"What if he pulls a gun on me? You want me to shoot 'im?"

"If he pulls his gun, Easy, then we all be dead."

# 7

AFTER EVERYONE WAS GONE I SAT DOWN BY THE PHONE. That was five minutes to three. If Lawrence had called me when he said he was I might have been okay. But the minutes stretched into half an hour and then to an hour. During that time I thought about all that I was going to lose; my property, my money, my freedom. And I thought about the way he called me *son* so easily. In those days many white people still took it for granted that a black man was little more than a child.

It was well after four by the time Lawrence called.

"Rawlins?"

"Yeah."

"I want you to come to my office at six-thirty this evening. I've notified someone downstairs so you shouldn't have any trouble getting in."

"Tonight? I cain't have all that by then, man."

But I was wasting my words, because he had already hung up.

I went to the garage and pulled out my box of papers. I had paid taxes on the money I paid myself through Mofass, but I didn't pay taxes on the stolen money because it was still hot in 1948 and after that it was already undeclared. Most of the profit from the rent went into buying more real estate. It was just easier to let the money ride without telling the government about my income.

Then I drove out to see Mofass. My choices were few and none of them sounded any too good.

On the drive over I heard a voice in my head say, "Mothahfuckah ain't got no right messin' like that, man. No right at all."

But I ignored it. I grabbed the steering wheel a little tighter and concentrated on the road.

"It don't look good, Mr. Rawlins," Mofass said behind his fat cigar.

"What about that thing you said with backdatin' them papers?" I asked. We were sitting in his office in a haze of tobacco smoke.

"You said it yourself, they ain't nobody got enough money for you to give it to."

"What about you?"

Mofass eyed me suspiciously and pushed back in his swivel chair.

He sat there, staring at me for a full minute before shaking his head and saying, "No."

"I need it, Mofass. If you don't do this I'm goin' to jail."

"I feel for ya but I gotta say no, Mr. Rawlins. It ain't that I don't care, but this is business. And when you in business there's just some things that you cain't do. Now look at it from my side. I work for you, I collect the rent and keep things smooth. Now all of a sudden you wanna sign ev'rything over t' me. I own it," he said, pointing all eight of his fingers at his chest. "But you get the money."

"John McKenzie do it with Odell Jones."

"From what you told me it sounds like Odell just likes his drink. I'm a businessman and you cain't trust me."

"The hell I cain't!"

"You see"—Mofass opened his eyes and puffed out his cheeks, looking like a big brown carp—"you'd come after me if you thought I was messin' wit' yo' money. Right now that's okay 'cause we got a legal relationship. But I couldn't be trusted if all that was yours suddenly became mines. What if all of a sudden I feel like I deserve more but you say no? In a court of law it would be mine."

"We couldn't go to no courts after we done faked the ownership papers, man."

"That's just it, Mr. Rawlins. If I say yes to you right now, then the only court of appeal we got is each other. We ain't blood. All we is is business partners. An' I tell ya this." He pointed his black stogie at me. "They ain't no greater hate that a man could have than the hate of someone who cheated him at his own business."

Mofass sat back again, and I knew he had turned me down.

"So that's it, huh?" I said.

"You ain't even tried t'lie yet, Mr. Rawlins. Go in there wit' yo' papers and yo' lie and see what you could get."

"He's talkin' court, Mofass."

"Sho he is. That's what they do, try an' scare ya. Go in there wit' yo' income papers an' ast'im where he think you gonna come up wit' the kinda cash it takes t'buy apartments. Act po', thas what you do. Them white people love t'think that you ain't shit."

"An' if that don't work," a husky voice in my head said, "kill the mothahfuckah."

I tried to shake the gloom that that voice brought on me. I wanted to drive right out to the IRS, but instead

I went home and dug my snub-nose out of the closet. I cleaned it and oiled it and loaded it with fresh cartridges. It scared me, because I would carry the .25 for a little insurance, but my .38 was a killing gun. I kept thinking about that clumsy white man, how he had a house and a family to go to. All he cared about was that some numbers made up zero on a piece of paper.

"This man is the government," I said in order to convince myself of the foolishness of going armed.

"Man wanna take from you," the voice replied, "he better be ready to back it up."

The front door of the government building was locked and dark, but a small Negro man came to answer my knock. He was wearing gray gardening overalls and a plaid shirt. I wondered if he owned any property.

"You Mr. Rawlins?" he asked me.

"That's right," I said.

"You could just go on upstairs then."

I was in such a state that all I paid any attention to was the blood pounding in my head. Loud and insistent. And what it was insisting on was more blood, tax man blood. I was going to tell him about the money I was paid and he was going to believe it or I was going to shoot him. If they wanted me in jail I was going to give them a good reason.

Maybe I'd've shot him anyway.

Maybe I would've shot the Negro in the overalls too, I don't know. It's just that sometimes I get carried away. When the pressure gets to me this voice comes out. It saved my life more than once during the war. But those were hard times where life-and-death decisions were simple.

I might have gone lighter if Lawrence had treated me with the same kind of respect he showed others. But I am no white man's *son*.

On approaching the door I threw off the safety on my gun. I heard voices as I pushed the door open but I was still surprised to see someone sitting with him. My finger clutched the trigger. I remember worrying that I might shoot myself in the foot.

"Here he is now," Lawrence was saying. He was the only man I had ever seen who sat in a chair awkwardly. He was tilting to the side and holding on to the arm to keep from falling to the floor. The man sitting across from him stood up. He was shorter than either Lawrence or I, maybe five-ten, and wiry. He was a pale-skinned man with bushy brown hair and hairy knuckles. I noticed these latter because he walked right up to me and shook my hand. I had to release hold of the pistol in my pocket in order to shake his hand; that's the only reason I didn't shoot Reginald Lawrence.

"Mr. Rawlins," the wiry white man said. "I've heard a lot about you and I'm happy to make your acquaintance."

"Yes, sir," I said.

"Craxton!" he shouted. "Special Agent Darryl T. Craxton! FBI."

"Pleased to meet you."

"Agent Craxton has something to discuss with you, Mr. Rawlins," Lawrence said.

When I took my hand off the pistol my chance for murder was through. I said, "I got the papers you wanted right here."

"Forget that." Craxton waved a dismissing hand at the shoe box under my arm. "I got something for you to do for your country. You like fighting for your country, don't you, Ezekiel?"

"I done it when I had to."

"Yeah." Craxton's smile revealed crooked teeth that had wide spaces between them. But they looked strong, like brown-and-white tree stumps that you'd have to dynamite to remove. "I've been discussing your case with Mr. Lawrence here. I've been looking for somebody to help me with a mission, and you're the best candidate I've seen."

"What kind of a mission?"

Craxton smiled again. "Mr. Lawrence tells me that you overlooked paying some taxes for the past few years."

"This man is suspected of tax evasion," Lawrence interrupted. "That is what I said."

"Mr. Rawlins here is a war hero," Craxton answered. "He loves this country. He hates our enemies. A man like that doesn't shirk his responsibility, Mr. Lawrence. I believe that he just made an error."

Lawrence pulled out a white handkerchief and dabbed at his lips.

Craxton turned back to me, "I could fix it so that you just pay your back taxes, by installment if you don't have the cash. All I need is a little help. No. No. Change that. All your country needs is a little help."

That set Lawrence up straight.

He said, "I thought you just wanted to talk with him?"

Before he could say any more I jumped in. "Well, you know I'm always ready to be a good citizen, Mr. Craxton. That's why I'm here this time of night. I want to show that I'm a good citizen." I knew how to be good too; LaMarque didn't have a thing on me.

"See, Mr. Lawrence, see? Mr. Rawlins is eager to help us out. No reason for you to pursue your current course. I tell you what. Mr. Rawlins and I will do some work together and then I'll come back and have his paperwork transferred to Washington. That way you won't have to worry about his settlement."

Reginald Lawrence grabbed on to the arm of his chair a little tighter.

"This is not proper procedure, Agent Craxton," the IRS man complained.

Craxton just smiled.

"I'll have to speak with my supervisor," Lawrence continued.

"You do what you think is appropriate, Mr. Lawrence." Craxton never stopped smiling. "I appreciate that a man has to do his job, he has to do what he thinks is right. If everybody just does that this country will be fine and healthy."

The blood rose to Lawrence's face. My heart was going like a bird in flight.

# 8

SPECIAL AGENT CRAXTON WAS SAYING, "NICE PLACE, Hollywood," as he sipped a glass of 7-Up.

I was nursing a screwdriver. We had driven to a small bar called Adolf's on Sunset Boulevard near La Cienega. Adolf's was an old place, established before the war, so it held on to that unpopular name.

When we got to the door a man in a red jacket and top hat barred our way.

"May I help you gentleman?"

"Stand aside," Craxton said.

"Maybe you don't understand, mister," the doorman replied, raising his hand in a tentative gesture. "We're a class place and not everyone can cut it."

He was looking directly into my face.

"Listen, bud." Craxton peeled back his left lapel. Pinned to the inside of the jacket was his FBI identification. "Either you open the door now or I shut you down—for good."

After that the manager came over and seated us

46

near the piano player. He also offered us free drinks and food, which Craxton turned down. Nobody bothered us after that. I remember thinking that those white people were just as afraid of the law as any colored man. Of course, I always knew that there was no real difference between the races, but still, it was nice to see an example of that equality.

I was thinking about that and how I had been suddenly saved from the gas chamber. Because it was a certainty that I would have murdered Agent Lawrence if the ugly man in front of me hadn't shaken my hand.

"What do you know about communism, Mr. Rawlins?" Craxton asked. His tone was like a schoolteacher's—I was being quizzed.

"Call me Easy. That's the name I go by."

He nodded and I said, "I figure the Reds to be one step worse than the Nazis unless you happen to be a Jew. To a Jew they ain't nuthin' worse than a Nazi."

I said that because I knew what the FBI man wanted to hear. My feelings were really much more complex. In the war the Russians were our allies; our best friends. Paul Robeson, the great Negro actor and singer, had toured Russia and even lived there for a while. Joseph Stalin himself had Robeson as his guest at the Kremlin. But when the war was through we were enemies again. Robeson's career was destroyed and he left America.

I didn't know how we could be friends with somebody one day and then enemies the next. I didn't know why a man like Robeson would give up his shining career for something like politics.

Agent Craxton nodded while I answered and tapped his cheekbone with a hairy index finger. "Lots of Jews are communists too. Marx was a Jew, grandfather to all the Reds."

"I guess there's all kindsa Jews just like ev'rybody else."

Craxton nodded, but I wasn't so sure that he agreed with me.

"One thing you have right is how bad the Reds are. They want to take the whole world and enslave it. They don't believe in freedom like Americans do. The Russians have been peasants so long that thas the way they see the whole world—from chains."

It was strange talk, I thought, a white man lecturing me about slavery.

"Yeah, some folks learn how to love their chains, I guess."

Craxton gave me a quick smile. In that brief second a shine of admiration flashed across his walnut eyes.

He said, "I knew we'd understand each other, Easy. Soon as I saw your police file I knew you were the kind of man for us."

"What kinda man is that?"

The pianist was playing "Two Sleepy People" on a bright and lively note.

"Man who wants to serve his country. Man who knows what it is to fight and maybe take a couple of chances. Man who doesn't give in to some foreign power saying that they have a better deal."

I had the feeling that Craxton didn't see the man sitting before him, but I'd seen pictures of Leavenworth in *Life* magazine so I pretended to be the man he described.

"Chaim Wenzler," Craxton said.

"Who?"

"One of those communist kind of Jews. Union persuasion. Calls himself a *worker*. Building chains is what he's doing. He's been organizing unions from Alameda County on down the line to Champion Aircraft. You know Champion, don't you, Easy."

The last real job I had was at Champion.

"I worked production there," I said. "Five years ago."

"I know," Craxton said. He pulled a manila folder from his jacket pocket. The folder was soiled, creased, and pleated down the center. He smoothed it out in front of me. The block red letters across the top said: "LAPD Special Subject." And below that: "subj— Ezekiel P. Rawlins, aka—Easy Rawlins."

"Everything we need to know in here, Easy. War record, criminal associations, job history. One police detective wrote a letter in 1949 saying that he suspected you of being involved in a series of homicides the previous year. Then in 1950 you turn around and help the police find a rapist working the Watts community.

"I'd been looking for a Negro to work for us. Somebody who might have a little trouble but nothing so bad that we couldn't smooth it over if somebody showed a little initiative and some patriotism. Then Clyde Wadsworth called about you."

"Who?"

"Wadsworth, he's Lawrence's head. Clyde saw an inquiry for your file go across his desk a few weeks back. He knew the neighborhood you lived in and gave me a call. Lucky for everybody."

He tapped the folder with a clean, evenly manicured fingernail.

"We need you to get to know this Wenzler, Easy. We need to know if it's the left or right leg he puts into his pants first in the morning."

"How could I do that and the whole FBI cain't do it?"

"This is a sly Jew. We know that he's up to his shoulders in something bad, but damned if we can do anything about it. You see, Wenzler never really gets involved with the place he's organizing. He won't work there. But he finds his fair-haired boy and grooms him to be his mouthpiece. That's what he did with Andre Lavender. Know him?"

Craxton stared me straight in the eye awaiting the answer.

I remembered Andre. A big, sloppy man. But he had the energy of ten men for all his weight. He always had a plan to get rich quick. For a while he sold frozen steaks and then, later on, he tried construction. Andre was a good man but he was too excitable; even if he made a couple of bucks he'd spend them just that quick. "Rich an' important men gotta spend money, Easy," he told me once. He was driving a leased Cadillac at the time, delivering frozen steaks from door to door.

"I don't remember him," I said to Special Agent Craxton.

"Well, maybe he wasn't so loud when you were at Champion, but now he's a union man. Chaim Wenzler's boy."

Craxton sat back for a moment and appraised me. He put his hand flat against my file like a man swearing on a sacred text. Then he leaned across the table and began to whisper, "You see, Easy, in many ways the Bureau is a last line of defense. There are all sorts of enemies we have these days. We've got enemies all over the world; in Europe, in Asia, everywhere. But the real enemies, the ones we really have to watch out for, are people right here at home. People who aren't Americans on the inside. No, not really."

He drifted off into a kind of reverie. The confusion must have shown on my face, because he added, "And we have to stop these people. We have to bring them to the attention of the courts and the Congress. So even if I have to overlook some lesser crimes . . ." He paused and stared at me again. ". . . like petty tax theft, I will do that in order to get the bigger job done."

"Listen, man," I said. "You got me by the nuts on this one, so I'ma do what you want. But get to it, alright? I'm a little nervous with all this talk an' these files an' shit."

"Okay," he said, and then he took a deep breath. "Chaim Wenzler has been organizing people through the unions. He's been giving them ideas about this country that are lies and unpatriotic. There's more to it, but I can't tell you what because we can't get anybody close enough to him to really find out what it is that he's up to."

"Why don't you just arrest him? Cain't you do that?"

"He's not what we want, Easy. It's what he represents, the people he works with—that's what we need to know."

"An' you cain't make him tell you all this stuff?" I was well aware of the persuasive powers of the law.

"Not this man." There was a hint of admiration in Craxton's tone. "And it's worth our time to find out who he's working with, without him knowing it, that is. You see, Wenzler is bad, but where you can see someone like him you know that there's serious rot underneath."

"Uh-huh." I nodded, trying to look like I was right up there with him. "So what do you need me for if you already know that this guy is the center of the problem? I mean, what could I do?"

"Wenzler is small potatoes. He's a fanatic, thinks that America isn't free and the Reds are. All by himself he's nothing, just a malcontent with a dull ax to grind. But it's just that kind of man that gets duped into doing the worst harm."

"But I don't even know this guy, how you expect me to get next to him?"

"Wenzler works in the Negro churches. We figure that he's making his contacts down there."

"Yeah?"

"He's working three places right now. One of them

is the First African Baptist Church and Day School. That's your neighborhood, right? You probably know some of that flock."

"So what does he do at the church?"

"Charity," Agent Craxton sneered. "But that's just a front. He's looking for others who are like him; people who feel that this country has given them a raw deal. He feels like that, doesn't hardly trust a soul. But the thing is, he'll trust you. He's got a soft spot for Negroes."

It was at that moment I decided not to trust Agent Craxton.

"I still don't see why you need me. If the FBI wants something on him why don't you just make it up?" I was serious.

Agent Craxton took my meaning and laughed. It sounded like an asthmatic's cough.

"I don't have a partner, Easy. Did you notice that?" I nodded.

"There's no crime here, Mr. Rawlins. We're not trying to put somebody in jail for tax evasion. What we are doing is shedding light on a group of people who use the very freedom we give them in order to burn down what we believe."

I wondered if Agent Craxton had political aspirations. He sounded like a man running for office.

"There is no crime to arrest him for. No crime that we know of, that is. But if you get next to him you might find out something. You might see where we could come in and arrest him for a crime the courts would recognize. You might be our means to his end."

"Uh-huh," I grunted. "But what do you mean about not havin' no partner?"

"I'm a special kind of agent, Easy. I don't just look for evidence. Some agents are in the business of solving crimes. My job is to avoid the damage before it's done."

"Yeah," I said, nodding. "But now lemme get this

straight. You want me to get to know this Wenzler guy, then get him to trust me so I find out if he's a spy?"

"And then you find out all you can, Easy. We let you pay your taxes and go back home."

"And what if I don't find out somethin' that you could use? What if it's just that he complains a lot but he don't do nuthin' really?"

"You just report to me. Say once a week. I'll know how to read it. And when you're through the IRS will let you alone."

"All that sounds good, but I need to know somethin' first."

"What's that?"

"Well, you talkin' 'bout my own people with this conspiracy stuff. An' if you want my opinion, all that is just some mistake. You know I live down there an' I ain't never heard that we some kinda communist conspiracy or whatever."

Craxton just smiled.

"But if you wanna believe that," I continued, "I guess you can. But you cain't get me t' go after my own people. I mean, if these guys broke the law like you say, I don't mind that, but I don't wanna hurt the people at First African just 'cause they run a charity drive or somethin'."

"We see eye to eye, Easy," Craxton said. "I just want the Jew, and whatever it is he's up to. You won't even know I was there."

"So what's this stuff about this other guy, Lavender?"

"You remember him?"

"No."

"We need to find Lavender. He's worked closer with Wenzler than anyone. If we could get him into custody I'm sure that he'd be able to help."

"You sound like he's missin'?"

"He quit Champion three weeks ago, and nobody has seen him since. We'd appreciate a line on him,

Easy. Finding Lavender would go a long way toward settling your taxes."

"But you just wanna talk to 'im?"

"That's right." Craxton was leaning so far across the table that he could have jumped down my throat.

I knew that he was lying to me, but I needed him, so I said, "Okay," and we shook hands.

The orange juice in my screwdriver was canned, it left a bitter metallic taste in my mouth. But I drank it anyway. Screwdriver was what I asked for; I guess I asked for Craxton too.

# 9

I LEFT ADOLF'S AND DROVE STRAIGHT TO JOHN'S BAR. I wanted a good-tasting drink in the bar of my own choosing.

That was about nine o'clock, so lots of people were there. Odell was at his regular seat, near the wall. Pierre Kind was with him. Bonita Smith danced slowly in the middle of the floor with Brad Winston in her arms. The bar was lined with men and women, and John worked hard meeting their demands. "Good Night, Irene," the original version by Leadbelly, played on the jukebox, and a haze of cigarette smoke dimmed the room.

I saw Mouse sitting at a table with Dupree Bouchard and Jackson Blue; as unlikely a trio as I could imagine.

Jackson had on jeans and a dark blue button-down shirt. He also wore a baby-blue jacket with matching pointy-toed shoes. Jackson's skin was so black that it glinted blue when in the full sun. He was a small man, smaller than Mouse even, and as cowardly as they come. He was a petty thief and a lackey to the various numbers runners and gangsters. He would have been what we called trash back then, but that wasn't all there was to Jackson Blue. He was the closest I ever came to knowing a genius. Jackson could read and write as well as anybody I knew, including the professors at Los Angeles City College. He'd tell you all kinds of things about history and science and things that happened in places elsewhere in the world. At first I didn't believe the things he'd tell me, but then I bought an old encyclopedia set from him. No matter how I tested him, Jackson knew every fact in those books. From then on I just took it on faith that everything else he said was true too.

But Jackson didn't just read and remember, he could also tell what people were thinking and what they were likely to do, by just talking to them. Jackson would walk into a room and come out the other side knowing everybody's secrets from just watching their eyes or hearing them talk about the weather.

He was a valuable asset to a man like me; even more so because Jackson never used his ability except to rat back and forth between factions of the criminal element. Give Jackson five dollars and he'd sell out his best friend. And you never had to worry about Jackson lying to you, because he was so cowardly and because he had great pride in the fact that he was right about whatever he said.

Dupree dwarfed his companions. He was a head taller than I and built to split stones. He was wide and burly with close-cropped hair and a great propensity for laughter. Right when I walked in he let go a terrific gust of guffaws. Mouse had probably been telling one of his grim tales.

Dupree wore drab green overalls with CHAMPION

sewn into the back in dull red thread. We both worked at the airplane manufacturer for some years, before the untimely death of his girlfriend, Coretta James, and my entrée into the world of real estate and favors.

But for all their showy qualities, Dupree and Jackson were dim lights compared with Mouse.

He wore a cream double-breasted suit with a felt brown derby and brown, round-toed shoes. His white shirt looked to be satin. His teeth were all aglitter with gold edgings, silver caps, and one lustrous blue jewel. He didn't wear rings or bracelets, because they got in the way of weapons handling. Mouse's color was a dusky pecan and his eyes were light gray. He was smiling and talking. People from other tables leaned away from their drinks to hear what he had to say.

"Yeah, man," Mouse drawled. "He waits till the bitch an' me was *in the bed,* not gettin' ready mind ya, but *in the fuckin' bed.* Then he jump out an' say, 'Ah-hah.'"

Mouse opened his eyes wide just the way the jealous lover must've done it. Everybody was laughing.

Jackson asked, "What you do then?" in a way that let you know he felt he might need that trick one day.

"Shit!" Mouse spat. "I kicked off the blankets an' jumped up t' face the mothahfuckah. I say, 'What the fuck is this shit?' That boy was rowdy, but you know he took out a moment t' look down at my big hard dick. 'Cause you know I got sumpin' give any man pause."

Mouse was a master storyteller. He had every man there wondering about his thing just like that jealous lover was supposed to have done.

"Then I go upside the dude's head wit' a lamp from the night table. Heavy clay job, man, it was so thick that it didn't even break. Shit. That boy hit the flo' hard."

"I bet you got yo' ass outta there in a hurry,"

Jackson laughed. You could tell that Jackson had his hand on his own business under the table; that's how some men maintain their security.

"Run? Hell no! Man, I was really ready t' fuck then. I pulled that bitch down in the bed an' got me some pussy like most men on'y dream of. Run? Shit."

Mouse sat back and drank his beer. The men around were all laughing. Most people there were from Texas originally, but many of them didn't know Mouse. They laughed because they loved a well-told lie. And Raymond didn't mind, because he liked to make people laugh. But I wasn't laughing. Neither was John behind his bar, or Odell over on his side.

Mouse never lied. That wasn't his way. I mean, he'd lie to you if it was business of some sort, but sitting around a bar Mouse told true stories.

What I wondered was how hard he hit that man.

"Easy." Mouse smiled at me out past the edge of his audience.

My heart thrilled and quailed at the same time. Mouse was the truest friend I ever had. And if there is such a thing as true evil, he was that too.

"Raymond," I said. I moved past the others to sit at the small table. "How ya doin', Jackson, Dupree?"

They both said my name and touched my hand.

"You heard I was here?" Mouse asked me.

"Yeah," I answered. "I wondered why you didn't come by t'see me."

Mouse and I were talking to each other. It was like no one else was in the room. Dupree was calling John to get more drinks and Jackson turned away, telling a story to somebody at another table.

"I been out at Dupree's house. I'm out there stayin' wit' him."

"You coulda come t' my house, Ray. I got room, you know that."

"Yeah, yeah. Coulda done, but . . ." He paused and

smiled at me. "But I don't like t' be surprised, Easy.
It's like that dude come bustin' in the bedroom. You
see, if I had seen my old lady fuckin' somebody in my
own bed, well, they both need the undertaker by
then."

I felt the weight of that .38 through my jacket and
on my right thigh. But my arms felt weak and I
remembered how awful it was for my Great-Uncle
Halley when he got so old that he couldn't even feed
himself.

"Ain't none of us gotta worry 'bout gettin' old,
Mouse," I said.

He laughed and slapped my thigh. It was a good
laugh. Happy.

"But," I went on, "that ain't no reason fo' you to go
to Dupree when I got room right in my own house."

"You seen Etta?"

I wanted to, but I couldn't lie in his face.

"She come yesterday, stayed the night, and moved
to a place t'day. Her an' LaMarque."

When I said LaMarque's name Mouse jerked his
head up. He looked me in the eye for a moment, and
what I saw there scared me.

Most violent and desperate men have a kind of
haunted look in their eyes. But never Mouse. He could
smile in your face and shoot you dead. He didn't feel
guilt or remorse. He was different from most men.
What he did, he did because of a set of rules that only
applied to him. He loved some people; his mother,
dead by then, Etta and LaMarque, and me too. He
loved us in the strange way that he felt everything.

So I was unsettled when I saw the remorse and
bitterness in Mouse's gaze. A man who is already
insane was frightening enough, but when he goes
crazy . . .

"Where she go?"

"She asked me not to tell ya, Raymond. She said

t'tell her how she could call you an' she'd do it—when she was ready."

Mouse just stared at me. His eyes were clear again. He might have killed me then. Who knows? Maybe if it all happened at a different time I would have acted differently. But I didn't know how to give in to my fear. In two days I had prepared to lose all my property and my freedom, I had settled on becoming a murderer, and I had become a flunky for the FBI. I decided to let fate hold my cards.

"You ain't gonna tell me where she is?"

"She upset, Raymond. If you don't let her do it her way she gonna blow up at you, an' me too."

Mouse watched me like a little boy might watch a butterfly. John hovered behind him while he put down short glasses filled with various amber liquors and ice.

"Easy got yo' number, Dupree?" Mouse asked at last.

"Ain't ya, Ease?" Dupree asked me.

"Yeah, yeah. I got it."

Mouse laughed. "Well then, that's business. Let's have some drinks.

Dupree got drunk and told stories after a while. Wholesome stories about foolish men at Champion Aircraft. The kind of stories that workmen tell. How somebody lost count when assembling a jet engine and how that engine blew the roof off of the construction bungalow. And when the boss asked what happened the perpetrator just opened his eyes and said something like "Somebody musta lit a match."

At one point I asked Dupree, "You seen Andre Lavender 'round there lately?"

"Uh-uh, man. He got the politics bug pretty bad there for a while. Union. But then he just disappeared one day."

"Disappeared?"

"Yeah, man. Gone. I think he stole sumpin', 'cause they had all kindsa cops there. But no one know what happened."

"Didn't his li'l girlfriend . . ." I snapped my fingers trying to remember.

"Juanita," Dupree said, frowning.

"Yeah. Juanita. Didn't she know where he was?"

"Nope. She come around the plant lookin' fo'im the next day, but nobody could help. But you know I did hear that Andre blew town with Winthrop Hughes' ole lady."

"You mean Shaker's girl?"

"Uh-huh. They say Andre took her, his bank book, an' his car."

"No shit?" I let it drop there. Andre could wait for a while.

When Dupree passed out (which is what he did whenever he drank) we carried him out to the car. We piled him in the back and Jackson jumped into the passenger's seat. Before Mouse pulled in behind the wheel he leaned very close to my face and said, "If you see'er, you tell'er that I give it a couple'a days. You tell'er that I won't be denied. I will not be denied." Then he grabbed my shirt with thin fingers that were hard as nails. "An' if you get in my way, Easy, or if you take her side, I kill you too."

As I watched them drive away I breathed a quiet sigh of relief that Etta had moved out of my house. I figured that EttaMae could handle Mouse, especially if she wasn't with me.

# 10

THE NEXT MORNING I CALLED ETTA TO TELL HER ABOUT MY talk with Mouse. She snorted once and had nothing else to say. I offered to escort her to church on Sunday. She accepted and excused herself, polite and cold.

As a kind of treat for my new freedom from the IRS and Raymond Alexander I decided to let myself loll in the sunny halls of the Magnolia Street apartments.

Mrs. Trajillo was at her window rolling out corn tortillas on a breadboard balanced on the windowsill. Her skin was a deep olive color dappled with various-sized freckles and one large mole at the center of her chin. Her long hair was salt and pepper and hung in one thick braid down to about the middle of her thigh. She was short but sturdily built, and though she had never had a job, her hands were strong from years of doing housework, raising children, and making food from scratch.

"Good morning, Mr. Rawlins," she greeted me.

"Hello, ma'am. How're you today?"

"Oh, pretty good I guess. My granddaughter had her confirmation last Sunday."

"That a fact?"

"You look good," she said. "I was worried about you and poor Mr. Mofass the other day. You weren't smiling at all, and that terrible girl . . ." She brought her fingers to her chest and made an O-shape with her lips. "The things she yelled at him. You know I was glad the children were still in school."

"I guess Poinsettia was upset. You know how she's sick and all."

"God gives you what you earn, Mr. Rawlins."

That seemed like a terrible curse coming from such a kind woman.

"What do you mean?" I asked.

"The way she was with men before. No girl of mine would be like that. I'm not telling you anything, Mr. Rawlins, but God knows."

It didn't bother me much. I know that older women often forget how it is to be loved by young men. Or maybe they do remember and hate it all the more.

I went upstairs and stood on the second floor for an hour or more just feeling the sun and looking at nothing. But after a while I picked up the trace of a foul scent.

The sun was shining in on the third floor too. It was beautiful but the smell was bad. The door to Apartment J was ajar; that's where the smell came from.

Really what I should call it is smells. There was the sweet smell of three or four kinds of incense that she used in her prayer altar and the odor of sickness that had been bottled up in her small rooms for the most part of six months. There were all kinds of rotting odors beyond that smell.

But now, I figured, she was gone, moved out after Mofass had threatened her with eviction. The door was open and I knew she had probably left me a major cleaning job.

Poinsettia had gone off for a vacation weekend six months before and come back two weeks later in a private ambulance. The attendants had told Mrs. Trajillo that Poinsettia had been in a bad car accident and that her boyfriend had paid to have her moved from the hospital back home. Her bones and bruises healed, but something happened to her nerves. She couldn't work anymore or even walk right. Somewhere in her late twenties, she had been a beautiful woman until that accident. It was a shame to see her come down so far. But what could I do about it? Mofass was hard but he was right when he said that I couldn't pay her rent.

The living room was a mess. The shades were drawn and the curtains pulled, so it was twilight in the musty rooms. Ghostly white cartons of Chinese food were open and moldering on the table, trash everywhere. I flicked the light switch, but the bulb had burned out. Against a far wall there sat an altar she had made from a small alcove. Inside she had glued a picture of Jesus. It was painted like a mosaic. He had a halo and held two fingers and a thumb above three saints who were bowing to receive his blessing. All around the painting there were old flowers wired to the walls. They were unidentifiable brown things that she'd probably brought home from mass or after a funeral.

At the foot of the painting was the bronze dish that she also used to burn the incense. The sweet smell was much stronger there. Little ashes, like white maggots, were littered around the brimming dish. And there was a black, gummy substance on the ledge and down the wall to the floor.

The bathroom was disgusting. All kinds of cosmetic bottles open and dried until the liquids had caked and cracked. Mildewed towels on the floor. A spider spun its web over the bathtub faucet.

The worst smells came from the bedroom, and I hesitated to go in there. It's a funny thing how smell is such an animal instinct. The first thing a dog will do is sniff. And if it doesn't smell right there's a natural reluctance to get any closer.

Maybe I should have been a dog.

Poinsettia was hanging from the light fixture in the middle of the ceiling. She was naked and her skin sagged so that it seemed as if it would come right off the bone any second. Directly under her was the cause of the worst smells. Even as I watched a thick drop of blood and excrement fell from her toe.

I don't remember going down to Mrs. Trajillo's apartment. I have a feeling that I tried to use Poinsettia's phone, but it had been disconnected.


"Sure," said Officer Andrew Reedy, a rangy and towheaded policeman. "She kicks over the chair after tying the knot." He was looking at the overturned chair that lay halfway across the room, then continued, "And bingo! She's hung. You said she was despondent, right, Mr. Rawlins?"

"Yeah," I answered him. "She was being evicted by Mofass."

"Who's that?" asked Quinten Naylor. He was Reedy's partner and the only Negro policeman I'd ever seen, up to that time, in plainclothes. He was also looking at that chair.

"He manages the place, collects the rent and the like."

"Who does he manage for?" Naylor asked me.

While I was considering how to answer, Reedy said, "Who cares? This is a suicide. We just tell 'em that she killed herself and that's that."

Naylor was of medium height but he was wide and so gave the feeling of largeness and strength. He was the opposite of his partner in every way, but they seemed to have a kind of rapport.

Naylor walked up to, almost under the hanging corpse. It seemed as if he were sniffing for something wrong.

"Aw, com'on, Quint," Reedy whined. "Who wants to murder this girl? I mean all sneaky-like, pretending she killed herself? Did she have any enemies, Mr. Rawlins?"

"Not that I know of."

"Look at her face, though, Andy. Those could be fresh bruises," Naylor said.

"Sometimes strangulation from hanging does that, Quint," Reedy pleaded.

"Hey listen," the fat ambulance attendant shouted from the hall. I'd called the hospital too, even though I knew she was dead. "When can we cut 'er down an' get outta here?"

He was not my favorite kind of white man.

"Hold up on that," Naylor said. "We got an investigation going here and we can't have the evidence disturbed. I want someone to photograph the room first."

"Aw, geez," Reedy sighed.

"Shit," the fat man said. Then, "Okay, we go, but who signs for the call?"

"We didn't call so you can't charge us," Naylor said.

"What about you, son?" the ambulance attendant asked me. He looked to be in his mid-twenties, almost ten years younger than I.

"Can't say that I know. I just called the police," I lied. It was a kind of warm-up lie. I was getting ready for the real lies I'd have to tell later.

The fat man glared at me but that's all he could do.

When the ambulance men left I turned away and saw Poinsettia hanging there. She seemed to be swaying slightly and my stomach started to move with her, so I turned to leave.

Naylor touched my arm and asked, "Who did you say that Mr. Mofass represented?"

"It's just Mofass. He don't go by no other name."

"Who does he represent?" Naylor insisted.

"Can't say I know. I just clean fo' him."

"Geez, Quint," Reedy said. He'd taken out a handkerchief and covered his mouth and nose. That seemed like a good idea, so I pulled out my own rag.

Reedy was an older man, past fifty. Naylor was

young, the ambulance attendant's age. He had probably been a noncommissioned officer in Korea. We got all kinds of things out of that war. Integration, advancement of some colored soldiers, and lots of dead boys.

"Don't look right, Andy," Naylor said. "Let's give it a little bit more."

"Who's gonna care about this one girl, Quint?"

"I care," was all the young policeman answered. And it made me proud. It was the first time I had ever seen civilian blacks and whites dealing with each other in an official capacity. I mean, the first time I'd seen them acting as equals. They were really working together.

"You need me for that?" I asked.

"No, Mr. Rawlins," Reedy sighed. "Just give me your address and phone number and we'll call you for a statement if we need to."

I gave him my address and phone. He wrote them down in a leather-bound notepad that he took from his pocket.

Downstairs, I told Mrs. Trajillo what was happening with the police. She was not only the burglar alarm but she was also a kind of newsletter for the neighborhood.

# 11

I LAMENTED POINSETTIA'S DEATH. SHE'D COME DOWN IN the world, but that was no reason to wish her ill. It was a senseless and brutal death whether she killed herself or somebody else did it. But if it was suicide I dreaded the thought that she did herself in over the threat of eviction; an eviction I knew was wrong. I tried to put that thought out of my mind but it burrowed there, in the back of my thoughts, like a gopher tunneling under the ground.

But, no matter how I felt, life had to go on.

I picked EttaMae up on Sunday morning. She was wearing a royal-blue dress with giant white lilies stitched into it. Her hat was eggshell-white, just a layered cap on the side of her head. Her shoes were white too. Etta never wore high heels because she was a tall woman, just a few inches shorter than I.

On the way I asked her, "You talk to Mouse?"

"I called him yesterday, yeah."

"An' what he say?"

"Just like always. He start out fine, but then he get that funny sound in his voice. Then he talkin' 'bout how he *will not be denied,* like I owe 'im sumpin'. Shit! I'ma have t'kill Raymond if he start comin' round scarin' LaMarque like he did in Texas."

"He say anything to LaMarque?"

"Naw. He won't even talk to the boy no more. Why you ask?"

"I dunno."

First African Baptist Church was a big salmon-colored building, built on the model of an old Spanish monastery. There was a large mosaic that stood out high on the wall. Jesus hung there, bleeding red pebbles and suffering all over the congregation. Nobody seemed to notice, though. All the men and women, and children too, were dressed in their finest. Gowns and silk suits, patent-leather shoes and white gloves. The smiles and bows that passed between the sexes on Sunday would have been scandalous anywhere else.

But Sunday was a time to feel good and look good. The flock was decked out and bouncy, waiting for word from the Lord.

Rita Cook came with Jackson Blue. He probably sniffed after her and moved in when Mouse got bored. That's the way most men do it, they let other men break the ice, then they have clear sailing.

Dupree and his new wife, Zaree, were there. She had once told me that her name was from Africa and I asked her from what part of Africa. She didn't know and was angry at me for making her look foolish—after that we never got along too well.

I saw Oscar Jones, Odell's older brother, on the stairs to the church. Etta was saying hello to all the people she hadn't seen yet, so I moved toward where Oscar stood.

As I suspected, Odell was there standing in the shadow of a stucco pillar facade.

"Easy," Oscar said.

"Howdy, Oscar. Odell."

They were brothers, and closer than that. Two men with slightly different faces whose clothes hung on them the same way. They were both soft-spoken men. I'd seen them talking but I'd never heard a word that one said to the other.

"Odell," I said. "I got to talk to you."

"Why don't you come over here."

I waved at Oscar and he bowed to me, that was about a year of conversation for us.

Odell and I walked around the side of the church, down a narrow cement path.

When we were alone I told him, "Listen, man, I got some business with a white man work here."

"Chaim Wenzler?"

"How you know 'bout it?"

"He the only white man here, Easy. I don't mean here today, 'cause he a Jew an' they worship on Saturday—or so I hear."

"I need to get next to 'im."

"What do you mean, Easy?"

"I gotta find out about him fo' the law. Tax man got me by the nuts on this income tax thing an' if I don't do this he gonna bust me."

"So what you want?"

"A li'l introduction is all. Maybe something like workin' fo' the church. I could take it from there."

He didn't answer right away. I know that he was uncomfortable with me nosing around his church. But Odell was a good friend and he proved it by nodding and saying, "Okay," when he had thought it out.

But then he said, "I heard about Poinsettia Jackson."

We stood before a small green door. Odell had his hand on the knob but he was waiting for my reply before he'd open up.

"Yeah." I shook my head. "Cops wanna chase it down, but I can't see that somebody killed her. Who'd wanna kill a sick woman like that?"

"I don't know, Easy. All I do know is that you talkin' 'bout all kindsa trouble you in an' the next thing I see one'a the people live in your buildin' is dead."

"Ain't got nuthin' to do with me, Odell. It's just a crazy coincidence is all." That is what I believed, and so Odell believed it too.

He led me down the stairs to the basement of the church, where the deacons gathered and suited up before the service. We came upon five men wearing identical black suits and white gloves. Above the left-hand breast pocket of each jacket was sewn a green flag that said *First African* in bright yellow letters. Each man carried a dark walnut tray with a green felt center.

The tallest man was olive brown and had a pencil-thin mustache. His hair was cut short but it was straightened so that he could comb a part on the left side of his head. He smelled of pomade. This man was handsome in a mean sort of way. I knew that the women of the congregation all coveted his attention. But once they got it, Jackie Orr left them at home crying. He was the head deacon at First African and women were only the means to his success.

"How ya doin', Brother Jones?" Jackie smiled. He came over to us and grabbed Odell's right hand with his two gloved ones.

"Brother Rawlins," he said to me.

"Mo'nin', Jackie," I said. I didn't like the man, and one thing I can't stand is calling a man you don't like "brother."

Odell said, "Easy say he wanna do some work fo' the church, Jackie. I tole'im 'bout Mr. Wenzler, you know how you said Chaim might need a driver."

It was the first I'd heard of it.

But Jackie said, "Yeah, yeah, that's right. So you wanna help out, huh, Brother Rawlins?"

"That's right. I heard that you been doin' some good work wit' old people an' the sick."

"You got that right! Reverend Towne don't believe that charity is just a word. He knows what the Lord's work is, amen on that."

A couple of the deacons seconded his amen.

Two of the deacons were just boys. I guess they had to join a gang one way or another, and the church won out.

The other two were old men. Gentle, pious men who could hold a jostling, impetuous baby boy in their arms all day and never complain, or even think about complaining. They'd never want Jackie's senior position, because that was something outside their place.

Jackie was a political man. He wanted power in the church, and being deacon was the way to get it. He might have been thirty but he held himself like a mature man in his forties or fifties. Older men gave him leeway because they could sense his violence and his vitality. The women sensed something else, but they let him get away with his act too.

I said, "I got a lotta free time in the day, Jackie, and I could get my evenings pretty free if I had t'. You know Mofass an' me got a understandin' so that I can always make a little time. An' Odell says that's what you need, a man who could make some free time."

"That's right. Why'ont you come over tomorrow, around four. That's when we have the meetin'."

We shook hands and I went away.

Etta was looking for me. She was ready for the word of God.

I could have used a drink.

# 12

FIRST AFRICAN WAS A BEAUTIFUL CHURCH ON THE INSIDE too. A large rectangular room with a thirty-foot ceiling that held two hundred chairs on a gently sloping floor. The rows of seats came down in two tiers toward the pulpit. The podium that stood up front was a light ash stand adorned with fresh yellow lilies and draped with deep purple banners. Behind the minister's place, slightly off to the left, rose thirty plush velvet chairs, in three rows, for the choir.

There were six stained-glass windows on either side of the room. Jesus at the mountain, John the Baptist baptizing Jesus, Mary and Mary Magdalen prostrate before the Cross. Bright cellophane colors: reds, blues, yellows, browns, and greens. Each window was about fifteen feet high. Giants of the Bible shining down on us mortals.

We might have been poor people but we knew how to build a house of prayer, and how to bury our loved ones.

Etta and I went to seats toward the middle of the room. She sat next to Ethel Marmoset and I sat on the aisle. Odell and Mary sat in front of us. Jackson and Rita stood at the back. People were coming in through the three large doors at the back of the church, and they were all talking, but in hushed tones so that there was a feeling of silence against the hubbub of voices.

When everybody was seated or situated in back, Melvin Pride came down the center aisle with Jackie Orr at his heel. Melvin was what First African called a senior deacon, a man who has paid his dues. While they came in I noticed that the other deacons had spaced themselves evenly along either side of the congregation. The choir, dressed in purple satin gowns, entered from behind the pulpit and stood before the red velvet chairs.

Finally, Winona Fitzpatrick came down the aisle, twenty feet behind Melvin and Jackie. She was the chairwoman of the church council. Winona was large woman in a loose black gown and a wide-brimmed black hat that had a sky-blue satin band. The room was so quiet by then that you could hear the harsh rasp of Winona's stockinged thighs.

As I watched her progress I noticed a large young man watching me from across the aisle. He was wearing a decent brown suit that had widely spaced goldenrod stripes. His broad-rimmed fedora was in his lap. His stony dull eyes were on me.

Jackie took his place as lead singer of the choir, and Melvin stood before the group with his hands upraised. Then he looked down behind him, and for the first time I saw a small woman sitting at a large organ just below the podium.

Then there was music. The deep strains of the organ and Jackie's high tenor voice. The choir sang in back of that.

"Angels," Etta muttered. "Just angels."

They sang "A Prayer to Sweet Baby Jesus." After Melvin was sure he'd guided them into harmony he turned to add his bass to Jackie's high voice.

Melvin was Jackie's height, but he was black and craggy. When he sang he grimaced as if in pain. Jackie seemed more like a suitor trying to talk his way into the bedroom.

The song filled the church and I loved it even though I was there for something else. Even though I was going to go against a member, or at least a helper, of that flock, still the love of God filled me. And that was strange, because I had stopped believing in God on the day my father left me as a child in poverty and pain.

"Brothers and sisters!" Reverend Towne shouted. I hadn't been looking when he came to the dais. He was a very tall man with a big belly that bulged out from his deep blue robes. He was dark brown with strong African features and dense, straightened hair that was greased and combed back away from his forehead.

He ran his left hand over his hair as the last members of the crowd went silent, then he looked out over the faces and grinned and shook his head slowly as if he had seen someone who had been missing for years.

"I'm happy to see you all here this Sunday morning. Yes I am."

No one spoke but there was a kind of shudder in the room.

He held his big open hands out toward us, relishing our human warmth as if he stood before a fire.

"Was a time once when I saw a lotta empty chairs out there."

"Amen," one of the elder deacons intoned.

73

"Was a time," the minister said, and then he paused. "Yes. Was a time that we didn't have no peanut gallery in the back. Was a time ev'rybody could sit and listen to the word of the Lord. They could sit and meditate on his spirit.

"But no more."

He looked around the room, and I did too. Everyone else had their eyes on him. The women had a kind of stunned look on the whole, their heads tilted upwards in order to bask in the peculiar and cool light that flowed from the stained-glass windows. The men were serious, by and large. They were concentrating every fiber of their wills to understand the ways of righteousness and the Lord in their everyday lives. All except the man in the brown suit. His stony glare was still on my profile, and I was wondering about him.

"No, no more," the minister almost sang. "Because now He is marching."

"Yes, Lord!" an old woman shouted from down front.

"That's right," the minister spoke. "We are going to have to go to the church council to expand the roof of the Lord. Because you know he wants all of you in his flock. He wants all of you to praise his name. Say it. Say, yes Je-sus."

We did, and the sermon started in earnest.

Towne didn't quote from the Bible or talk about salvation. The whole sermon was aimed at the dead and maimed boys coming back home from Korea. Reverend Towne worked in a special clinic that tended to the severely wounded. He spoke especially long and poignantly about Wendell Boggs, a young man who'd lost his legs, most of his fingers, one eye, the other eyelid, and his lips in the service of America. Bethesda Boggs, a member of the congregation, wailed as if to underscore his terrible litany.

Together they, mother and minister, had us all squirming in our chairs.

After a while he started talking about how war was a product of man and of Satan, not God. It was Satan who waged war against God in his own home. It was Satan who had men kill when they could turn the other cheek. And it was Satan who led us in war against the Koreans and the Chinese.

"Satan will take on the guise of a good man," Reverend Towne intoned. "He will appear as a great leader, and you will be blinded by what looks like the fireworks of glory. But when the smoke clears and you squint around to see, you will be surrounded by the wages of sin. Dead men will be your steppingstones and blood will be your water. Your sons will be wounded and dead, and where will God be?"

He had me back on the front lines. I was choking the life out of a blond teenage boy and crying and laughing, and ready for a woman too.

He ended the sermon like this:

"My question to you is, what are you going to do about Wendell Boggs? What can you do?" Then he made a gesture toward the choir, and Melvin lifted his hands again. The organ started up and the choir rose in song. The music was still beautiful but the sermon had turned it sour. There was a collection by the deacons, but many people left even before the plate got to them.

Everywhere people were grumbling.

"What do he mean? What can I do?"

"A minister ain't no politician, that's illegal."

"We cain't hep it."

"Communists are against God. We gotta fight 'em."

Etta turned to me and took hold of my hand. She said, "Take me home, Easy."

# 13

TOWNE WAS OUT IN FRONT OF THE CHURCH WITH WINONA, Melvin, Jackie, and a couple I didn't know. The couple were older and they looked uncomfortable. They'd probably shaken the minister's hand every Sunday for twenty or more years and they weren't going to stop just because Towne gave one sour sermon.

"Easy," Melvin said. We knew each other from the old days back in the fifth ward, in Houston, Texas.

"Melvin."

Jackie was wringing his hands. Winona was gazing at Reverend Towne. It was only then that I noticed Shep, Winona's little husband, standing in the doorway. I hadn't seen him in church.

"That was a powerful and brave sermon, minister," Etta said. She walked up to him and shook his hand so hard that his jowls shook.

"Thank you, thank you very much," he replied. "It's good t'have you up here, Sister Alexander. I hope you're planning to stay for a while."

"That all depends," Etta said, and then she stole a quick glance at me.

Winona stepped up and said something to Towne, I couldn't make out what, then Etta asked, "How is that boy's folks? You think I could he'p 'em?"

I had to laugh at those women fighting over the minister. I think Etta was doing it just because she didn't like to see Winona flirting there in front of her own husband.

I saw Jackie and Melvin move to the bottom of the stairway. There they began to argue. Jackie was waving his hands in the air and Melvin was making placating gestures, holding his palms toward the handsome man as if he were trying to press Jackie's anger down.

I would have liked to know what they were fighting about, but that was merely curiosity, so I turned back to EttaMae.

She had linked arms with the minister and they were walking away. Etta was saying, "Why don't you introduce me to the poor woman, I could maybe do the cooking on some days."

I got to look over my shoulder to see Melvin and Jackie still arguing at the bottom of the stair. Melvin was stealing glances up at me.

"Go get the car, Shep," Winona said, casual and cruel.

"Okay," he answered. Then little brown Shep, in his rayon red-brown suit, went away to the parking lot.

"Etta with you, Easy?" Winona asked before Shep disappeared around the building.

"Say what?"

"You heard me, Easy Rawlins. Is EttaMae your woman?"

"Etta ain't rightly nobody's, Winona. She don't hardly even like t'think she belongs t'Jesus."

"Don't fool with me," she warned. "That bitch is givin' the minister the eye, an' if she free it's gonna have t'stop."

"He married?" I asked, shocked.

"'Course not!"

"Well, Etta ain't neither."

I shrugged and Winona gnashed her teeth. She went down the stairway in a huff.

I looked down at the bottom of the stairs, but Jackie

and Melvin were gone, so I turned to enter the church. I found myself at about chest level with a brown suit that had goldenrod stripes. He was standing on a higher stair but even if we stood toe to toe he would have towered over me.

"You Rawlins, ain't you?" he asked in a voice that was either naturally rough or husky with emotion.

"That's right," I said, taking a step backward so I could see his face and move out of range.

His brown face, which clashed with his suit, was smallish, perfectly round, childlike and mean.

"I want you t'take me to yo' boss."

"And why is that?" I asked.

"I got business with'im."

"This is Sunday, son. On today we s'posed t'rest."

"Listen, man," he threatened. His voice cracked. "I know all about you . . ."

"Yeah?"

"You di'n't lift a finger." He was quoting someone. "She tole me 'bout how he used her, how he took her fo' money an' then he just let her slide when she got sick. She could just die an' all you care 'bout was yo'self."

"What's your name, man?"

"I'm Willie Sacks." He puffed up his shoulders. "Now let's go." He put his hand on my shoulder but I brushed it off.

"You Poinsettia's boyfriend?" I asked. I wasn't going anywhere.

He threw a punch at me that would have put a hole in a brick wall. I crouched down under it though, grabbing his wrist as I did, and came up behind him twisting his arm and wrenching his giant thumb.

Willie said, "Oh!" and knelt on the stair.

"I don't wanna hurt ya, boy," I whispered in Willie's ear. "But you make me damage this suit an' I'm a do some damage on you."

"I kill you!" he shouted. "I kill all'a you!"

I let him go and moved down a few stairs.

"What's your problem, Willie?"

"Take me t'Mofass!"

He stood up. In that shade I felt like David without his slingshot.

It's hard for a big man to throw a punch downward. I let his fist snap somewhere off to the west and then I gave him one and two in the lower gut. Willie folded like a peel bug and rolled down the stairs.

He got right up though, so I ran down and hit him again, on the side of his head that time. I hit him hard enough to hurt a normal man, but Willie was more like a buffalo. I hit him as hard as I could and all he did was sit down.

"I don't wanna hurt you, Willie," I said, more to distract me from the pain in my hand than to worry him.

"When I get up from here we gonna see who gonna be hurt." There were patches of bloody flesh on his face, scrapes from the granite stairs.

"Poinsettia ain't nobody's fault, Willie," I said. "Let it go."

But he lurched to his feet and came shambling up the stair. I lost patience and broke his nose. I could feel the bone give under my knuckle. I was considering his left ear when I felt a blow to my back. It wasn't hard, but I was tensed for a fight, so I swung around, only to be hit in the face with something like a pillow. A tiny woman in a frilly pink dress was swinging her woven string purse at my head. She didn't say a word, saving all of her energy for the fight.

She might have kept it up, but when Willie yelled, "Momma!" she forgot about me and ran to his side.

He was cupping his hands under the bloody faucet of his nose.

"Willie! Willie!"

"Momma!"

"Willie!"

She pushed him until he was up off his knees and then dragged him away, down the street.

Twice the pink-and-brown woman glared at me. She was tiny and wore white-rimmed glasses. Her lips caved inward where teeth once held them firm. Mrs. Sacks couldn't lift her son's arm, but I was more frightened of those killer stares than I would have been of a whole platoon of Willies.


"Sit down on the couch here next to me, honey, not way over there." Etta patted the green fabric next to her.

We were in her new apartment on Sixty-fourth Street. It was a nice six-unit apartment building. Her place had two bedrooms, a shower, and blue wall-to-wall shag carpets. LaMarque was with Lucy Rideau and her two girls. They had all gone to Bible school and now they were having Sunday supper.

"I should really get on to work, Etta."

"On Sunday?"

"I'ma be doin' some extra work fo' the church so I gotta make up my time on the weekend."

"Now what you gonna be doin' fo' the Lord, Easy Rawlins?"

"We all do our li'l piece, Etta. We all do our li'l piece."

"Like you makin' so LaMarque an' me ain't gotta pay no rent to that terrible man?"

"Mofass ain't so bad. He lettin' you stay here, ain't he?"

"He give me this furniture too?"

"We had an eviction last year an' this stuff been in my garage. I tole'im I'd haul it off to the dump."

"You coulda sold this stuff, Easy. That bed in there is mahogany."

When I didn't answer she said, "Come here, baby, sit down."

I did.

"What's wrong, Easy?"

"Nuthin', Etta, nuthin'."

"Then why you ain't come by. You got me a house an' furniture. You must like us t'do all that."

"Sure I like you."

"Then why'ont you come over an' show me how much?"

Her hand was on my neck. She was much warmer than I was.

Etta's dress was silken and flimsy under her jacket. The bodice was low-cut and her breasts bulged upward when she leaned toward me.

"I thought you didn't wanna see me no mo'," I said.

"I's jus' mad, honey," she said as she leaned toward me. "Thas all."

For some reason I imagined what Wendell Boggs must have looked like on his deathbed. There was fresh blood on his half-face and a whitish scab where one of his eyes should have been.

"Easy?"

"Yeah, Etta?"

"I got the papers to my divorce in the other room."

She shifted slightly to bring her left knee over her right one, nudging my leg. Her dress looked very tight, like it wanted to burst.

"I don't need to see 'em," I said.

"Yes you do."

"No."

"Yes, Easy. You need to see that I'm a free woman and that I can have what I want."

"It ain't you, Etta, it's me," I said, but I kissed her anyway.

"You got me all riled up though, honey." She kissed me back. "Gettin' my house an' my bed, takin' me t' church, mmm, I love that."

We didn't talk for a little while then.

When she leaned back, and I got a moment to breathe, I asked, "But what about Raymond?"

Etta took my hand and put it on her chest, then she gazed at me with eyes that I dream about to this very day.

"Do you want me?" she asked.

"Yeah."

She pressed a finger against my shirt, where my nipple was.

"Then I tell you what," she whispered.

"What?" Just that one word drained all the breath out of me.

"You don't talk about him now an' I won't say nuthin' 'bout him when we wake up."

# 14

I GOT HOME IN THE EARLY EVENING. THE PHONE WAS RINGing as I got to the door. I tried to get the key into the lock but I was too much in a hurry and dropped it in a pile of fallen passion-fruit leaves. The phone kept ringing, though, and it rang until I rummaged around, found the key, and made it inside the door. But I tripped on the doormat and by the time I got off the floor and limped to the coffee table the ringing had finally ceased.

Then I massaged my bruised knee and went to the bathroom. Just as I began to relieve myself the phone started ringing again. But I had learned my lesson. The phone rang while I rinsed my hands and dried them. It rang until I had made it back to the coffee table and then it stopped again.

I was in the kitchen with a quart bottle of vodka in

one hand and a tray of ice in the other when he called again. I considered yanking the line out of the wall, thought better of it, and finally I answered the phone.

The first thing I heard was a child screaming. "No! No!" he, or she, yelled. And then, "No," still a yell but muted as if someone had closed a door on a torture room.

"Mr. Rawlins?" IRS Agent Reginald Lawrence asked.

"Yeah?"

"I wanted to ask you a couple of questions and to give you some advice."

"What questions?"

"What was the deal that Agent Craxton offered you?"

"I don't know if I can really say, sir. I mean, he said that it was government business and that I had to be quiet on that."

"We all work for the same government. I'm a government man too."

"But he's the FBI. He's the law."

"He just represents another *branch* of the government. And his branch doesn't have anything to do with mine."

"Then why you askin' 'bout what he wants?"

"I want to know what he's offered you, because he cannot offer anything on behalf of the Internal Revenue. Once our office commits itself we have to see an investigation through. We have no other choice. You see, I have to follow this investigation or my records" —he paused for a moment, looking for the right words—"my records will be incomplete. So you see, no matter what anyone says, I will have to draw up papers for the court case tomorrow morning."

"What can I do about that?" I asked. "He got me on a federal case an' I'm doing' it. If I tell you his business I'll be in even more trouble than I am already."

"I cannot speak for the FBI, all I can tell you is that if you attempt to avoid paying your taxes, even by working for the FBI, we will still be there when everything is over. I have spoken to my supervisor and he agrees with me on this point. You will have to submit your tax records to me by Wednesday of next week or we will have to subpoena you."

"So you talked this over with Wadsworth, huh?" I asked when he'd run out of wind.

"Who told you . . ." he started to ask, but I guess the answer came to him.

"I'm sorry, but I can't help you, Mr. Lawrence. I got my cards and you got yours. I guess we'll just have to play it out."

"I know that you think you're helping yourself, Mr. Rawlins, but you're wrong. You cannot escape your responsibilities to the government." He sounded like a textbook.

"Mr. Lawrence, I don't know about you, but I take Sundays off."

"This problem won't go away, son."

"Okay, that's it. I'm puttin' the phone down now."

Before I could Mr. Lawrence hung up in my ear.

I went back to the kitchen and put the vodka away. I got my bottle of thirty-year-old imported Armagnac from behind a loose board in the closet. There was a snifter sitting next to it. I learned how to drink good liquor from a rich white man I worked for once. I found that if you could savor the booze, I mean if you took longer to drink it, then the intoxication was more pleasurable. And I liked drinking alone when I wanted to be drunk. No loud stories or laughing; all I wanted was oblivion.

The tax man wanted to send me to jail, it was personal with him. And Craxton was lying, I was sure about that, so I had no idea what it was he really wanted. I might not find a thing on his communists, and then he'd just throw me back to the dogs, he might have done so anyway. I considered trying to sign my property over to someone in the meanwhile, just to cover my bases. But I didn't like that idea because I wanted to put my name on the deeds. I wanted EttaMae. I wanted her with all my heart. If she was to be mine then I had to be a man of substance to buy her clothes and make her home.

Of course, that meant that either Mouse or I had to die, I knew that. I knew it but I didn't want to admit it.

On Monday I went to Mofass' office. He was sitting behind the desk glowering at a plate of pork chops and eggs. A boy in the neighborhood brought up his breakfast every morning at about eleven. Mofass stared at the food for sometimes up to half an hour before eating. He never told me why, but I always imagined that he was afraid that the boy spat in it. That's the kind of insult that Mofass always feared.

"Mornin', Mofass."

"Mr. Rawlins."

He picked up a chop by its fatty bone and took a bite out of the eye.

"I ain't gonna be 'round much for the next three or four weeks. I got business t'take care of."

"I'm doin' business ev'ry day, Mr. Rawlins. I cain't take no vacation or you'd go broke," he chided through a mass of mashed meat.

"That's why you get paid, Mofass."

"Yeah, I guess," he said. He scooped a good half of the scrambled egg into his mouth.

"Anything happenin' that I need to know about?" I asked.

"Not that I know of. The police come and asked about Poinsettia." A brief shadow worked its way across Mofass' face. I remember thinking that even a hard man like that could feel pain at a young woman's demise. "I told 'em that I only knew that she was five months behind on the rent. That Negro cop didn't like my attitude, so I advised him to come back when he had a warrant."

"I wanted to talk to you about her," I said.

He looked at me with only mild interest.

"Her boyfriend, Willie Sacks, tried t'knock my head off in front of First African Sunday."

"How come?" Mofass asked.

"He wanted you, and I didn't wanna tell'im where you was."

Mofass took a mouthful of egg and nodded. As soon as he got the mess down to the size of a golf ball he said, "Okay."

"But he was sayin' somethin' like whatever happened to her, I mean like her accident, had sumpin' t'do with you."

"That boy's jes' grievin', Mr. Rawlins. He done left'er when she got sick and now he wanna blame somebody else when she up and kills herself." He shrugged slightly. Harder than diamonds is right.

Mofass was contemptuous but I still felt bad. I knew what it was to be the cause of another human being's demise. I had felt that guilt myself.

"You want me to hire somebody to take care of the work 'round the places while you on vacation?" Mofass asked.

He knew I didn't like to be called lazy.

"I'm just doin' some extra work, man. Somethin' gotta do with that tax thing."

"What?"

He stopped eating and picked up a cigar that had been in a glass ashtray on his desk.

"They got me doin' 'em a li'l favor. I do that right an' the taxes get easier."

"What could the IRS need from you?"

"Not them exactly." I didn't want to tell him that I was working for the FBI. "Anyway they want me t' find a guy gotta do with the minister down at First African. Maybe he owes 'em mo' taxes than me."

Mofass just shook his head. I could tell he didn't believe me.

"So you be at church the next couple of weeks?"

"More or less."

"I guess you gonna be *prayin'* off them taxes instead'a payin' 'em."

He made a sound like coughing. At first I thought he was choking but then as it got louder I realized that Mofass was laughing. He put his cigar down and pulled out the whitest pocket handkerchief I'd ever seen. He blew his nose and wiped tears from his eyes and he was still laughing.

"Mofass!" I yelled, but he just kept on laughing.

"Mofass!"

He added a little catch in his throat, sort of like a far-off goose calling her mate. The tears flowed.

Finally I gave up and walked out.

I stood outside for a few minutes, listening behind the closed door; he laughed the whole time I stood there.

In the late afternoon, I went to First African.

The front of the church was on 112th Street and went all the way through the block to 112th Place. The back entrance was just a door in a rough stucco wall, like a small office building, maybe a dentist's office. On the first floor there was an entrance and a short hall with a few plywood doors on either side. At the end of the tan-carpeted hall was a stairwell that went up and down. Odell had told me that the minister had his office and apartment on the upper floor and that there was a kitchen and cafeteria space in the basement.

I went down to the basement.

There I saw a scene that had been a constant in my

life since I was a small boy. Black women. Lots of them. Cooking in the industrial-size kitchen and talking loud, laughing and telling stories. But all I really saw was their hands. Working hands. Laying out plates, peeling yams, folding sheets and tablecloths into perfect squares, washing, drying, stacking, and pushing from here to there. Women who lived by working. Brushing the hair of their own children, or brushing the hair of some neighborhood child whose parents were gone, either for the night or for good. Cooking, yes, but there was lots of other work for a Negro woman. Dressing wounds of the men they started out being so proud of. Punishing children, white and black. And working for God in His house and at home.

My own mother, sick as she was, made sweet-potato pies for a church dinner on the night she died. She was twenty-five years old.

"Evenin', Easy," Parker Lamont said. He was one of the elder deacons. I hadn't seen him when I walked in.

"Parker."

"Odell and the others are out in the back," he said and began to lead me through the crowd of working women.

Many of them said hello to me. I moved around the neighborhoods quite a bit in those days and if I saw that one of the ladies needed some help I was happy to oblige; there's all kinds of truth and insight in gossip, and the only key you need is a helping hand.

Winona Fitzpatrick was there. She was bright and full of life even though she didn't smile at me. She was wearing a flattering white dress that wasn't made for the kind of work people were doing. But she wasn't working either. The chairwoman of the church council, she was the power behind the throne, as it were.

"What's goin' on here?" I asked Parker.

"What?"

"All this cookin' an' stuff."

"Gonna be a meetin' of the N double-A C P. Ev'ry chapter in southern California."

"Tonight?"

"Yeah."

He led me through a maze of long dining tables and through an open doorway in the back. This led to a closed door. I could smell the smoke even before we went in.

There I found a room full of black men. All of them smoking and sitting in various positions of ease.

It was a smallish room with a threadbare light green carpet and a few folding tables that the men used to hold their ashtrays. There were checkerboards and dominoes out but nobody was playing. There was a sour smell under the smoky odor. The smell of men's breath.

Odell rose to meet me.

"Easy," he said. "I want you to meet Wilson and Grant."

We nodded at each other.

"Pleased t'meetcha," I said.

Dupree was there and some other men I knew.

"Melvin and the minister be down in a few minutes. They upstairs right now," he said. "And this here is Chaim, Chaim Wenzler."

The white man had been sitting on the other side of Dupree, so I hadn't seen him. He was short and hunched over in a serious conversation with a man I didn't know.

But when he heard his name he straightened up and looked at me.

"This is Easy Rawlins, Chaim. He's got some free time in the week an' wants t' help out."

"Wonderful," Chaim said in a strong voice. He stood up to shake my hand. "I need the help, Mr. Rawlins. Thank you."

"Easy. Call me Easy."

"We are doing work in the neighborhood," he said. He indicated a chair for me and sat himself. We'd gone right to work. I liked him even though I didn't want to.

"Food for old people, some driving maybe. I don't drive and it's hard to get a ride when you need it. Sometimes my daughter drives me, but she works, we all work." He winked on that. "And sometimes we need to take messages about meetings here at the church and some other places."

"What kinda meetin's?"

He hunched his thick shoulders. "Meetings about work. We do lots of work, Mr. Rawlins."

I smiled. "Well, what kind of work you want from me?"

He gave me the once-over then and I took him in. Chaim was short and powerful. His head was bald and I would have put his age at about fifty-five. His eyes were gray, about the same color as Mouse's eyes, but they looked different in Chaim. Chaim's eyes were piercing and intelligent but they were also generous, rather than cruel. Generosity was a feeling that Mouse only had after someone he didn't like had died.

You could see something else in Chaim's eyes. I didn't know what it was at the time but I could see that there was a deep pain in that man. Something that made me sad.

"We need to get clothes," he said at last.

"Say what?"

"Old clothes for the old people. I get people to donate them and then we have a sale."

He leaned toward me in a confidential manner and said, "You know we have to sell it to them because they don't like to be given wit'out paying."

"What you do with the money?"

"A little lunch wit' the sale and it's gone." He slapped his hands together indicating breaking even.

"Yeah, okay," I said. But there must've been a question in my voice.

"You have something to ask, maybe?" He smiled into my eyes.

"Naw, not really . . . it's just that . . ."

"Yes?"

There were people around us but they weren't listening.

"Well, it's like this," I said. "I cain't see why somebody ain't even from down there wanna do all this an' they ain't even bein' paid."

"You are right, of course," he said. "A man works for money or family or," he shrugged, "some men work for God."

"That what move you? You a religious man?"

"No." He shook his head grimly. "No, I'm not a religious man, not anymore."

"So here you don't even believe in God but you gonna do charity for the church?"

I was pushing him and wishing I wasn't. But something bothered me about Chaim Wenzler and I wanted to find out what it was.

He smiled again. "I believe, Mr. Rawlins. Even more—I know. God turned his back on me." The way he looked at me reminded me of something, or someone. "He turned his back on all the Jews. He set the demons on us. I believe, Mr. Rawlins. There could not be such evil as I have seen wit'out a God."

"I guess I could see that."

"And that's why I'm here," Wenzler said. "Because Negroes in America have the same life as the Jew in Poland. Ridiculed, segregated. We were hung and burned for just being alive."

It was then that I remembered Hollis Long.

Hollis was a friend of my father. They used to get together every Saturday afternoon on the front porch. Being the only two black men in the parish that could read, they would smoke pipes and discuss all the newspaper articles that they had read in the past week.

Hollis was a big man. I remember him laughing and bringing me presents of fruit or hard candy. I'd sit on the floor between the two men and listen to them talk about events in New Orleans, Houston, and other southern capitals. Sometimes they'd talk about northern cities or even foreign lands like China or France.

Then one weekday I came home from school to find my mother standing over the wood stove crying. My father stood next to her with his arm around her shoulders. Hollis Long was sitting at the table drinking straight whiskey from a clay jug. The look in his eye, the same look that Chaim Wenzler had when he was talking about God, told of something terrible.

No one spoke to me, so I ran out of the house down to the sugarcane field that bordered our land.

That night Hollis slept at our house. He stayed there for two weeks before going away to Florida for good. And every night I could hear him moaning and crying. Sometimes I'd be wrenched out of sleep because Hollis would get from his bed hollering and smashing the walls with his fists.

After the first night my mother told me that there was a fire while Hollis was gone lumbering with my father. His wife and sons and mother all perished in the flames.

"When I had given up everything," Chaim said, "men came and saved me. They helped me to take vengeance. And now it is my turn to help."

All I could do was nod. When God abandoned Hollis Long there was no one to save him.

"We must help each other, Easy. Because there are men out there who would steal the meat from your bones."

I thought about agents Lawrence and Craxton and I looked away.

He put his hand on my shoulder and said, "We will work together."

I said, "All right."

"You got time tomorrow?" he asked, and then he touched the back of my hand the way John had when he was concerned for me.

"Maybe not tomorrow, but in a couple'a days."

And it was done. Chaim and I were partners working for the poor and elderly. Of course, I was trying to hang him too.

Towne and Melvin came in with a beautiful young woman. Her black skin and bright white dress were a shocking contrast. Tall and shapely, she had straightened brown hair that was shot through with golden strands. Her lips were bright orange and her big brown eyes were on Towne. It was the passion of her gaze that made her beautiful. You could see that she held nothing back.

The minister said a few words to Parker, and then he turned to whisper something to the girl. The way he put his palm against her side I knew they were lovers. It wasn't much but it was very familiar. When I looked away from them I saw Melvin staring hard at me.

They left almost immediately. I could see that this disturbed the men. They expected the minister to represent their church at the meeting. But he had other fish to fry. I did too.

Odell asked me, "You stayin', Ease?"

I said, "No, man, I got some calls t' make."

When I turned to go he grabbed me by the arm. That was only time he'd ever done anything like that. He said, "Don't be messin' wit' us now, Ease. Get what you want from that man, but don't hurt the church."

I smiled as reassuringly as I could and said, "Don't

worry, Odell, all I need is some information. That's all. You won't even notice I was here."

The phone only rang once before he answered.
"Craxton."
"I met 'im."
"Good. What did he say?"
"Nuthin' really. He wants me to get clothes for old people."
"Don't fall for it, Mr. Rawlins. He's only helping those people for his own ends."
Just like I am, I thought. "So what next?"
"String him along for a few weeks, see if he brings you to the others. Milk him for information. Try to sound like you're unhappy with white people and America, he eats that stuff up. Maybe find out if he knows where Andre Lavender is."
I made sounds like I'd do what he wanted and then I asked, "Mr. Craxton?"
"Yes?"
"I got a call from Agent Lawrence the other day."
"About what?"
"He wanted to know what am I going to do about my taxes."
"He did?" Craxton laughed. "You have to hand it to him, the man is loyal to his work."
"His loyalty be my jail term."
"Don't worry, Mr. Rawlins. J. Edgar Hoover pulls every string in Washington. If he says you're all right, then you are."
Mr. Hoover hadn't said a thing to me, but I didn't mention it.
"What was Wenzler doing at the church?" Craxton asked.
"Helpin' with the N double-A C P meeting."
"Yeah, I thought so."
I could almost hear him nodding.

"You thought what?"

"NAACP. That's one of them. One of the so-called civil rights organizations that are full of Reds and people who will one day be Reds."

I thought that he was crazy and then I thought, I'm working for him, so what does that make me?

# 15

CHAIM WENZLER WAS A STRANGE ONE. BUT HE CALLED UP memories in me and I found myself hoping that he wasn't the bad guy Agent Craxton claimed. I figured that as long as Craxton didn't know where to find Andre, that's what I should concentrate on. I suspected that the FBI man wasn't telling me the whole story about what had happened at Champion. And it didn't make sense that he would go to all the trouble springing me from the IRS just to see what might be happening with some union organizer. I needed more information and Andre was my best bet, but getting to him was a crooked road.

Craxton was smart to get a man like me, because the FBI couldn't really mount an investigation in the ghetto. The colored population at that time wasn't readily willing to tell a white man anything resembling the truth; and the FBI was made up exclusively of white men.

I also had the added advantage of knowing Andre and the company he kept.

Andre had gotten a little girl, Juanita Barnes, pregnant and Juanita had a baby boy. I knew that she was living in a little place off Florence and that she wasn't working. Andre was proud of his son and so I figured he went off with Linda because she flattered his manhood, such as it was, and because he could get a few dollars away from her to send for his son. Not to mention whatever trouble he had gotten into with Champion Aircraft and Chaim Wenzler.

Winthrop Hughes, Linda's husband, knew most of that too, but he wouldn't get one word out of Juanita.

It was the kind of job I liked.

I dropped by Juanita's filthy one-room efficiency apartment the next morning with some patch-up work. Juanita liked to think she was good with needle and thread. She told everybody that she earned her board and keep by sewing, but I didn't believe that lie.

Anyway, I went over there with some torn clothes and asked her could she fix them up.

"You might as well throw this stuff out, Easy," she said, holding the crotch up to the window. You could see the birds congregating on the telephone line through the holes in those pants. "They ain't hardly worth the work," she said.

"You mean you don't need t'work?"

"Naw, it ain't like that."

"Look like it t'me. Here I bring you my work pants and you cain't even be bothered with it."

She cowered a little under my gaze. "I just sayin' that you could maybe buy sumpin' better fo'almost much as you gonna pay me."

"Why'ont you let me say how the money goes," I said. I was standing over her. She had little Andre Jr. in her arms.

Andre Jr. was about fourteen months old. He was walking by then and showing some individuality. His mother was a small, hard-looking girl, about the color of a cougar. She was eighteen with small eyes and skinny legs. But even though she was ugly, Juanita had

96

the dazed look of love in her eyes. The look that many women have with their firstborn.

I took Andre Jr. from her and cuddled him to my chest.

"I'll look after the baby while you fix my clothes," I said. I tried to sound like a father and she played the obedient child. When I think on it now I realize that I must've been almost twice her age.

Little Andre and I had a good time. I let him walk on me and sleep on me, I even heated his bottle, letting Juanita check it to see that I wasn't going to scald her baby's tongue. She gave me a few shy smiles while I sat in her padded chair and she sat on the kitchen counter, working at my rags. But what really got her to glow was when I changed his diapers. I laid him out on the counter next to her and played with him so he didn't even cry.

I showed her that I knew how you could put Vaseline on a baby to keep him from chafing. While I was rubbing the stuff on Andre's buttocks Juanita uncrossed her legs, licked her sliver lips, and asked, "You hungry, Easy?" and before I could answer, "'Cause I'm starved."

I couldn't see where I was doing anything wrong.

Juanita didn't have any close family, so she was alone with Andre Jr. most of the time. And everybody knows how a gabbling baby will drive the strongest will to distraction after a while. All I did was keep her company when she needed a man around.

I got steaks, cornbread mix, and greens from the Safeway and made dinner, because Juanita couldn't really cook. After dinner she put Andre Jr. in a cardboard box on a table next to the couch, which she proceeded to unfold into a bed.

Then Juanita took the bottle of Vaseline and showed me some things she knew how to do. She might have been eighteen, and unacquainted with many ways of the world, but Juanita was full of love.

Powerful love. And she had the ability to call forth the love in me.

She pushed me down in that bed and wrapped her arms around me and told me all the things she had dreamed since Andre Sr. had left.

In the middle of the night the baby cried and Juanita tended to him. Then she whispered something to me and before long I was on my knees begging and praying to her like she was a temple and a priestess rolled up into one.

At four in the morning I woke again. I didn't even know where I was. Every tender spot on my body was sore and when I looked at that little girl I felt a kind of awe that verged on fear.

The shades were torn. Light from the granite-columned streetlamp shone on Andre Jr. in his card-board cradle. I could see his tiny lips pushing in and out.

I looked around the rest of the house. Even in the dark it felt dirty. Juanita never really cleaned the floors or walls. There was dirt in that house that had been there before her; it would be there after she had gone.

When I saw the drawers in the kitchen counter I remembered what I was doing there.

In the very bottom drawer, under a few rolls of wrapping paper, was a stack of envelopes held together with a wide rubber band. The postmark, which was all but impossible to make out in the dim light, was from Riverside, and Juanita's name and address were written in a junior high school scrawl. But it was the return address that interested me. I tore off the upper left corner of one letter, shoved it back into the middle of the stack, and pushed the drawer closed.

"What you want, Easy?"

"Tryin' t'get some water but I didn't wanna turn on

the light and wake ya," I said, straightening up quickly.

"You lookin' on the floor fo'some water?"

"I kicked my damn toe!" I tried to sound angry so that she'd let it go.

"Glasses in the cabinet right over your head, honey, get me some too."

When I climbed back into bed Juanita reached for the jar of Vaseline again.

"I'm a little tired, baby," I said.

"Don't worry, Easy, I'ma get you up."

A few hours later sunlight came in through the shade. Juanita was sitting up against the head of the couch with a knowing look in her eye. She had the baby, suckling on his bottle, in her arms.

"How long Andre's father been gone?" I asked.

"Too long," she said.

I lit a cigarette and handed it to her.

"You hear from him at all?"

"Uh-uh. He just gone, thas all." Then she smiled at me. "Don't worry, honey, he ain't gonna come in here. He ain't even in L.A."

"I thought you didn't even know where he was?"

"I heard he was gone."

"From who?"

"I just heard it, thas all."

Her mouth formed a little thin-lipped pout.

I took her foot and rubbed it until she smiled again. Then I asked, "You think you might want him back?"

She said no. But she didn't say it right away. She looked at her baby first and she made like she wanted to pull her foot away from my hand.

I got up and put on my pants.

"Where you goin'?" asked Juanita.

"I gotta meet Mofass at one'a his places at eight," I said.

* * *

I went home and napped for a few hours, then I drove out to Riverside.

Riverside was mainly rural then. No sidewalks or street signs to speak of. I had to go to three gas stations before I found out how to get to Andre's address.

I staked out their place until early evening, when I saw Winthrop's Plymouth coming up the road. It was a turquoise job.

Linda was a big woman, heftier than EttaMae and looser in the flesh. Her skin color was high yellow, that's why Shaker, that is to say Winthrop, took to her in the first place. Her face was lusty and sensual, and poor Andre didn't seem as if he could bear the weight of her arm around his shoulders. His shirttails flapped behind him and I could see the lace string of his right shoe dancing freely. Andre Lavender was a bug-eyed, orange-skinned man. He wasn't fat but he was meaty. He had a good-natured and nervous air about him; Andre would shake your hand three times at any one meeting.

I watched them stagger up the dirt driveway to the house. Linda was singing and Andre sagged sloppily in the mud.

I could have gone up against him then, but I wanted him to talk to me. I needed Andre to be scared, but not of me, so I drove back to L.A., back to a little bar I knew.

# 16

THAT NIGHT I WENT TO THE COZY ROOM ON SLAUSON. IT was a small shack with plaster walls that were held together by tar paper, chicken wire, and nails. It stood in the middle of a big vacant lot, lopsided and ungainly. The only indication you got that it was inhabited was the raw pine plank over the door. It had the word *Entrance* painted on it in dripping black letters.

It was a small room and very dark. The bar was a simple dictionary podium with a row of metal shelves behind it. The bartender was a stout woman named Ula Hines. She served gin or whiskey, with or without water, and unshelled peanuts by the bag. There were twelve small tables hardly big enough for two. The Cozy Room wasn't a place for large parties, it was there for men who wanted to get drunk.

Because it wasn't a social atmosphere Ula didn't invest in a jukebox or live music. She had a radio that played cowboy music and a TV, set on a chair, that only went on for boxing.

Winthrop was at a far table drinking, smoking, and looking mean.

"Evenin', Shaker," I said. Shaker Jones was the name he went by when we were children in Houston. It was only when he became an insurance man that he decided he needed a fancy name like Winthrop Hughes.

Shaker didn't feel very fancy that night.

"What you want, Easy?"

I was surprised that he even recognized me, drunk as he was.

"Mofass sent me."

"Wha' fo'?"

"He need some coverage down on the Magnolia Street apartments."

Shaker laughed like a dying man who gets in the last joke.

"He got them naked gas heaters, he could go to hell," Shaker said.

"He got sumpin' you want though, man."

"He ain't got nuthin' fo'me. Nuthin'."

"How 'bout Linda an' Andre?"

My Aunt Vel hated drunks. She did because she claimed that they didn't have to act all sloppy and stupid the way they did. "It's all in they minds," she'd say.

Shaker proved her point by straightening up and asking, in a very clear voice, "Where are they, Easy?"

"Mofass told me t'get them papers from you, Shaker. He told me t'drive you out almost to 'em an' then you give me the papers an' I take you the whole way."

"I pay you three hundred dollars right now and we cut Mofass out of it."

I laughed and shook my head.

"I'll see ya tomorrow, Shaker." I knew he was sober because he bridled when I called him that. "Front'a Vigilance Insurance at eight-fifteen."

I turned back to look at him before I went out of the door. He was sitting up and breathing deeply. I knew when I saw him that I was all that stood between Andre and an early grave.

I was in front of his office at the time I said. He was right out there waiting for me. He wore a double-breasted pearl-gray suit with a white shirt and a maroon tie that had dozens of little yellow diamonds printed on it. His left pinky glittered with gold and diamonds and his fedora hat had a bright red feather in its band. The only shabby thing about Shaker was his briefcase, it was frayed and cracked across the middle. That was Shaker to a T: he worried about his appearance but he didn't give a damn about his work.

"Where we headed, Easy?" he asked before he could slam the door shut.

"I tell ya when we get there." I smiled at his consternation. It did me good to see an arrogant man like Shaker Jones go with an empty glass.

I drove north to Pasadena, where I picked up Route 66, called Foothill Boulevard in those days. That took us through the citrus-growing areas of Arcadia, Monrovia, and all the way down to Pomona and Ontario. The foothills were wild back then. White stone and sandy soil knotted with low shrubs and wild grasses. The citrus orchards were bright green and heavy with orange and yellow fruit. In the hills beyond roamed coyotes and wildcats.

The address for Linda and Andre was on a small dirt road called Turkel, just about four blocks off the main drag, Alessandro Boulevard. I stopped a few blocks away.

"Here we are," I said in a cheery voice.

"Where are they?"

"Where them papers Mofass wanted?"

Shaker stared death at me for a minute, but then, when I didn't keel over, he put his hand into the worn brown briefcase and came out with a sheaf of about fifteen sheets of paper. He shoved the papers into my lap, turning a few pages back so he could point out a line that said "Premiums."

"That's what he wanted when we talked last December. Now where's Linda and Andre?"

I ignored him and started flipping through the documents.

Shaker was huffing but I took my time. Legal documents need a close perusal; I'd seen enough of them in my day.

"Man, what you doin'?" Shaker squealed at me. "You cain't read that kinda document. You need to have law trainin' for that."

Shaker was no lawyer. As a matter of fact, he hadn't finished the eighth grade. I had two part-time years of Los Angeles City College under my belt. But I scratched my head to show that I agreed with him.

I said, "Maybe so, Shaker. Maybe. But I jus' got a question t'ask you here."

"Don't you be callin me Shaker, Easy," he warned. "That ain't my name no mo'. Now what is it you wanna know?"

I turned to the second-to-the-last sheet and pointed to a blank line near the bottom of the page.

"Whas this here?"

"Nuthin'," he said quickly. Too quickly. "The president of Vigilance gotta sign that."

"It says, 'the insurer or the insurer's agent.' Thas you, ain't it?"

Shaker stared death at me a little more, then he snatched the papers and signed them.

"Where is she?" he demanded.

I didn't answer but I pulled back into the road and drove toward Andre and Linda's address.

Shaker's Plymouth was in the yard, hubcap-deep in mud.

"There you go," I said, looking at the house.

"All right," Shaker said. He got out of the car and so did I.

"Where you goin', Easy?"

"With you, Shaker."

He bristled when I called him that again.

Then he said, "You got what you want. It's my business here on out."

I noticed that his jacket pocket hung low on the right side. That didn't bother me, though. I had a .25 hooked behind my back.

"I ain't gonna leave you t'kill nobody, Shaker. I ain't no lawyer, like you said, but I know that the police love what they call accessory before the fact."

"Just stay outta my way," he said. Then he turned toward the house, striding through the mud.

I stayed behind him, walking a little slower.

When he pushed through the front door I was seven, maybe eight, steps behind. I heard Linda scream and Andre make a noise something like a hydraulic lift engaging. The next thing I heard was crashing furniture. By that time I was going through the door myself.

It was a mess. A pink couch was turned on its back and big Linda was on the other side of it, sitting down and practicing how wide she could open her eyes. She was screaming too; loud, incoherent shrieks. Her wiry, straightened hair stood out from the back of her head so that she resembled a monstrous chicken.

Shaker had a blackjack in one hand and he had Andre by the scruff of the neck with the other. Poor Andre sagged down trying to protect himself from the blows Shaker was throwing at him.

"Lemme go!" Andre kept shouting. Blood spouted from the center of his forehead.

Shaker obliged. He let Andre slump to the floor and dropped the sap. Then went for his jacket pocket. But by that time I was behind him. I grabbed his arm and pulled the pistol out of his pocket.

"What? What? What?" he asked.

I almost laughed.

"You ain't gonna kill nobody t'day, Shaker."

"Get get get." His eyes were glazed over, I don't think he had any idea of what was happening.

"You got some whiskey?" I asked Andre.

"In the kitchen." Andre blinked his enormous eyes

at me and made to rise. He was so shaken it took him two attempts to make it to his feet. Blood cascaded down his loose blue shirt. He was a mess.

"Get it," I said.

Linda was still screaming. Her voice was already gone, though. Instead of a chicken she'd begun to sound like an old, hoarse dog barking at clouds.

I grabbed her by the shoulders and shouted, "Shut up, woman!"

I heard something fall, and when I turned around I saw Shaker going at Andre again. He had him by the throat this time.

I boxed Shaker's ears, then I sapped him with the barrel of his gun. He hit the ground faster than if I had shot him.

"He was gonna kill me." Andre sounded surprised.

"Yeah," I said. "You spendin' his money, drivin' his car, an' fuckin' his wife. He was gonna kill you."

Andre looked like he didn't understand.

I went over to Linda and asked, "How much of Shaker's money you got left?"

"'Bout half." The fear of death had knocked any lies she might have had right out of her head.

"How much is that?"

"Eighteen hundred."

"Gimme sixteen."

"What?"

"Gimme sixteen an' then you take two an' get outta here. That is, 'less you wanna go back with him?" I motioned my head toward Shaker's body.

Andre got the money. It was in a sock under the mattress.

While I counted out Linda's piece she was throwing clothes into a suitcase. She was scared because Shaker showed signs of coming to. It didn't fluster me, though. I would have liked to sap him again.

"Come on, baby," Linda said to Andre once she was packed. She wore a rabbit fur and a red box hat.

"I just come from Juanita, Andre," I said. "Li'l Andre want you back, an' you know this trick is over."

Andre hesitated. The side of his face was beginning to swell, it made him resemble his own infant son.

"You go on, Linda," I said. "Andre already got a family. And you cain't hardly take care of both of you on no two hundred dollars."

"Andre!" Linda rasped.

He looked at his toes.

"Shit!" was the last word she said to him.

I said, "There's a bus stop 'bout four blocks up, on Alessandro."

She cursed me once and then she was gone.

"My car is the Ford out front," I said to Andre after I watched Linda slog through the mud toward the end of their street. "You go get in it an' I'll talk to the man here."

Andre took a small bag from the closet. I laughed to myself that he was already packed to leave.

I sat and watched Shaker writhing on the floor and rolling his eyes. He wasn't aware yet. While enjoying the show I took three hundred dollars from the wad that Linda left. He came to his senses about fifteen minutes later. I was sitting in front of him, hugging the back of a folding chair. He looked up at me from his knees.

"Thirteen hundred was all they had left. Here you go," I said, throwing the sock in his face.

"Where Linda?"

"She had somewhere to go."

"Wit' Andre?"

"He's wit' me. I'ma take him home to his family."

"I'ma kill that boy, Easy."

"No you not, Shaker," I said. "'Cause Andre is under my protection. You understand me? You best to understand, 'cause I will kill you if anything happens to him. I will kill you."

"We had a deal, Easy."

"An' I met it. You got your car, you got all the money that's left, an' you' wife don't want you; killin' Andre ain't gonna stop that. So leave it be or we gonna have it out, an' you know you ain't gonna win that one neither."

Shaker believed me, I could see it in his eyes. As long as he thought I was a poor man he'd be scared of me. That's why I kept my wealth a secret. Everybody knows that a poor man's got nothing to lose; a poor man will kill you over a dime.

# 17

WINTHROP HUGHES GOT TO HIS FEET AND I WALKED HIM TO his car. I kept his pistol and his blackjack in case he saw Linda or he decided to come against me and Andre.

He drove off, cursing and threatening to complain to Mofass. Andre and I took off about twenty minutes later.

"Thank you, Easy," Andre said as we pulled onto the highway. The fright had made him courteous. "You really saved my butt back there."

I didn't say anything. Andre held my handkerchief to the gash in his forehead as he looked from side to side like a dog who needed to be let out.

After a while I asked him, "Where you wanna go, Andre?"

"Um, well." He hesitated. "Maybe you could drop me off at my auntie's over on Florence."

I shook my head. "Police already got that covered, man."

"Say what?"

I was quiet again. I wanted Andre to be scared for his life.

"What you mean 'bout the cops, Easy?"

"They been lookin' for you, Andre. They been askin' 'bout you."

"Who?"

"The police," I said.

Andre seemed to relax.

"And some man from the FBI."

I might as well have thrown hot oil in his face.

"No!"

"It's the truth, man," I said. "You know Shaker got me to look for you 'cause he wanted Linda back and he told me the government might pay somethin' for you. You lucky that I didn't want to play his game. I went over t'ask Juanita what I should do an' she said that you' boy needed his daddy."

"Thanks," Andre said, but he was looking out of the window. Maybe he was thinking of throwing himself into the road.

"What them cops want?" I asked.

"I dunno, man. They musta made some mistake or sumpin'."

"You gonna tell me?"

"Tell you what? I ain't seen no cops. I just been out here wit' Linda, that's all."

"You want me to drive you to the cops, Andre? 'Cause you know I will."

"Why you wanna mess wit' me, Easy? I ain't done nuthin' t'you."

There were cows leaving a pasture we passed. Black-and-white cows winding their way up a narrow pathway cut into the side of the hill. Their hold on the ground seemed precarious, but they were standing on bedrock compared to the cow-eyed man sitting next to me.

"You tell me what's up an' maybe I could help ya," I said.

"How could you help me?"

"I could find you a place t'stay. Maybe I could get your girlfriend and her baby out to you. I might even buy you some groceries until this thing blows over."

"Ain't nuthin' gonna blow over."

"Tell me the story," I said in a low, reassuring voice.

Andre sat back and wiped his palms against his pants. He was grimacing, showing a mouthful of teeth and moaning.

"I got set up!" he shouted. "Set up!"

"By who?"

"Them people at Champion, man. They put them papers in a envelope that wasn't marked. It was in a blue folder, the same color folder they use for the distribution list."

"What you talkin' 'bout, man?"

"They set me up!" he shouted again. "Mr. Lindquist's secretary told me I could wait fo'im in his office. I'm shop steward an' I meet wit' the VP every other month. But we been talkin' strike out in the yard 'cause they gonna lay off a hundred and fifty men."

He stopped talking as if everything should have been clear.

"So this list was the men they were going to lay off?"

"That's what I thought. I grabbed it an' took it out wit' me. It's only later that I seen the seal."

"What seal?"

"Top Secret, man." Andre started tearing. "Top Secret."

"Why not just take it back?"

"I swear, man, I got outta there quick 'cause I didn't want no one t'see me. It wasn't till I got home and opened it up that I seen that government seal. Then I was too scared t'bring it back." Andre mixed his fingers together to show the complexity of his situation.

"But the envelope was the kind they used for the distribution list?" I asked.

"Yeah."

"Could be a setup," I said, noncommittally.

Andre looked at me hopefully. "I tole you."

"Or you could just be a poor fool," I said. "What you do with them papers?"

"I ain't sayin' nuthin' 'bout that."

It was Andre's turn to be quiet. We drove on toward the outskirts of L.A. proper. It was high noon. The desert sun was so bright that even the blue in the sky seemed to fade.

I pulled off the road at a restaurant called Skip's. I gave Andre a pullover sweater I kept in the trunk to hide the blood on his shirt. We couldn't do anything about his head, though. At first I thought the waitress wasn't going to serve us. We ordered chicken-fried steaks and beer. Andre was polite, but other than that he was silent.

I didn't want to push too hard, because Andre was high-strung and he had been through quite a lot already.

When the waitress left the check Andre just stared at it.

"What's it gonna be, Andre?"

"What do you mean?"

"I mean, you gonna tell me about Chaim Wenzler or what?"

It was a pleasure surprising Andre. He face registered emotion like mercury gauging a match.

"How'd you know that?"

"I got my ways. I need to know about you an' this dude."

"Why you gotta know?"

"I'm working' fo'a man, okay? Leave it at that an' you might stay outta jail."

Andre huffed and clenched his fists, but I could tell that he was broken.

"He's a guy I met, that's all."

"How?"

"When I was elected steward. This white guy, Martin Vost, district union president, introduced me at a monthly meetin'. Chaim was there as a adviser."

"Yeah? So he advise you t'go steal top secrets."

"Man, he was just like a friend. We go out drinkin' an' talkin' an' aftah while he took me t'this study group he got."

"An' what they be studyin'?"

"Union newspapers an' like that."

"So he didn't tell you t'steal them papers?"

"He said that strikin' was a war. He said that we gotta do ev'rything we could t'win fo'our side. So when I seen that distribution list I took it. It's kinda like he told me to; like he primed me fo'it."

"What he say when you bring it to 'im?"

"Who said I did?"

"Com'on, man, I ain't got time fo'this play shit."

"His eyes got all wide an' he asked me where I got it from. I told'im. He said that stealin' that document was a fed'ral charge. He told me t'disappear."

"That's it?"

"All I gotta say, man."

"But there's one more thing," I said.

"What's that?"

"Where's what you stole?"

It was then that I noticed the sweat on Andre's upper lip. Maybe it was there the whole time.

"You gotta swear you ain't gonna tell where you got this from."

"Where is the shit, man?" I was losing patience with Andre's fears.

"You know the brick-walled car graveyard down at the far end of Vernon?"

"Yeah."

"We went down there. They got this emerald-green Dodge truck down along the back wall. We put the papers 'hind the seat."

"Wenzler go with you?"

"Yeah, man, we went there together. I said that we was lookin' fo'a muffler and then we snuck back there an' hid it."

"What if they sell it?"

"Shit, man, that ole thang is just a wreck. It's been back there fo'years."

When we got back in the car I told Andre that I'd try to help him.

"I work for a guy named Mofass. He manages a few 'partment buildin's," I said.

"Yeah?"

"I'ma call him an' ask him to put you up in one of his Mexican buildin's. I'll call Juanita too, send her over there." I took the three hundred dollars from my shirt pocket and handed it to Andre. "Use it slow, man. You might have to be gone for a while."

I let Andre off at a hotel on Buena Vista Boulevard. When I got home I called Mofass and told him to prepare a room somewhere for Andre.

"Who gonna pay me?" Mofass asked.

"I will."

"Ain't good business, Mr. Rawlins. Landlord should never pay nobody's rent."

Then I called Juanita.

"That you, Easy?" she said, softening when she heard my voice.

"Andre's in a hotel downtown, honey," I said, and then I gave her the address. "He got a little money an' he pretty scared too."

"You want me to go to him?" she asked, as if I had a say in how she spent the rest of her life.

113

"Yeah," I said. "And, Juanita?"

"Huh, Easy?"

"Maybe you could go easy on the boy an' not tell'im 'bout us."

"Don't worry, honey, I'ma keep that secret right in here."

I couldn't see her but I could imagine where her hand was.

# 18

I CAME HOME TO LOUD HAMMERING. THERE WERE THREE men on my porch. Two of them were doing the carpentry. Boards had already been laced over the windows; there were bright yellow ribbons of paper across them. Right then the men were driving nails into fresh timbers across my front door.

"What the fuck you think it is you doin' here!" I shouted.

All of the men were white and wore dark suits. When they turned around I recognized only one of them, but that was enough.

Agent Lawrence said, "We're sealing the house against the threat of you liquidating property that may rightfully belong to the federal government."

"What?"

Instead of talking Lawrence tore off a sheet of paper that had been tacked to the wall. He handed me the federal marshal's warrant. It said that my property was temporarily confiscated by the federal marshal until such time that my tax responsibility had been determined; I made that much out. Two judges had signed the document; also the tax agent involved, Reginald Arnold Lawrence.

I ripped the warrant in half and pushed my way past the tax man. I went up to the closest marshal and said, "Brother, I don't know what you'd do if a man threatened to take your house, but I've been told by the FBI that I don't have to worry 'bout this until I done some work for them."

The marshal was short. He had blue eyes and thinning sandy hair that lay down and stuck to his scalp because of the sweat he'd built up driving nails into my walls.

"I don't know anything about that, Mr. Rawlins. All I know is that I got this warrant to execute."

"But this is my house, man! All my clothes are in there. My shoes, my address book, I don't have anything."

The two officers looked at each other. I could see that they sympathized with me. Nobody likes to kick a man out of his home. Nobody decent, that is.

"Come on, Aster," Agent Lawrence said. "I have to get home."

"He's got a right to hear something," Aster complained. "I mean, here we are locking up his house and he doesn't have anything but what's on his back."

"This is the law, mister," Lawrence said. "All we have is the law, that's why I'm here. I'm doing my job. And that's what I want from you."

Lawrence gave the men a hard stare and they turned back to their hammers.

I watched them for a minute. And while I did my breath came up short. Something started shaking in my chest.

"You cain't do this, man." I said it because I was afraid of what might happen if I didn't talk.

Lawrence ignored me, though. He took the two halves of the warrent and tacked them back up against the wall.

"I said, you cain't do this, man!"

The tone of my own voice in my ears reminded me of Poinsettia; her crying to Mofass that she needed another chance.

The marshals were almost done with their job, so I put my hand on Lawrence's shoulder.

He didn't bother with the hand. He drove his fist into my temple and followed with an uppercut that I managed to avoid. The adrenaline was already pumping, so I hit him somewhere in the chest and then in the side of his head. When he doubled over I pushed him down the stairs.

I was just ready to go after him when I remembered the two men behind me. I was about to turn but then they grabbed me by both arms.

As they dragged me down the stairway Lawrence cried, "He hit me! He assaulted me!" He said that over and over. He didn't sound outraged, though. It was more like he was glad that I had assaulted him.

The marshals wrestled me to the fence and forced me to my knees before handcuffing me to one of the metal posts. I was struggling and fighting, and maybe screaming a little. There may have been tears in my eyes and my voice as I warned those men to stay away from my house.

A small crowd of my neighbors gathered at the front gate. A few men even entered and approached the white peacekeepers.

The marshal who had talked to me approached the men. He had a calmness about him and was holding up his identification. As I watched him I felt a blow to the side of my head. When I looked around I saw the other marshal holding Agent Lawrence back.

"Stop it!" the black-haired, Mediterranean-looking man ordered.

". . . we're just doing our job," Marshal Aster was saying to the men. He was backing them up. No guns were drawn. "Everybody go on home. Mr. Rawlins will explain himself after we're gone. . . ."

"I want him arrested for attacking a federal agent!" Lawrence shrieked. His lips stuck straight out and he shook as if he were freezing.

"Next time I'll kill your ass!" I shouted from my knees.

The black-haired marshal dragged Lawrence out to the gate and the other man came to my side.

"You cain't do this to me, man!" I said to him. "I ain't gonna lose my house, my clothes . . ."

"Shut up, man!" he ordered. He must have been an officer somewhere, because the tone of his voice demanded obedience.

He knelt there beside me and reached for the cuffs.

"We're going off duty after this, Mr. Rawlins. If you break the seal we'll have to come by tomorrow and arrest you, if you're still here, that is."

He took off the cuffs and I jumped to my feet. I advanced on the two men at the gate with Aster at my heel.

"What's goin' on, Easy?" Melford Thomas, my across-the-street neighbor, asked.

"I want you to arrest him," Lawrence said again.

"Why?" Aster asked. "All I saw was you fall on your ass."

"I won't take this!" Lawrence said, spitting over all of us.

Aster wiped his face. "We're going home now. You want to come with us you better get in the car, or else you can stay here and arrest him yourself."

Lawrence looked as if he might try it. But when he saw all of my angry-looking black neighbors he backed down.

"Don't break that seal, Rawlins," he said. "That's an official barrier."

And then they were off in their car.

I had the planks pulled off my door before they turned the corner.

Craxton was working late that night. Maybe he worked late every night, sitting up in some vast office plotting strategies against the enemies of America. I didn't need to worry about communists, though—the police were enough for me.

"What's that?" he laughed. "He had the federal marshal out there?"

"I don't find it too funny. He kicked me upside the head."

"Sorry, Easy. It's just that you've got to admire a man who wants to do the job right."

"What about me? I'm supposed to work for you and I don't even have a place to sleep or clothes to wear."

"I'll make some calls. You just climb into your bed, Easy, and get ready to work tomorrow. Agent Lawrence will not bother you again."

"Okay. Just as long you keep that man away from my house. I don't want him in here again."

"You got it. I thought Lawrence had more sense than that. My request for your help was informal. I didn't want to have to step on him. But I'll do that now."

I was satisfied with that much. There was a moment when we were both quiet.

Finally I asked, "So you still want me to look into this Wenzler thing?"

"Certainly do, Easy. You're my ace in the hole."

"Well then, I was thinkin' . . ."

"Yes?"

"About this, um, Andre Lavender guy."

"What about him?"

"Well, I asked a couple'a guys I still know down there about him. They said that he got in trouble with the law down there and disappeared."

"What kind of trouble was that?"

I was pretty sure that he already knew the answer, so I said, "I don't know."

"Well, Easy, I don't know about any trouble he had. I know that he's working with Wenzler and we'd like to talk to him. If you get a line we'd sure appreciate it. As a matter of fact, if you could lead us to Lavender we might not need you anymore at all."

It was a tempting offer. Andre didn't mean anything to me. But he was innocent of anything but being a fool and Craxton wasn't promising me anything anyway. So I said, "Nobody seems to know where he's gone to, but I'll keep my eyes peeled."

I paced the rooms of my tiny house all night. I walked and cursed and loaded all my pistols. When the sun came up I sat out on the front porch, waiting for marshals.

They didn't come, though. That was better all the way round.

# 19

MY LIFE WAS PRETTY CRAZY IN THE DAYS I WORKED FOR THE FBI. I spent most of my late evenings in the arms of EttaMae. Those nights I spent exploring Etta's body and her love; either one was worth dying for. Being with EttaMae was the most exciting and dreadful time I ever had. I had to overcome my guilt and my fear of Mouse to be with her. I'd come to her apartment in the late evening looking all around to make sure that no one saw me. LaMarque would be sleeping in his little room and Etta would come to me slowly like a horse trainer trying to tame a skitterish buck. My heart was always racing from fear when I got there, but the fear soon turned to passion. Sometimes in the middle of our lovemaking Etta would hold me behind my neck and ask, "Do you really love me, Easy?" And I'd cry out, "Yeah, yeah, baby!" in a powerful surrender to the forces that built in me.

In the daytime I worked with Chaim Wenzler. He was a hard worker and a good man. We'd go from door to door in Hollywood and Beverly Hills and Santa Monica. I'd wait in the car and Chaim would go beg for clothes and other items. I offered to go up with him once but he said, "These people wouldn't put it in your hand, my friend. They wanna give maybe, but not direct. Give it to the kike and then he could give to the *schwartze*, that's what they're thinking." Then he spat.

We always went to coffee-shop restaurants for lunch. Chaim paid one day and I would pay the next. The people running the restaurants were willing to take our money, but you could see that they were bothered by us. It was probably because we were so boisterous and intimate.

Chaim liked to tell stories and laugh, or cry. He told me about his childhood in Vilna. I had heard about Vilna because I had gone through Germany *liberating* the death camps. When I told Chaim about my experiences he talked to me about his times among the Germans, Poles, and Jews. In that way we grew close. We shared experience through memories that, although we were never in the same place, had the very real feelings of desperation and death that consumed us both during World War Two.

Chaim had been part of the communist underground during the German occupation of Vilna. He organized and fought against the Nazis. When the frightened Jewish population denounced the underground he and his comrades fled the city and formed a Jewish platoon that slew Nazis, blew up trains, and liberated every Jew that they could.

"We fought side by side with the Russian guerrillas," Chaim told me once. "They were soldiers of the people," he said, and he touched his chest with one hand and my arm with the other. "Like you and me."

I knew that the Russians abandoned the Warsaw Ghetto and I was sure that Chaim knew it too, but I couldn't say anything because I never knew a white man who thought that we were *really* the same. When he touched my arm he might as well have stuck his hand in my chest and grabbed my heart. Agent Craxton might have liked what I was doing for him, but he didn't think I was on his level.

Chaim carried a steel hip flask full of vodka. He liked to chip at it during the day. His high was pleasant and his friendliness was real. Sometimes he'd bring up his "organizing" at Champion. Once he even mentioned Andre Lavender. But whenever he did that I changed the subject. I acted like I was afraid to know about politics or unions. And I was afraid; afraid of what I might do to save myself from jail.

"What you do for money, Chaim?" I asked him one day. We were sitting at a tiny strip of park that overlooked the Pacific Ocean.

He looked out over the blue air and blue water for a long time before saying, "They won't let me work."

"Who?"

"America. They come and they tell the weak boss that I'm a bad man and he fires me. They wouldn't let me wash shit from the floor. So my friends help me, and my family."

"Who you talkin' 'bout?"

"The Cossack," he spat. "The Nazi, the FBI."

"You mean they come out to yo' job an' tell the boss that you did sumpin'?"

"They say I am not American. They say I am communist."

I found myself shaking my head. "Don't you know that's some shit."

"That is why I work for charity, for First African. The white people don't understand being treated like this. They think that they are free because nobody comes to their job. They see that I am bad because the police follow me. They have no idea." Chaim pointed at his head. "In here they are stupid with what they are told."

"You could say that again. You all the time hearin' 'bout how free America is, but it ain't."

"No. But they are free. They have a job and they keep it. When things get bad, my friend, it is you and I that are out of work."

I nodded. There had been many a time I'd seen the Negro staff of a company laid off when money was tight. It didn't always happen like that, but it did often enough.

Chaim grabbed my hand in viselike grip. There were tears in his eyes. We sat there holding hands and looking at each other until I got a little uncomfortable. Then he said, "I saw them hang my brother when I was a child. He was accused of spitting in a soldier's path. They hung him and burned down my mother's house."

I won't say that those few words alone made us friends, but I understood Chaim Wenzler then.

I talked to Agent Craxton later that same night. He asked all sorts of questions about where we picked up clothes and who handled the money. He was looking for spies everywhere. If I hadn't talked to Andre Lavender I would have thought the FBI man was crazy.

But even though I had the proof I needed to set myself free I balked at bringing down Chaim Wenzler.

"What is it that you want on the man?" I asked Craxton.

"I'll know it when you tell me, Easy. Has he invited you to any meetings?"

"What kinda meetin's?"

"That's what I'm asking you."

"Uh-uh, no. All we do is collect clothes and then give 'em away."

"Don't you worry, Mr. Rawlins, he'll slip up. And then we'll have him."

There wasn't much consolation for me in that.

"I talked to your friend the other day, Easy," Agent Craxton said.

"Who's that?"

"Lawrence. He's singing a new tune now that Washington called his boss. He says that everything's okay and that he would be happy to process a schedule of payments when this thing is over."

"You not gonna let him do that, are you?"

"No, I don't think so. I told him that Washington should have your paperwork by the end of next week."

I sighed, "Thanks."

"You see, Easy, we're helping each other."

I could still feel that powerful grip on my hand.

# 20

I KNEW THAT I WAS BOUND TO SUFFER A FALL. IN A PERFECT world I would have had Etta for my bride and Chaim for my best man. But after that last talk with Craxton my hopes for a happy life just sank. Everything I was doing seemed wrong. The police were suspicious. The IRS wanted me in jail. Even Craxton was lying to me, and I didn't know why. There was no room for escape, so I turned to alcohol. I had a drink or two and went through the motions of cleaning up. But the bath didn't cleanse and the whiskey didn't work.

I wasn't only worried about Mouse and what he might do to exact vengeance on me. I'm not a meek man and I will fight for what I believe is right, regardless of the odds. If I'd felt it was right for me to love Etta, then I wouldn't have cared about what Mouse might do; at least I would have been at peace with myself. But Mouse was my friend and he was in pain; I knew that when I looked into his eyes at Targets. But I hadn't worried about him at all. All I cared about was how I felt. The fact that I was so selfish sickened me.

It was same with Chaim Wenzler. He might have been a communist but he was a friend to me. We'd drink out of the same glass sometimes, and we talked from our hearts. Craxton and Lawrence had me so worried about my money and my freedom that I had become their slave. At least Mouse and Chaim acted

124

from their natures. They were the innocent ones while I was the villain.

Finally, when I succumbed to the whiskey, I began to think about Poinsettia Jackson.

All I could think about was that young woman and how my cold-heartedness had caused her to take her own life. I liked what the detective Quinten Naylor was doing, but I didn't agree with him. Why would someone want to kill a woman whose every moment was torture and pain? If it was someone who wanted to put her out of her misery they wouldn't have hung her. A bullet in the head would have been more humane. No. Poinsettia took her own life because she lost her beauty and her job, and when she begged me to let her at least have a roof over her head I took that too.


I was in a foul mood when I went down to First African that evening. I was more than a little drunk and willing to blame anybody else for the wrong that was in me.

I'd promised Odell that I'd come down to the elementary school that the church ran and do something about their ants. They had a problem with red ants.

Los Angeles had a special breed of red ant. They were about three times the size of the regular black ant and they were fire-engine red. But the real problem with them was their bite. The red ant's bite was painful, and on many people it made a great welt. That would have been bad enough, but children seemed to be especially bothered by the ants. And little kids loved to play in the dirt where red ants made their nests.

I had a poison that killed them in the hive. And I was so upset about everything, and so drunk, that I didn't have the sense to stay home.

I used the key Odell had given me and went down to

125

the basement of the church, looking for a funnel. When I got to the cafeteria I saw that the lights were on. That didn't bother me, though. There were often people working in the church.

I got the funnel from a hopper room, then headed for the exit at the back of the basement. When I walked through the main room I saw them. Chaim Wenzler and a young woman who had black hair and pale skin.

"Easy," Chaim said with a smile. He rose and crossed the room to shake my hand.

"Hi, Chaim," I said.

He pulled me across the room by my hand, saying, "This is my daughter, Shirley."

"Pleased to meet you," I said. "But listen, Chaim, I got some work I gotta do an' there's a problem back home."

I must have sounded sincere, because Chaim and Shirley both frowned. They had identical dimples at the center of their chins.

I wanted to get away from there. The room seemed to be too dark and too hot. Just the idea that I was there to fool those people, the same way I fooled Poinsettia with my lies about being a helpless janitor, made my stomach turn. Before they could say their words of concern I threw myself toward the exit.

The schoolyard was a vast sandy lot that had three bungalows placed end to end at the northern side. The ants dug their nests against the salmon brick walls at the back. I set up my electric torch and took out the amber bottle of poison. I also had a flask of Teachers. I took a sip of my poison and then poured the ants a dram of theirs through the funnel.

What followed was a weird scene.

I'd never watched to see what happened after the poison hit a hive. Under electric light the sand looked like a real desert around the mound. At first there was just a wisp of smoke rising from the hole, but then about twenty of the ants came rushing out. They were frantic, running in widening arcs and stamping on the sand like parading horses held under a tight rein. These ants ran off into the night but were followed by weaker, more confused ants.

I saw no more than four of them actually die, but I knew that the hives were full of the dead. I knew that they had fallen where they stood, because the poison is very deadly in close quarters. Like in Dachau when we got there, the dead strewn like chips of wood at a lumberyard.

There were six holes in all. Six separate hives to slaughter. I went through the ritual, drinking whiskey and staring hard at the few corpses.

They were all the same except for the last one. For some reason, when I gave that one the dose of poison the ants flooded out of there in the hundreds. There were so many that I had to back away to avoid them swarming over me. I was so scared that I ran, stumbling twice.

I ran all the way back to the church. Before I went in, I drained the scotch and threw the bottle in the street.

I made it down into the basement, tripping on my own feet and the stairs. Chaim and his daughter were still there. The way they looked at me I wondered if I had been talking to myself.

Chaim gazed into my face with almost colorless eyes. I imagined he knew everything. About the FBI and Craxton, about the ants, about Poinsettia and daddy Reese. He probably knew about the time I fell asleep and when I woke up my mother was dead.

"What's wrong, Mr. Rawlins?" he asked.

"Nuthin'," I said. I took a step forward. The impact

of my foot on the floor sounded in my head like a giant kettle drum. "It's just that . . ."

"What?" Chaim grunted as he caught me by my arms. I realized that I was falling and tried to regain a foothold.

I kept talking too. "Ain't nuthin', I said." I tried to back away but the wall stopped me.

Shirley, his daughter, moved in close behind Chaim. There was concern in her porcelain face.

"Stand still, Easy," Chaim was saying. Then he laughed, "I don't think you'll be sorting clothes tomorrow morning."

I laughed with him. "You be better off wit' somebody else helpin' you anyways, man."

He shook me the way people do when they're trying to awaken someone. "*You* are my friend, Easy." His somber look saddened me even more. I thought of the victims I had seen. Men wasted to the size of boys, mass graves full of innocence.

"I ain't no friend'a yours, man. Uh-uh. Th'ew her outta her own place. Th'ew her out an' now she's dead. You cain't trust no niggah like me, Chaim. You do better jus' t' shine me on."

With that I leaned against the wall and slid down to the floor.

"We can't just leave him here, Poppa," Shirley said. He said something back, but it sounded like music to me, a song that I forgot the words to. I thought for a moment that he understood my confession, that he intended to kill me in the church basement.

But instead they got me to my feet, and pushed me toward the door. I walked under my own steam for the most part but every now and then I tripped.

There was a loud drumming in my head and lamplights hanging against a completely black sky. I could hear the moths banging against the glass covers in between the thunder of my footsteps.

The light snapped on in the car and I fell into the backseat; Chaim pushed my legs in behind me.

I remember motion and soothing words. But I don't remember going into the house. Then I fell again, this time into a soft bed. I had been crying for a long time.

# 21

I HEARD A DOOR SLAM SOMEWHERE BELOW ME. SOMETIME after that I opened my eyes.

The window had a lace curtain over its lower half. There were big white clouds moving fast across a perfectly blue sky in the upper panes. Watching that sky helped my breathing. I remember how deeply I inhaled, not even wanting to let it out.

"Good morning, Mr. Rawlins." It was a woman's voice. "How are you feeling?"

"What time is it?" I asked, sitting up. I wasn't wearing a shirt and the blankets came down to my stomach. Shirley Wenzler's eyes were fast to my chest.

"Ten, I guess."

She wore a no-sleeve one-piece cotton dress that had slanting stripes of blue, green, and gold, all very bright. Squinting at those bright colors let me know that I had a hangover.

"This your house?" I asked.

"Kind of. I rent. Poppa lives all the way in Santa Monica so we thought we'd take you here for the night."

"How'd I get in bed?"

"You walked."

"I don't remember." It was partially true.

"You were kind of drunk, Mr. Rawlins." She giggled and covered her mouth. She was a very pretty young woman with extremely pale skin against jet-black hair. Her face was heart-shaped, everything seemed to point at her smile.

"Poppa just shouted at you, and told you where to go, and he kept on shouting until you did it. You . . ." She hesitated.

"Yeah?"

"You were kind of like crying."

"Did I say anything?"

"About a dead woman. You said she killed herself because you made her leave. Is that true?"

"No, no it's not. She got evicted from a place I clean for. That's all."

"Oh," she whispered and then looked at my chest. I liked the attention, so I left the blankets alone.

"Is Chaim here?" I asked.

"I took him to the church. I just got back. He said that you'd come later if you weren't too sick."

"Is this your room?" I asked, looking around.

"Uh-huh. But I stayed in the spare room in the attic. It has a bed and I like to go up there and read sometimes. Especially in the spring or fall when it isn't too hot or too cold.

"Poppa slept on the couch," she added. "He does that sometimes."

"Oh," I said, partly because I didn't know what to say, and partly because my head hurt.

I watched her watching me for a few moments until she finally said. "I've never seen a man's chest, I mean, like yours."

"All it is is brown, honey. Ain't that different."

"Not that, I mean the hair, I mean you don't have much and it's so curly and . . ."

"And what?"

Just then the doorbell rang. Three short chimes that

sounded like they were in some other world. Shirley, who had turned bright red, made to leave. I guess that she was kind of flustered. I was too.

When she was gone I looked around the room. The furniture was all hand-crafted from a yellowish-brown wood that I couldn't identify. Not a surface was flat. Everything curved and arced, from the mirrored bureau to the chest of drawers.

There was a thick white carpet and a few upholstered chairs. It was a small, feminine room; just exactly the right size and gender for my hangover.

After a while I heard men's voices. I went to the window and saw Shirley Wenzler standing outside of a wire fence in front of a well-manicured little yard. She was talking to two men who were wearing dark suits and short-brimmed hats. I remember thinking that the men must have gone shopping together to get clothes that were so similar.

Shirley got angry and shouted something that I couldn't make out. Finally she walked away from them, turning every now and then to see if they'd gone. But they just stared at her attentively, like sentinels of a wolf pack.

While I watched I hustled on my pants. When I heard the door slam I wanted to go ask her what had happened, but the twins interested me. They walked slowly across the street and got into a dark blue or black Buick sedan. They didn't start the car and drive away; they just sat there, watching the house.

"So you're up?" Shirley Wenzler said from the doorway. She was smiling again.

I turned from the window and said, "Nice neighborhood you live in. Hollywood?"

"Almost." She smiled. "We're near La Brea and Melrose."

"That's a long drive from where you got me."

She laughed, a little too loudly, and came into the room. She sat in a plush-bottomed chair across from the bed. I sat down on the mattress to keep her company.

"Did some woman really die?" she asked.

"Woman over where I clean couldn't pay the rent and she killed herself."

"You saw it?"

"Yeah." But all I could remember was Poinsettia's dripping toe.

"My poppa saw things like that." There was a strange light in her eyes. Not haunted like Chaim's, but empty.

"Many Jews," she continued, as if reciting a prayer she'd gone to bed with her whole life. "Mothers and sons."

"Yeah," I said, also softly.

At Dachau I'd seen many men and women like Wenzler; small and slight from starvation. Most of them were dead, strewn across the paths between bungalows like those ants, I imagined, stretched out in their hives.

"You think you could have saved her?" she asked. I had the crazy feeling that I was talking to her father, not her.

"What?"

"The woman who died. You think you could have saved her?"

"I know it. I got the ear'a the man run the place. He'da let 'er stay."

"No," she said simply.

"What you mean, no?"

"We are all of us trapped, Mr. Rawlins. Trapped in amber, trapped in work. If you can't pay the rent you die."

"That ain't right," I said.

Her eyes brightened even more and she smiled at me. "No, Mr. Rawlins. It is wrong."

It sounded so true and so final that I couldn't think

of anything to say. So I held my peace, staring at her pale delicate hands. I could see the trace of blue veins pulsing just under the white skin.

"Come on down when you're ready," she said, rising and moving toward the door. "I'm making breakfast now."

As if she'd conjured it, I suddenly smelled coffee and bacon.

She sat at a maple table in an alcove that looked out onto a very green backyard. There was a tangerine tree right out the window. It was covered with waxy white blossoms. The flowers were being picked over by dozens of hovering bees.

"Come have a seat," she said to me. She got up and took my arm just above the elbow. It was a friendly gesture, and it gave me a pang of guilt in the chest.

"Thanks," I said.

"Coffee?" Shirley asked. She wouldn't meet my eye.

"Love it," I said as sexy as I could with a hangover.

She poured the coffee. She had long, lovely arms and skin as white as the sandy beaches down in Mexico. White-skinned women amazed me back in those days. They were worth your life just to look at in the south. And anything that valuable held great allure.

"Before the war started my father sent me out of Poland in a box," she said as if continuing a conversation.

"He's a pretty smart guy, your father."

"He said that he could smell it—the Nazis coming." She looked like a young girl. I had the urge to kiss her but I held it in check.

"That's why my father works with you, Mr. Rawlins. He knows that the trouble he felt in Poland is just like what you feel here." There were tears in Shirley's eyes.

I thought of why I was there and the toast dried on my tongue.

"Your father is a good man," I said, meaning it. "He wants to make things better."

"But he has to think of himself too!" she blurted out. "He can't keep doing things that will take him away from his family. He has to be here. He's getting old, you know, and you can't keep taking things out of him."

"I guess he might spend a little too much time out on his charities, huh?"

"And what if no one worries about him? What happens when the Cossack comes to his door? Is anybody going to stand up for him?"

I could feel her tears in my own eyes. Nothing had changed since the night before. I was still traitorous and evil.

Shirley got up and went into the kitchen. Actually she ran there.

"Would you like some more toast, Mr. Rawlins?" Shirley asked when she'd come back in from the kitchen. Her eyes were red.

"No thanks," I said. "What time you got?"

"Almost twelve."

"Damn. I better get down there to help your father or he's gonna wonder what we been doin'."

Shirley smiled. "I can drive you."

It was a nice smile. I shuddered to see her trust me, because her father's ruin was my only salvation.

"You're pretty quiet," Shirley Wenzler said in the car.

"Just thinkin'."

"About what?"

"About how you got the advantage on me."

"What do you mean?"

I leaned over and whispered, "Well, you got to give

your opinion on my chest but the jury still out on yours."

She focused her attention back on the road and blushed nicely.

"I'm sorry," I said. "I always like to flirt with pretty girls."

"I think that was a little bit more than flirting."

"'Pends on where you come from," I said. "Down here that was just a little compliment from an admirer." That was a lie, but she didn't know it.

"Well, I'm not used to men talking to me like that."

"I said I'm sorry."

She let me out at First African. I shook her hand, holding it a little longer than I should have. But she smiled and was still smiling as she left.

I watched the little Studebaker drive away. After that I noticed the dark Buick with the two dark-suited men. They were parked across from the church then. Just sitting there as if they were salesmen breaking for an afternoon lunch.

# 22

FIRST AFRICAN HAD AN EMPTY LOOK TO IT ON WEEKDAYS. Christ still hung over the entrance but he looked like more of an ornament when the churchgoers weren't gathered around the stairs. I always stopped to look up at him, though. I understood the idea of pain and death at the hands of another—most colored people did. As terrible as Poinsettia's death was, she wasn't the first person I'd seen hung.

I'd seen lynchings and burnings, shootings and stonings. I'd seen a man, Jessup Howard, hung for looking at a white woman. And I'd seen two brothers who were lynched from two nooses on the same rope because they complained about the higher prices they were charged at the county store. The brothers had ripped off their shirts and gouged deep scratches in each other's skin in their struggles to keep from strangling. Both of their necks, broken at last, were horribly enlongated as they hung.

Part of that powerful feeling that black people have for Jesus comes from understanding his plight. He was innocent and they crucified him; he lifted his head to tell the truth and he died.

While I looked at him I heard something, but it was like something at the back of my mind. Like a crackle of a lit match and the sigh of an old timber in a windstorm.

Chaim was down in the basement, already working on boxes of clothes. He was holding up an old sequined dress, squinting at the glitter.

"Looks good," I said.

"Not bad, eh, Easy? Maybe Mrs. Cantella could find a new husband?" His smile was conspiratorial.

"Probably won't be no better than the last nine men she had."

We both laughed. Then I started helping him. We moved clothes from one box to another while putting prices on them with little eight-sided paper tags and safety pins. For plain dresses we charged a dollar and for a fancy one we charged one seventy-five. All pants were sixty-five cents, and hats and handkerchiefs ran about a quarter.

"Shirley's a good girl," Chaim said after a while.

I nodded. "I guess so. Takes a generous woman to take in some drunk that she don't even know."

"Sometimes you have to drink."

"Yeah, I guess that's true too."

"You're a good man, Easy. I'm glad to have you in my daughter's house."

We moved boxes around for another few minutes in silence.

I was just beginning to think seriously about how I could stay out of jail without getting Chaim in trouble when we heard the scream. It sounded far off but you could tell that it was full of terror.

Chaim and I looked at each other and then I headed for the stairs. I was halfway to the second floor when Winona Fitzpatrick came at me. She was running down with her arms out so I couldn't avoid her. She was crying and yelling and one of her shoes was off.

"Winona!" I cried. "Winona!"

"Blooddead," she moaned and then she fell into my arms.

Winona weighed at least two hundred pounds. I did my best to slow her fall till we came to the first floor. Then I let her down as gently as I could, but I still had to put her on the floor.

"Dead," she said.

"Who?"

"Dead. Blood," she said.

I decided that Chaim would come and take care of her and so I sprinted up the stairs. When I got to the minister's apartment on the second floor I slowed a bit. I began to wonder, at that very moment, what was happening to me. I gazed at the plywood door and thought about the Texas swamplands southeast of Houston. I thought about how a man could lose himself in those swampy lands for years and nobody could find him. I knew things had to be bad if I was missing that hard country.

Reverend Towne was sprawled back on the couch. His pants were down around his ankles and his boxer shorts were just below his knees. His penis was still half erect and I'm sure the pious men and women of the congregation would have been surprised that it was so small. You think of a Baptist minister as being a virile man, but I'd seen little boys that had more than him.

Another strange thing was the color of his skin. Most black men's skin gets darker in the genital area, but his was lighter, some strange quirk in his lineage.

The blood on his white shirt and his stunned expression told me that he was dead. I would have run to him to check it out but my way was blocked by the woman doubled over her own lap, sitting on her heels, at his feet. There was blood at the back of her head.

Nothing seemed to be out of place other than the two corpses. It was a modern apartment, there were no walls separating the rooms. The pine kitchen to the left had an electric range and a window that looked out the front of the church. On the right the bedroom, all made up and neat, sported African masks, shields, and tapestries on the far wall. A bright red blanket lay at the foot of the bed. The center of the apartment had a floor that was lower than the rooms that flanked it.

The center room was carpeted in white. The dead man reclined on a white leather couch. Towne's empty gaze lay on the modern fireplace that was shielded by a golden screen.

Everything was clean and made up except in a corner by the door; there was a pile of vomit. The murderer had eaten cole slaw and meatloaf for lunch. The strong smell of alcohol emanated from that corner.

When I looked out of the kitchen window I saw the stairs where I'd stood not fifteen minutes before; I remembered the crackle and sigh. I wondered if it could have been a volley of small-caliber shots. Could have been.

I went back to the lovers, if that's what you could

call them. It looked more like the convenience that we GIs enjoyed across Europe when there wasn't much time or money. She was still fully dressed, she even wore her shoes. It was the same woman I had seen him with in the basement.

Then I wondered who would be investigating the case. Magnolia Street wasn't that far away.

While I considered the telephone and the east Texas swamps, Chaim entered.

"What's this?" he stammered.

"Dead."

"Who?" he asked back. In real life you don't need very much language.

"I dunno, man. Winona was comin' down an' yellin' an' here they was."

"She kill them?"

"You wanna call the police, Chaim?"

"Where?" he asked. I was happy that he didn't ask why.

I pointed out the phone and looked around while he dialed. When he'd finished talking to the police dispatcher I asked him if he'd seen anything strange downstairs. He said no. Then I asked if he'd seen anyone other than me. He said that he saw one of the younger deacons, Robert Williams, earlier in the day.

The uniformed police came in around ten minutes. They called in the same report that Chaim had made, then they separated us and began asking questions.

Winona was led upstairs. She sat on the floor just outside the apartment crying and mumbling about blood.

My cop asked if Winona had known the minister. I said that I didn't know what their relationship was, and he got suspicious.

"You don't know her? Then how do you know her name?"

"I know her to say hello, I just don't know if she

knew the minister. I mean, she's on the church council, so she knew him, but I don't know what they had to do with each other."

"How long was she up there with him?"

"Beats me."

He started pacing and clenching his fists. He was a fat man with a red face and bright blue eyes. He was taller than I was, and he had a habit of talking to himself.

"He knows her name," he said. "But after that he's stupid."

I said, "I was down in the basement," but he didn't even hear it.

He went, "Something wrong with that. Yes, something wrong."

Then he asked me, "You know where she lives?"

"No."

That started him pacing again.

"Boy's fooling around here, hiding something. Yeah, hiding something."

It was said that there were still crocodiles deep in the Texas swamps. I would have preferred a cuddly reptile right then.

"Fine," someone said from the door.

The crazy policeman turned as if someone had called him. It was Andrew Reedy.

"What's happening here?" Reedy asked.

"Two spooks blasted and salt-and-pepper here acting like it was God done it. Girl out in the hall found them."

Quinten Naylor came in behind Reedy. I don't know if he heard what the crazy cop had said but you could see that there was no love lost between the two. They didn't even acknowledge each other.

"Well, well, well," Reedy was saying. "Here you are again, Mr. Rawlins. Were they evicting these two?"

"That's the minister of the church on the couch. I don't know the girl."

I could see the mood shift in Reedy's face. A dead minister was a political problem, no matter what color he was.

"And why were you here?"

"Just workin' downstairs, that's all."

"Working?" Naylor said. "People always turn up dead when you're working?"

"No sir."

"Did you know the minister?"

"To speak to, that's all."

"You a member of this church?"

"Yes sir."

Naylor turned his head to the uniforms.

"Cover them up," he said. "Don't you guys know procedure?"

The fat cop made like he was going to go at Naylor but Reedy grabbed him by the arm and whispered to him. Then the uniforms left with the fat cop swaggering through the door.

On the way out the fat one said to Naylor, "Don't worry, son, lotsa killin's on nigger patrol. Wait till you see how the nigger bitches cut up on each other." Then he was gone.

"I'll kill that son of a bitch," Naylor said.

Reedy didn't say anything. He'd gone up to the bedroom and gotten sheets to cover the dead.

"What about you?" Naylor asked Chaim.

"I am Wenzler, officer. Easy and I are working in the basement and we hear the screams. He runs up, I come in, and poor Dr. Towne was here, and the girl. It's terrible."

"Mr. Rawlins work for you?"

"Together," Chaim said. "We do charity for the church."

"And you were down there when you heard the screams?"

"Yes."

"What about shots?"

141

"No shots, just screams. Weak little screams like she was far away, in a hole."

"Let's take 'em all down and get statements, Quint," Reedy said. "I'll call for more uniforms and we'll take 'em. I'll call the ambulance and the coroner, too."

# 23

I HADN'T BEEN TO THE SEVENTY-SEVENTH STREET STATION for *questioning* in many years. It looked older in the fifties but it smelled the same. A sour odor that wasn't anything exactly. It wasn't living and it wasn't dead, it wasn't food and it wasn't excrement. It wasn't anything I knew, but it was wrong, as wrong as the smells in Poinsettia's apartment.

The last time I was taken there I had been under arrest and the police put me in a raw-walled room that was made for questioning prisoners. The kind of questioning that was punctuated by fists and shoes. This time, though, they sat me at a desk with Quinten Naylor. He had a blue-and-white form in front of him and he asked me questions.

"Name?"

"Ezekiel Porterhouse Rawlins," I answered.

"Date of birth."

"Let's see now," I said. "That would be November third, nineteen hundred and twenty."

"Height."

"Close to six feet, almost six-one."

"Weight."

"One eighty-five, except at Christmas. Then I'm about one ninety."

He asked more questions like that and I answered freely. I trusted a Negro, I don't know why. I'd been beaten, robbed, shot at, and generally mistreated by more colored brothers than I'd ever been by whites, but I trusted a black man before I'd even think about a white one. That's just the way things were for me.

"Okay, Ezekiel, tell me about Poinsettia, Reverend Towne, and that woman."

"They all dead, man. Dead as mackerel."

"Who killed them?"

He had an educated way of talking. I could have talked like him if I'd wanted to, but I never did like it when a man stopped using the language of his upbringing. If you were to talk like a white man you might forget who you were.

"I'ont know, man. Poinsettia kilt herself, right?"

"Autopsy report on her will be in this evening. You got something to say about it now?"

"They ain't got to that yet?" I was really surprised.

"The coroner's working a little hard these days, Mr. Rawlins. There was that bus accident on San Remo Street and the fire in Santa Monica. Up until now we were only half sure that this was even a case," Quinten said. "He's been butt-high in corpses, but your turn is coming up."

"I don't know nuthin', man. I know the minister and the girl was murdered 'cause I seen the blood. I'ont know who killed 'em an' if I get my way I ain't gonna know. Murder ain't got nuthin' t'do wit' me."

"That's not how I hear it."

"How's that?"

"I hear that there were quite a few murders that you were intimate with a few years ago. Your testimony put away one of the killers."

"That's right! Not me." I pointed at my chest. "Somebody else did a killin' an' I told the law. If I knew today I'd tell you now. But I was dumb-assed in the basement, movin' some clothes, when I heard Winona yell. I went up to help but I could see that they was beyond what I could do."

"You think Winona did it?"

"Beats me."

"You see anybody else around?"

"No," I said. Chaim had mentioned Robert Williams, but I hadn't seen him.

"Nobody?"

"I seen Chaim, an' Chaim seen me. That's it."

"Where were you before you got to work?"

"I was at breakfast, with a friend'a mines."

"Who was that?"

"Her name was Shirley."

"Shirley what?"

"I don't know the girl's last name but I know where she lives."

"How long were you at the church before you went down to the basement?"

"I went right down."

So we started from the top again. And again.

One time he asked me if I heard the shots.

"Shots?"

"Yeah," he answered gruffly. "Shots."

"They were shot?"

"What did you think?"

"I'ont know, man, they coulda been stabbed fo'all I know."

That was it for officer Naylor. He got up and left in disgust. A few minutes later he returned and told me I could go. Chaim and Winona had been gone for hours. The police didn't suspect them. Winona was too hysterical to be faking it, and nobody knew that Chaim was part of the Red Terror.

I went out on the street and caught a bus down Central to the church, then I drove home. Nothing seemed quite right. Everything was off. It was strange enough that so much had happened. But now people were dying and still it didn't make sense.

As if to prove my fears, Mouse was on my swinging sofa on the front porch, drinking whiskey. I could smell him from ten feet away.

He was usually a natty dresser. He wore silk and cashmere as another man might wear cotton. Women dressed him and then took him out to show the world what they had.

He told me once that a woman had the pockets in his pants taken out and replaced them with satin so that she could stroke him under the table, or at a show, the way she did at home.

But it wasn't the smooth dresser I saw on my porch. He hadn't shaved in days, and Mouse had that kind of sparse beard that looked ratty on a man. His clothes were soiled, his disposition was taciturn. And he was drunk. Not the one-night kind of drunk but a drunk that you can only get from days of booze.

"Hiya, Easy."

"Mouse."

I sat down next to him and all of a sudden I had the feeling that we were young men again, as if we'd never left Texas. I guess that's what I was hoping for, simpler times.

"I ain't got my gun, man," Mouse said.

"No?"

"Naw."

"How come?"

"Might kill somebody, Easy. Somebody I don't wanna kill."

"Whas wrong wit' you, Ray? You sick?"

He laughed, hunching forward as if he were having a seizure.

"Yeah," he said. "Sick. Sick t' death of all this pain."

"What pain is that?"

He looked into my eyes with a steely gray gaze. "You seen my boy?"

"Yeah, when Etta come she brought him."

"He's a beautiful boy, ain't he?"

I nodded.

"He got big feet and a big mouf. Shit, that's all you need in this world. That's all you need."

Mouse stopped talking, so I said, "He's a great boy. Strong, and he's smart too."

"He's the devil hisself," Mouse whispered to his left arm.

"What's that you said?"

"Satan. Evil angel'a hell. You could tell the way his eyebrows goes up, makin' like horns."

"LaMarque kinda mischievous, but he ain't bad, Raymond."

"Satan in hell. Black cats and voodoo curse. You 'member Mama Jo?"

"Yeah."

I'd never forget her.

Mouse had conned me into driving him, in a stolen car, to a small bayou town in eastern Texas called Pariah. We were barely in our twenties but Mouse's true nature was already fully developed. He wanted a dowry his mother had promised him before she died. He was to marry EttaMae and he said, "I will get that money or daddyReese will be dead." Reese was Mouse's stepfather.

But before we ever got to Pariah, Mouse had me drive to a place out in the middle of the swamplands. There we came to a house hidden on all sides by pear trees that doubled as pillars. And in that house lived the country witch, Mama Jo. She was a six-foot-six witch who lived by her wits out beyond the laws of normal men. She was twenty years older than I, and I was barely twenty. But she put a spell on me when we stayed with her for a night. Mouse was out planning the murder and Mama Jo had me by the hair. I was screaming love for her and talking out of my head. I remembered the smell of her breath: sweet chili and garlic, bitter wine and stale tobacco.

"She always told me," Mouse said, "that sometimes evil come down on ya when you live bad. Evil come out in your chirren if you don't pay fo' what you done."

"LaMarque ain't like that, Ray."

"How you know?" he shouted, rearing up belligerently. "That boy done give me the eye, Easy. He tole me hisself that he hates me. He tole me hisself that he wisht I was dead. Now tell me it don't take a evil son to make that kinds wish on his own daddy."

I was thinking about Etta. I was trying to figure out how I thought I could get away with being her lover and Mouse's friend too.

"He don't hate you, Ray. He just a boy an' he mad that you an' Etta cain't be together."

"Devil outta hell," he whispered again. Then he said, "I did what a daddy's s'posed, Ease. I mean, I ain't ever seen my own daddy, an' you know I killed Reese."

Mouse had finally murdered his stepfather despite my attempts to stop him.

"Yeah," Mouse continued. "Kilt 'im dead. But you know him an' his son Navrochet beat me reg'lar an' laughed on it too."

Mouse had also killed his stepbrother, Navrochet.

"LaMarque don't think'a you like that, Ray," I said.

"Yes he do. Yes he do. An' you know I ain't given him no reason, man. You know I loved that boy an' I done right by him." There were tears streaming down his face. "You know sometimes I pick him up an' take 'im down t' Zelda's big-timin' house. The ho's there love it when you bring a boy. They jus' fuss over him an' give 'im chocolates. An' I shows 'im how t'gamble an' dance. But you know he start t'actin' shy an' scared an' shit. Embarrass me in front'a Zelda herself.

"But you know he always runnin' after me t'go t'the bafroom at the same time." Mouse smiled then. "He look at Dick like he ain't never seen nuthin' that big. Then, right after the las' time we went, he tole me that he don't wanna go nowhere wit' me no mo'. He won't even talk to' me an' if I try an' make 'im he scream like a demon, right out there in the middle'a the street just like I was a bad man, like Reese."

Before Mouse got the drop on Reese the old farmer had us on the run through the swamp. Raymond had killed one of his hunting dogs, but he had two more and they were chasing us down through the trees. We finally escaped, but by then it was nightfall and we had to stay outside for the night. I had the grippe and Mouse curled around me like a momma cat, keeping me warm through the night. I might have died if he hadn't cared for me.

I reached out my hands and held him by the forearms while he cried. It was loud and embarrassing but I didn't let go.

"I'm sorry, Raymond," I said after he stopped. He looked up at me, his eyes were red and his nose was running.

"I love that boy, Easy."

"He loves you too, man. That's your son, your blood. He loves you."

"Then why he act like that?"

"He just a li'l boy, that's all. You go down wit' all them wild folks you know an' he get so scared an' worked up that he wanna get outta there. He cain't stand it."

"Why don't he tell me that? I take 'im fishin'."

"He prob'ly don't know, man. You know kids don't really think, 'cept 'bout what feel good, and what don't."

Mouse sat back and stared at me as if I had just pulled a rabbit out of my ear. I could see the change come about in him. He sat up a little straighter, his eyes cleared.

I said, "Why don't you come on in? You get a shower and a good night's sleep. I'll talk wit' LaMarque the next time I'm over there."

I made the call while Mouse was in the shower.

"How's it going, Mr. Rawlins?" Special Agent Craxton asked.

"Minister and his girlfriend got killed."

"What?"

I told him about the murders. He asked all sorts of questions about the room.

Finally he said, "Sounds like a professional job."

"Could just be a good shot."

"Then why wasn't anything moved around, messed up?"

"She was down on his peter, man, maybe her husband found 'em. Maybe Winona found 'em and she thought Towne was hers."

"Maybe. Hear me," he said. "I'll look into things on my end. Meanwhile, you find out what you can about the minister. Who has he been seeing, what kind of political connections does he have?"

Craxton was the boss, so I said, "Okay."

Raymond came out of the shower with a towel around his hips and a smile on his face.

"You look better," I said.

"And you look like you just swallowed a pig. What's wrong, Easy?"

"You might as well ask what's right."

"You gonna talk to LaMarque fo' me?"

"Soon as I can, man."

He laughed like a small boy, younger even than his son.

"Then tell me what's wrong."

"I owe a man some money an' he holds the deed

149

t'my houses. He want me to find some stuff on some men work down at First African."

I lied to Mouse because I was afraid that if I told him the truth he might decide to do me a Louisiana kind of favor, like burning down the IRS office, records and all.

"Yeah?"

"So then the minister, Reverend Towne, and some girl gets killed and I was there when it happened. And another man work for the first man's company still wants my houses and a girl live in one'a my places hung herself on account of I wanted t' throw her out. Or maybe she was murdered."

"You talk wit' the boy an' I kill the men, Easy."

"Naw, man. They work fo' big companies. You know, cut off one an' two take his place."

"White men?"

"Yeah."

"You think about it, man. If you want sumpin' just call me."

He dressed in the bathroom and left soon afterwards. He didn't stay, because his good clothes were at Dupree's and he was ready to look good again.

After he'd gone I went to my bed and drank three glasses of whiskey too fast. I passed out thinking that I should call EttaMae.

# 24

THE FAT AMBULANCE ATTENDANT STOOD AWKWARDLY ON A high kitchen chair, a butcher's knife in his hand. He was sawing at the rope Poinsettia hung from. The sound was loud, like two men hacking at a tree. Finally she fell to the floor. The dead weight hit with a terrible impact. Her body had become soft and so punky that one of her arms and her head flew off. But it was the sound as she hit the floor that was the worst. The floorboards started rattling and the walls shook. The whole house vibrated with the power of an earthquake.

When I started awake it was barely dawn. The sky out my window had that weak blue of the early sun, but the racket hadn't stopped. For a moment I thought that I was really in an earthquake. But then I realized that it was someone knocking at the door.

When that someone shouted, "Police!" I thought that I would rather it be a natural disaster.

"Hold on!" I shouted back. I hauled on some slacks and a T-shirt and stepped into a beat-up pair of slippers.

When I opened the door Naylor and Reedy each took hold of an arm.

"You're under arrest," Naylor said, then he spun me around and put on the handcuffs.

I wasn't surprised, so I didn't say anything. If somebody had taken me out behind the house and put a bullet in my head I wouldn't have been surprised.

151

There was nothing I could do, so I just hung my head and hoped I could ride out the storm.

I rode it out to the Seventy-seventh Street station. There they put me in a small room with the handcuffs still on. After a while the fat policeman with the red face, Officer Fine, came in to keep me company.

I asked him, "Am I under arrest?"

He showed me a mouth full of bad teeth.

"Well if I am I should be allowed a call, right?"

That didn't even get him to smile.

After a short while Reedy came in and asked the fat man to sit in the hall. He looked at me with sad green eyes and said, "Do you want to confess, Mr. Rawlins?"

"I wanna make a call is all."

Naylor came in then. They pulled up chairs on either side of me.

"I don't have much patience with murderers, Mr. Rawlins, especially when those murderers have killed a woman. A Negro woman at that," Naylor said. "So I want to know what happened or Reedy and I are going to go for coffee and we're going to leave Fine to ask the questions."

"That's mighty white'a you, brother," I grinned.

He slapped my face, not too hard though. I got the feeling that Quinten Naylor was trying to save me from real injury.

"Wanna get Fine?" Reedy asked while stifling a yawn.

"Who killed the minister and the girl?" Naylor asked me.

"I'ont know, man, I'ont know."

"Who killed Poinsettia Jackson?"

"She killed herself, right?"

They both were looking at me hard.

"I found 'er hangin' there, thas it, hangin'. I ain't killed nobody."

"But somebody hit her on the head, Easy. They knocked her unconscious and hung her from the light fixture," Naylor said. "Then they knocked the chair over to make it look like she'd used it to hang herself, but the chair was too far from the body, that's how we got onto them. They murdered her, Easy. Now do you know why anybody would want to do that?"

Philadelphia! It came to me just that fast. Quinten was an eastern Negro from Philadelphia, I'd've bet anything.

"Mr. Rawlins," Reedy said.

"How should I know?"

"Maybe you know someone who had a motive, a reason," Reedy continued. Naylor sat back and stared.

"Why anybody wanna kill a sick girl?"

"Maybe to get her ass outta that apartment."

"How should I know? Why don't you ask the owner?"

"I'm asking," Reedy said. He was looking me in the eye.

I pretended that I was alone on a raft in a rough sea. The policemen were sharks cruising my craft. I was safe for the moment, but I was taking on water.

"I wanna lawyer, I wanna make some calls."

"Why'd you lie to us, man?" Naylor asked. He sounded embarrassed, as if my little trick made him look bad at the station.

"Just gimme a phone, all right?"

"We'll give you Officer Fine," Reedy said.

"Send the mothahfuckah in then," the voice in my head said. "Let's see us some blood."

I didn't say a word but stared bullets at the cops instead. I knew how to take a beating. My old man used to take me out behind the house many a time before he finally left for good. Sometimes, when I was still a boy, I missed his whipping stick.

Reedy said, "Shit!" and walked out. Officer Fine replaced him by the door.

Naylor leaned close to me and said, "This could turn ugly, Ezekiel. I can't protect you if you don't give."

"Cut that shit out, man. You one'a them. You dress like them an' you talk like them too."

"Detective Reedy wants you in the hall, Naylor," Fine said. He was almost polite.

"Let me get a call or two, man," I hissed at Naylor. "You wanna save my ass, gimme some rights."

I held my breath while the black cop thought. Fine would have liked to kill me, I could tell that by the way he smelled.

"Come on," Naylor finally said.

"Hey wha . . ." Fine started to say, but Quinten stood up to him, and Quinten Naylor looked to be made from bricks.

"He's going to make a call. That's his right," Naylor said.

Naylor unlocked my handcuffs and led me down the hall toward a small area that was partitioned off by three frosted glass walls. Each one was about six feet high. There was a phone on a wooden stool in the cubicle.

"There you go," Naylor said to me, then he stood back to show me some privacy. Reedy came down with Fine and the three men started to haggle. I was a dead longhorn and those men were vultures, every one of them.

I dialed Mofass' office. No answer.

I dialed the boardinghouse he lived in. On the third ring Hilda Bark, the owner's daughter, answered. "Yeah?"

"Mofass there?"

"He gone."

"Gone where?"

"Gone. Don't you understand English?" she scolded me the way her mother must have scolded her. "He left."

"You mean he moved out?"

"Uh-huh," she grunted and then she hung up.

The men were still haggling over my bones, so I quickly dialed Craxton's number.

"FBI," a bright male voice said.

"Yeah, yeah, right. Can I talk to Agent Craxton?"

"Agent Craxton is in the field today. He'll be back tomorrow. Would you like to leave a message?"

"Is he gonna call in?"

"Hard to say, sir. Agent Craxton is a field agent. He goes where he wants to and calls when he feels like it."

"Please tell him that this is Ezekiel Rawlins calling from the Seventy-seventh Street police station. Tell him that I need to see him down here right away."

"What's the nature of your business?"

"Just tell 'im, man."

He hung up on me too.

The next place I dialed was First African Day School. The phone was ringing when Fine came up and grabbed me by the shoulder.

"Nobody else was home," I told him.

"Okay," he smiled. He'd wait until I was finished with this call and then he'd see how loud I could scream.

"Hello?" a voice I didn't recognize said.

"May I speak to Odell Jones, please?"

There was a long wait but Odell finally came on the line.

"Yes?"

"Odell?"

"Easy?"

"Man, I'm in trouble."

"That's how you was born, man. Born to trouble an' bringin' everybody else down wit' you."

"They got me in jail, Odell."

"That's where criminals belong, Easy, in jail." He even raised his voice!

"Listen, man, I ain't had nuthin' t' do wit' Towne. It wasn't me, not at all."

"If it wasn't you then tell me this," he said. "If you didn't go out there to the church in the first place would he be dead now?"

It was a good question. I didn't have an answer.

"So what you want?" he asked curtly.

"Come get me outta here, man."

"How'm I gonna do that? I ain't got no money. All I got is God."

"Odell," I pleaded.

"Call on someone else, Easy Rawlins, this well is dry."

Three strikes and Fine took me by the arm.

"I'm off duty now, Mr. Rawlins," Quinten Naylor said. "Officer Fine will continue your interrogation."

# 25

OFFICER FINE WAS A PATIENT MAN. PATIENT AND DELI-cate. He and his partner, a wan-faced rookie called Gabor, taught me little secrets like how far an arm can be twisted before it will break.

"All you gotta do is take your time," Fine said to no one in particular, as he twisted my right hand toward the base of my skull. "I could get these here fingers over the head and into the mouth and he'd probably bite 'em off t' stop the hurt."

"Don't give in, Easy!" the voice screamed in my head.

"Why'd you kill her?" Gabor asked me. I wanted to hit him but my feet and my left hand were manacled to the chair.

We'd been playing the game for over an hour. I'd been slapped, kicked, beaten with a rolled-up magazine, and twisted like a licorice stick.

When I grimaced from the arm twisting I felt dry blood crack across my cheek.

That nearly broke me. I was almost ready to confess, confess to anything they'd say. But the voice kept screaming for me.

The door opened and a tall silver-haired man walked in. I was grateful for the respite, but when Fine released me it felt as if he'd torn the arm from its socket.

I moaned, humiliated and in pain as I gazed at those shiny black shoes.

"Captain," Gabor said.

Then I saw a second pair of shoes that were as bright as polished onyx.

"This is what you call questioning, John?" Special Agent Craxton asked.

"It's a hard case, uh, Agent Craxton," the silver-haired man answered. Then he said to Fine, "Agent Craxton here is with the FBI. He needs Mr. Rawlins for a case he's working on."

"What about the murders?" Fine asked.

"Unchain him and apologize or I tear off your prick and shove it down your throat," Craxton said simply, almost sweetly.

Fine didn't like that, he brought his fists up to his chest and pushed his body forward a little, but when he peered into Craxton's eyes he backed down. He even unlocked my manacles, but he didn't apologize and he looked defiant, like a child angered at his father.

Craxton just smiled. The spaces between his teeth made him look like an alligator that had evolved to human form.

"Send me this officer's file, John."

"Apologize, Charlie," Captain John said.

The fat cop who had caused me so much pain said, "I'm sorry." And even though I was so hurt, that sounded good to me. His humiliation was like sweet, cold ice cream on hot apple pie.

I rubbed the dried blood from my face and said, "Fuck you, mothahfuckah. Fuck you twice."

It wasn't smart but I never imagined that I'd live to be an old man.

Agent Craxton was with two men who looked like real FBI. They wore dark suits and ties with white shirts and short-brimmed hats. They had black shoes and white socks and small bulges on the left side of their bulky jackets. They were clean-shaven and silent as stones.

They were also the same men that I saw Shirley talking to in front of her house.

The twins got in the front seat of a black Pontiac. Craxton and I got in behind. We headed out into the street, turning every three blocks or so. I don't think we had a destination; at least not a place we were going to.

"They think you killed all of them, Easy. Killed the girl at your place and killed the minister too."

"Yeah, I know."

"Did you?"

"Did I what?"

"Kill your tenant?"

"What for? Why I wanna kill her?"

"You tell me. She was your tenant. She wasn't paying your rent."

"Ain't nuthin to' tell. I found Poinsettia dead and I found the minister too. Bad luck, that's all."

"I can understand why they suspect you, though. If I hadn't sent you into that church myself I'd think it pretty strange."

"Yeah, that's how things happen—strange. I seen all kindsa things happen you wouldn't believe."

"Somebody's on to you, Mr. Rawlins. Somebody knows you're working with us."

"Why you say that?"

"Because this murder in the church was professional. Either they hired it out or one of the Russians did it themselves."

"Did? You mean shot them? Why would anybody wanna come kill Towne?"

"The reverend must've been involved. They thought they could cover their tracks by killing him."

"Why not just kill me?"

"Kill a weed at its root, that's what they do. He could have been their prize pupil but they cut him short if they think he'd jeopardize even one thing."

I decided to take a chance with Craxton.

"Man, they gotta be sumpin' you ain't tellin' me."

He paused, looking at me for a few moments before speaking.

"Why do you say that?"

"Well, I been on Wenzler for some days now an' I cain't see where he's any big thing. So I gotta wonder why you wanna get me out of a fed'ral charge just to spy on some small-time union guy. Then, on top'a that, this man gets himself killed an' you sure it's got somethin' t'do with what I'm doin'. Like I said— sumpin' don't add up."

Craxton leaned back against the window and began to outline his jaw with a hairy index finger. He started from the center of his chin and worked his way up the left side of his face. As his finger progressed a smile began to form. It was a full-fledged grin by the time he'd reached the earlobe.

"You're a smart one, eh, Rawlins?"

"Yeah," I said. "So smart that I'm here with you worryin' 'bout my liberty, my money, and my life. If I was any smarter I wouldn't even have to breathe."

"Wenzler's got something," Craxton said.

"Yeah? What's that?"

"You don't really need to know that, Easy. All you need to know is that we're playing for high stakes here. We're playing for keeps."

"You sayin' I could get killed?"

"That's right."

"So why the fuck didn't you say that before?" One of the robots in the front seat cocked his head a little. But I didn't let that bother me. "Here you lettin' me walk around like everything is goin' on accordin' t'plan an' really they's people drawin' a bead on me."

Craxton wasn't bothered by me, though.

"You want to go to prison, Easy?" he asked. "Just say the word and we can hand you back to Agent Lawrence."

"Listen," I said. "If you know what it is that Wenzler has got why don't you just take him?"

"We have, Easy. We arrested him and interrogated him. But he gave us nothing and we haven't got any proof. We don't have a fiber of evidence. I can't tell you what it is that we think he has but I can tell you that it's something important. I can tell you that it would hurt America to let it slip through our fingers."

"So you ain't gonna tell me what it is I'm lookin' for?"

"It's better if you don't know, Easy. Believe me, you don't want to know."

"Okay then, tell me this," I said. "Does whatever this is have to do with Andre Lavender?"

"I can tell you that if you know where Lavender is you should tell us. This isn't about race, Easy, it's about your country."

"So I should go out there with a bull's-eye on my back 'cause you say so?"

"You can pull out anytime."

He knew the chances of me doing that. "So you want me to stay on Wenzler?"

"That's right. And now you have the knowledge that Towne was somehow linked. We already have his involvement with the antiwar people. You can work from his relationship with Wenzler. For all we know Wenzler is the one who killed him."

Chaim had been a killer in Poland. The war wasn't so far back that a good soldier would forget his trade.

"What about Poinsettia? You think the Russians killed her?"

He gave me a hard look then.

"You could have killed her, or maybe somebody else did. I don't know and I don't care, because I don't have that job."

"You better believe those cops care."

Craxton shifted in his seat and gazed out the window.

"When this is over I'll explain why you were at the church," he said, leaning so close to the glass that steam clouded his already dim reflection. "I'll tell them that you're a hero. If they have no physical evidence you did the girl, then . . ." He hunched his shoulders and turned from the window to look at me. I felt a trickle of blood come down the side of my face.

"Ever been out in a cold foxhole, Ezekiel?"

"More times than I'd like t' remember."

"It's cold and alone out there, but that sure makes coming home sweet."

I didn't say anything, but I could have said, "Amen to that."

"Yeah," he continued. "Pain makes men out of scared little boys."

The sun was a big red ball just over the city. The underbellies of the clouds over our heads were long black hanging things, like stalactites in a great cave, but above those clouds was a bright orange that was almost religious it was so warm. I could almost hear the church organs.

"Yeah, Ezekiel, we have a real job to do. And it might get kind of painful."

I couldn't twitch my baby finger without a jolt going through my arm, but I asked, "How you figure?"

"We got to get Wenzler. He's a tough man and he's in with people worse than that. I know that you're taking a chance, but we need that to get this job done."

"What if I do all this you say an' I still don't find nuthin'?"

"If I don't get what I want, Mr. Rawlins, then my job isn't worth a cent. If I can't make this case you'll be shit out of luck along with me."

"And if you do find it?"

"Then I help you, Easy. Sink or swim."

"I have your word, Mr. Craxton?"

Instead of answering me he asked, "Home?"

"Yeah."

On the ride all he talked about was how he was going to buy some bonita, cut the fish in chunks, scald it, and then marinate it in a vinegar and soya sauce. It was a dish he'd learned to make while on duty in Japan.

"Nips know how to do fish," he said.

# 26

"WHAT YOU THINKIN' 'BOUT, EASY?" ETTA ASKED.

We were lying back in her bed. I had my hands together behind my head and she was running her fingers along my erection, under the covers. I felt strange. It was one of those feelings that doesn't quite make sense. My body was excited but my mind was calm and wondering about the next move I should make. If Etta hadn't kept her fingers going like that I would have been nervous, unable to think about anything.

I came to her house in the evening, after LaMarque had gone to bed. She bathed me and then I loved her, again and again until it was close to sunrise. I don't think there was much pleasure in it for her, except maybe the pleasure of helping me dull the fear and pain I felt.

"'Bout them people. 'Bout how they dead but still I gotta worry 'bout 'em. That's what makes us different from the animals."

"How's that?" she whispered and, at the same time, she gave me a little squeeze.

"If a dog see sumpin' dead he just roll around on the corpse a few times an' move on, huntin'. But I find a dead man an' it's like he's alive, followin' me around an' pointin' his finger at me."

"What you gonna do, baby?"

"FBI man thinks Reverend Towne was mixed up in

163

somethin'. He thinks that Towne was messed up wit' communists."

"What com'unists?"

"Uh, that feels good," I said. "The Jew I been workin' for, communist."

"What they gotta do wit' Towne?"

She sat up a little.

I said, "Put your hand back, Etta, put it back."

She grinned at me and settled back against my chest.

"That's why the government got me outta jail. They want the Jew," I said, clearheaded again.

"So? Let them do it. You ain't gotta go out an' do they job."

"Yeah," I said. Then I sat back and smiled because so much pleasure could come after pain.

"Mofass is gone," I said after a while.

"Gone where?"

"Nobody knows."

"Outta his house?"

"Uh-huh. He left some kinda half-assed note at the office. Said his mother was sick down in New Orleans and he was going to care for her. He let his room go too. That's some strange shit."

"Ain't nuthin' wrong wit' that."

"I guess. But I cain't see Mofass runnin' out without a word."

"People change when it comes t' family."

"But that's just it, Mofass never even liked his momma."

"You just cain't tell, Easy, blood is strong."

I knew she was right about that. I loved my father more than life even though he abandoned me when I was eight years old.

"But you know it is funny," Etta said.

"What?"

"You know that boy tried to beat up on you after church?"

"Willie Sacks?"

"Uh-huh. His momma, Paulette, come by here today."

"Why's that?"

"I asked her 'cause I wanted her to know how Willie had come after you. I told her but she already knew it. She said Willie had gone bad after he met Poinsettia."

"Bad how?"

"She had'im runnin' after her an' spendin' all his money. Willie used t'take his money home. He ain't got no father an' Paulette relied on him t'pay the rent."

"Boys grow up, Etta. LaMarque do the same thing when some girl get him to feelin' like this." I touched her hand.

"But you know Willie never made enough an' Mofass was payin' fo' that girl too."

"What?"

"Mofass been payin' her rent the last year. Poinsettia told Willie 'bout it. She said how sometimes she had to go out with him but that they never did any more than kiss."

"No lie?" I never thought Mofass chased the ladies.

"But she also said how Mofass had her go out with other men sometimes."

"You mean like he was her pimp?"

"I don't know, Easy. I just know what Paulette said. Now you know she heard it from her son an' he got it from Poinsettia. Willie broke up with her when he found out. At least that's what Paulette thought. But after her accident she started callin' again. Maybe Mofass did somethin' to that girl."

"I don't know," I said. "But I can't see it. What could she have on him to make him wanna do that?"

"You'll find out."

"What makes you think so?"

"I just know it, that's all. You're a smart man, and you care too."

"Yeah?"

"Uh-huh."

She tossed back the blankets so that I could see her handiwork. She watched it too.

"I want some more, baby." She said it loudly and bold as if she were announcing to an audience.

I knew she didn't but I asked, "You do?"

"Yeah." It was almost a growl in my ear.

"Where?"

And she guided me. And I turned into a rutting pig again, trying to rut myself to safety.

I woke up with a start. There was a sound somewhere in the apartment. I worried that Mouse was in the other room with his revolver but at the same moment I looked at EttaMae. I looked at her feeling how spent I was and I realized that I wanted her more than just for sex. That was new to me. Usually sex was the first and last thing with me, but I wanted her with the same ardor when I was all used up.

I snaked out of bed and slithered into my pants. There was no light from outside or from the other room. I eased the door open and saw him sitting in the living room. He was swinging his head back and forth and kicking the heels of his feet against the couch.

"LaMarque!"

"Hi, Unca Easy," he said, looking around me to the room I came from.

"What you doin' up?"

"You sleep wit' my momma?"

"Yeah." I couldn't think of anything else to say. I could only hope that he would never repeat it to Mouse. I would have liked to ask him to keep it quiet, but it was a sin, I thought, to make a child lie.

"Oh."

"Why you up?" I asked again.

"Dreams."

"What kinda dreams?"

"'Bout a big ole monster wit' a hunert eyes."

"Yeah? He chase you?"

"Uh-uh. He ax me if I wanna ride an' then he take me flyin' so high an' then he start fallin' like we gonna crash."

LaMarque's eyes opened wide with fear as he spoke.

"Then," he went on, "he stop jus' fo' we crash an' he laugh. An' I ax 'im t' let me go but he jus' keep on flyin' high an' scarin' me."

I sat next to him and let him crawl into my lap. He was panting at first.

I waited until he'd calmed down and then I asked, "Do you like it when your daddy takes you to Zelda's?"

"Uh-uh, it's smelly there."

"Smell like what?"

"Dookey an' vomick." He stuck out his tongue.

"You tell your momma 'bout what it smells like there?"

"Uh-uh, I never telled. I's ascared ta."

"How come?"

"I'ont know."

"You think that they might fight if you told?"

"Uh-huh, yeah."

He'd grabbed a fistful of the fabric of my pants and wrung it.

"You know if you told your daddy that you didn't wanna go there no more he wouldn't take you."

"Yeah he would. He like to be gamblin' an' gettin' pussy."

When LaMarque said the last word he ducked down as if I might hit him.

"No, honey," I said and I patted his head. "Your daddy wanna see you more than them folks. He wants to play ball wit' you, an' watch TV too."

He didn't say anything to that, so we just sat for a

while. He was wringing my pants hard enough to pinch me.

"Your daddy gonna come visit you an' Etta in a coupla days," I said after a long while.

"When?"

"Prob'ly day after tomorrow, I bet."

"He gonna bring me a present?"

"I bet he does."

"Are you gonna be in my momma's bed?"

I laughed and hugged him to my chest.

"No," I said. "I got work to do."

We sat there and watched the sun come up. Then we both fell asleep. I dreamed about Poinsettia again. The flesh was coming off her. She was deteriorating in my dreams from one night to the next; soon she'd just be bones.

I awoke maybe half an hour after we'd gone to sleep. LaMarque was snoring. I carried him to his room and then I looked in on Etta. She was in the same position, one powerful hand thrown up next to her beautiful, satin-brown face. I still wanted her the way I had for so many years, but for the first time in my life I considered marriage.

I left a note in the kitchen telling Etta that Mouse would be by to visit his son in a couple of days. I told her that everything was fine. I signed it, "I love you."

# 27

FROM ETTAMAE'S I WENT OVER TO MERCEDES BARK'S house on Bell Street. Bell was a short block of large houses with brick fences and elaborate flower gardens. During Christmas everyone on Bell put out thousands of colored lights around their trees and bushes and along the frames of their houses. People lined up in their cars to see that street for three weeks either side of Christmas Day. It was just that kind of a neighborhood. Everybody worked together to make it nice.

It was all good and well but there was a down side to the Bell Street crowd; they were snobs. They thought that their people and their block were too good for most of the rest of the Watts community. They frowned on a certain class of people buying houses on their street and they had a tendency to exclude other people from their barbecues and whatnot. They even encouraged their children to shun other kids they might have met at school or at the playground, because it was the Bell Street opinion that most of the black kids around there were too coarse and unsophisticated.

Mercedes had a three-story house in the middle of the block. The walls were painted white and the trim was a deep forest green. There were chairs and sofas set out along the porch and a bright green lawn surrounded by white and purple dahlias, white sweetheart roses, and dwarf lemon trees.

Mercedes' husband, Chapman, had been a dentist

and could afford the upkeep on so large a domicile. But when he died the widow was quick to realize that his life insurance wasn't enough to maintain the family in the way they had lived before. So she took the money and turned the upper floors into a boardinghouse. She could accommodate as many as twelve tenants at one time.

The neighborhood association took Mercedes to court. They complained that their beautiful street would be ruined by the kind of riffraff that had to live in a single room for weekly rent. But the county court didn't agree and Mrs. Bark started her rooming house.

Mofass was her first and most long-lasting tenant. He didn't need a kitchen because he took his meals at the Fetters Real Estate Office. And he certainly didn't want to be bothered with leaky roofs and shaggy lawns after doing that kind of work all day.

I got to the Bell Street Boardinghouse at about nine-thirty that morning. I knew that Mrs. Bark was sitting in a stuffed chair just inside the front door but I couldn't see her. She was hidden in the shadow of a stairwell and by the screen door, but she still had a good view of whoever came to visit.

I waited patiently ringing the bell even though I knew damn well that she could see me. I carried a tan rucksack in which I had two quart bottles of Rainier Ale.

"Who is that?" Mrs. Bark asked after the fourth ring.

"Easy Rawlins, ma'am. On some business for Mofass."

"You too late, Easy Rawlins. Mofass done moved out already."

"I know that, ma'am, that's why I'm here. Mofass called me from down south and said that I should get some papers that he left in his room by mistake."

I wasn't taking much of a chance. If Mofass had

moved out all of a sudden he might have left something that would give me an idea about his relationship with Poinsettia. If he'd moved out clean I would have just been caught in a white lie by one of the snobs of Bell Street.

"What?" she cried. The audacity of Mofass forced Mercedes Bark to her feet, which was no easy task. She waddled her great body to the door and then rested by leaning her upper arm against the jamb. Mercedes wasn't tall, and if you only looked at her bespectacled face you would never have guessed how large she was. Even her shoulders were small, you might have called them slender. But from there on down Mercedes Bark was a titan. Her breasts and buttocks were tremendous. She took up the entire lower half of the doorway.

"He got some nerve," she said. "Sendin' you here when he left me a room fulla mess and now I cain't even rent the place until I hire somebody to clean it out."

"But that's just it, ma'am. Mofass told me that he was sorry but that his mother got sick so fast that he didn't have time to think things out. He don't wanna move outta this place. He told me to pay you the sixty dollars for his next month's rent."

I had the money in my hand. Mrs. Bark turned from a snapping wolf to a loon, crooning her sorrows for Mofass' poor mother and complimenting a son's deep love.

She got the key, after taking my money, and even came out of her apartment to point me on the way. Mofass' room was far from being a mess. It was neat as a pin and as orderly as a pharaoh's tomb. In the center drawer of his desk were his pencils, pens, pads of paper, and ink pads. In the righthand drawers were all of the receipts of his bills for his entire life. He still kept ticket stubs for movies he'd seen in New Orleans twenty years before. In the lower left drawer he kept folders detailing his daily business. One folder was for expenses, another for expenditures, and like that.

He also had a drawer full of cigars. I knew something was wrong when I saw them. For Mofass to leave fifty good cigars he must have been really shaken.

I searched the rest of the place without finding very much. Nothing under the bed or between the mattresses or even in his clothes. No loose boards or envelopes taped under the drawers.

Finally I sat down at his desk again and put my hand flat on top of it. Really it wasn't flat because there was a blotter there. I lifted it but there was nothing underneath so I let it fall back. And it made a little sound: flap flap. Not a single flap but two, as if there were two blotter sheets.

Mofass had slit his blotter in two and then taped it back together so he could keep things in there secret without calling any attention to them. But the tape had worn thin and the pages had separated.

I found a few items of interest there. First there was a receipt signed by William Wharton (Mofass' real name) from the Chandler Ambulance Service of Southern California. The bill was $83.30, issued for the transmission of a patient from Temple Hospital to 487 Magnolia Street on January 18, 1952. There was another hospital bill for $1,487.26 for two weeks of hospitalization of a P. Jackson. I couldn't imagine Mofass spending twenty dollars on a date and here he was spending six months' salary for a girl he urged me to evict.

The last two items were both envelopes. One had a hundred dollars in twenty-dollar bills and the other had a list of eight names, addresses, and phone numbers. The addresses were widely spread around the city.

While I was trying to make sense of what I'd found I

sensed someone, or maybe I heard him there behind me.

Chester Fisk was standing in the doorway. A tall and slender elderly gentleman, Mr. Fisk was Mercedes' father and a permanent resident of the Bell Street Boardinghouse. His skin color was somewhere between light brown and light gray highlighted in certain places, like his lips, with a brownish yellow.

"Mr. Rawlins."

"Hey, Chester. How's it goin'?"

"Oh." He contemplated a few seconds. "All right. Sun's a li'l too strong and the night's a li'l too long. But it beats the hell outta bein' dead."

"Maybe I could take a little of that heat off," I said. Then I pulled out the two bottles of ale.

For a moment I thought Chester might cry. His eyes filled with gratitude so docile that it was almost bovine.

"Well, well, well," he said. He rested his hand around the neck of the closest bottle.

"You seen Mofass just before he moved out, Chester?"

"Sure did. Everybody else was asleep but old men hardly need t'sleep no more."

"Was he upset?"

"Powerful." Chester accented his answer with a nod.

"Did you talk with him?"

"Not too much I didn't. He just had this one li'l bag packed. Prob'ly just had a toothbrush and a second pair a drawers in it. I ast'im was somethin' wrong an' he said that things were bad. Then he said that they was *real* bad."

"That's it? Did he say anything about his mother?"

"Nope. Didn't say nuthin' else 'bout nuthin'. Just rush in in a hurry an' run out the same way."

\* \* \*

On the drive back to my house I tried to figure what it all meant. I knew that Mofass had paid for Poinsettia's hospital bill and probably for her rent, maybe for a year or more. I also had some names that I didn't know all around L.A.

Maybe his mother was sick.

Maybe he killed Poinsettia. Maybe Willie did. Everything was just cockeyed.

# 28

THE PHONE RANG EIGHT TIMES BEFORE ZAREE BOUCHARD answered. "Hello?"

She sounded bored or fed up.

I said, "Hey, Zaree, how you doin'?"

"Oh, it's you, Easy." She didn't sound happy. "Which one of 'em you want?"

"Which one you wanna part wit'?"

"You could have 'em both fo'a dollar twenty-five."

I could see that we weren't going to play, so I said, "Let me have Dupree."

I heard her yell his name and then I winced at the hard knock of the receiver as she dropped it.

After a minute of quiet the phone started banging around again until finally Dupree said, "Yeah?"

"Mr. Bouchard," I exclaimed. "Easy here."

"Well, well, well." His voice reminded me of an alto sax going down the scale. "Mr. Rawlins. What can I do for you?"

"You heard about Towne?"

174

"Ain't done nuthin' but hear about it. That was a shame."

"Yeah. I was the one found the body, at least the one after Winona."

"I heard that, Easy. I heard that an' it made me think all over again how you was the last one saw Coretta 'fore Joppy Shag did her in."

Dupree always blamed me for his girlfriend's death. I never got mad at him, though, because I always felt a little responsible for it myself.

"Cops brought me in and I'm scared they might try an' pin it on me."

"Uh-huh," Dupree said. Maybe he wouldn't have minded the police finding me dirty.

"Yeah. Anybody know who the girl was they found with'im?"

"Couple'a folks I heard said that her name was Tania, somethin' like that. But nobody said where she come from, or where she been."

Dupree was a good man. No matter how he felt about me we were still friends. He wouldn't lie.

"What's goin' on with Zaree?" I asked.

"She mad on Raymond."

"How come?"

"First he all wild over Etta. Then he start drinkin' an' get all slouchy an' filthy. Then, just yestiday, he gets all dressed up an' last night he come in wit' two white girls."

"Yeah?"

"I tell ya, Easy." The old friendliness returned to Dupree's voice. "I couldn't sleep wit' the kinda racket they was makin'. I mean he had'em beggin' fo'it! An' if they asted fo' a little more in a soft voice he'd say, 'What you say?' and they had to scream."

"That got to Zaree?"

"Well, yeah," Dupree chuckled. "But what really got to'er was that I got hard up ev'ry time he got one of 'em, and then I'd go after her. I told'er that if she didn't want it then one'a them girls out there would."

Mouse was a bad influence on anything domestic.

"Lemme talk to'im, okay, Dupree?"

"Yeah." Dupree was still laughing when he got off the phone.

"Whas happenin', Ease?" Mouse asked in his cool tone.

"You gotta call Etta, Ray."

"Yeah?" You could hear the satisfaction in his voice.

"Yeah. Call'er an' take LaMarque out, to the park or somethin'."

"When?"

"Soon as you can, man, but you gotta remember somethin'."

"What's that?"

"LaMarque ain't hardly more than a baby, Ray. Don't go showin' him yo' business or takin' him out wit' one'a yo' girlfriends."

"What should I do?"

"Take him swimmin', or fishin'. Take 'im to the park an' play ball. What did you do when you was a boy?"

"Sometimes I'd sneak up on one'a them big river rats sunnin' hisself on the pier. You know I'd grab'im by the tail and swing the mothahfuckah 'round till I smash his ass on the pilin'."

"LaMarque is sensitive, Ray. He wanna play little kid games. All you gotta do is remember that an' he ain't gonna want you dead."

Mouse was quiet for a few moments, and then he said, "Okay," softly.

"So you gonna call?" I asked.

"Yeah."

"An' you gonna play wit' him?"

"Uh-huh, yeah, play."

"Okay then," I said.

176

"Easy?"

"Yeah?"

"You all right, man. You might got a nut or sumpin' loose, but you all right."

I didn't know just what he meant but it sounded as if we had become friends again.

# 29

I WAS STILL LAUGHING ABOUT DUPREE AND ZAREE WHEN I got off the phone. A good story or joke seems funnier when you're surrounded by death. I never laughed harder than when I rode along with Patton's army into the Battle of the Bulge.

I don't know how long he'd been knocking at the front door. Whoever it was he was a patient man. Knock knock knock, then a pause, then three more raps.

I can't say I was surprised to see Melvin Pride standing there. He wore black cotton pants, a white T-shirt, and a black sweater vest. It had been years since I had seen Melvin informally dressed.

"Melvin."

"Could I come in, Easy?"

There was an occasional twitch in his right cheek. A large nerve that connected his bloodshot eye with his ear.

I offered him coffee instead of liquor. After I'd served it we sat opposite each other in the living room, white porcelain cups cradled in our laps.

Then, instead of talking, we lit cigarettes.

After a long while Melvin asked, "How long you been living here?"

"Eight years."

Melvin and I were both serious men. We stared each other in the eye.

"Do you want something from me, Melvin?" I asked.

"I don't know, Brother Rawlins. I don't know."

"Must be somethin'. I'm surprised that you even knew my address."

Melvin took a deep draw on his cigarette and held it for a good five seconds. When he finally spoke, wisps of smoke escaped his nostrils, making his craggy face resemble a dragon.

"We do a lot of good work at First African," he said. "But there's lotsa pressure behind that good work. And you know all men don't act the same under pressure."

I nodded while gauging Melvin's size and strength.

"Who you been talkin' to, Melvin?" I asked. A spasm ran through the right side of his face.

"I don't need to be talkin' t'nobody, Easy Rawlins. I know *you*. Fo' years you been stickin' yo' nose in people's business. They say you got Junior Fornay sent up to prison. They say you'n Raymond Alexander done left a trail'a death from Pariah, Texas, right up here to Watts."

Even though what he said was true I acted like it wasn't. I said, "You don't know what you talkin' 'bout, man. All I do is take care'a some sweepin' here and there."

"You smart." Melvin smiled and winced at the same time. "I give ya that. I seen you cock your ear when me an' Jackie was talkin' on the church stair. Then I see you gettin' tight wit' Chaim Wenzler. You don't be givin' stuff away, Easy. Ev'rybody knows you a horse trader, man. So whatever you doin' up

there I know it ain't gotta do wit' no Christian love.
An' this time somebody talked. This time I *know* it's
you."

"Who said?"

"Ain't no need fo'me t'tell you nothin', man. I
know, and that's all gotta be said."

"There's a name fo'the shit you talkin', Melvin," I
said. "I learned it at LACC. They call it paranoid. You
see, a man wit' paranoia be scared'a things ain't even
there."

Melvin's cheek jumped and he smiled again.

"Yeah," he said. "I be scared all right. An' you
know it's the scared animal you gotta watch out for.
Scared animals do things you don't expect. One
minute he be runnin' scared an' the nex' he scratchin'
at yo' windpipe."

"That's what you gonna do?"

Melvin stood up quickly, setting his cup on the arm
of his chair. I matched him, move for move.

"Let it be, Easy. Let it be."

"What?"

"We both know what I'm talkin' 'bout. Maybe we
made some mistakes but you know we did some good
too."

"Well," I said, trying to sound reasonable. "Let's
just lay it out so we both know what's happening."

"You heard all I got to say."

Melvin was finished talking. He didn't have a hat so
he just turned around and walked away.

I went after him to the door and watched as he went
between the potato and strawberry patches. His gait
was grim and deliberate. After he'd gone I went to the
closet, got my gun, and put it in my pocket. An hour
later I was pulling up to a house on Seventy-sixth
Street. The house belonged to Gator Wade, a plumber
from east Texas. Gator always parked his car in the
driveway, next to his house, so he had no use for the
little garage in the backyard. He floored the little

shack, wired and plumbed it, and let it out for twenty-five dollars a month.

Jackie Orr, the head deacon at First African, had been living there for over three years.

Gator was at work. I parked out front and made my way back to Jackie's house. Nobody answered my knock, so I pried open the lock and let myself in. Jackie worked during the daytime as a street sweeper for the city. I was fairly sure that he wouldn't interrupt me. And even if he did I doubted if he'd be armed.

The place was a mess but I couldn't be sure if someone had searched it or if Jackie was just a poor housekeeper, like most bachelors.

Next to his bed was a thick sheaf of purple-printed mimeographed papers. The title line read, "Reasons for the African Migration." It was a long rambling essay about Marcus Garvey and slavery and our ancestors back home in Africa. It wasn't the kind of literature I expected Jackie to read.

His clothes surprised me too. He had at least thirty suits hanging in the closet, and a different-color pair of shoes to match each one. I noticed a nice ring on his nightstand and a good watch too. I knew his salary wouldn't have covered the payments, and a woman would have to hear wedding bells to lay that kind of cash on a man's back.

Underneath the bottom drawer of his bureau was a thick envelope that contained more than a thousand dollars in denominations of twenty or less. There was also another list of names. This one included amounts of cash:

L. Towne,  -0-

M. Pride, 1,300

W. Fitzpatrick, 1,300

J. Orr, 1,300

S.A., 3,600

There was money changing hands. And in Jackie's case the money turned into clothes. I didn't know who S.A. was but I had it in mind to find out.

I left the money but I took the list with me. Sometimes words are worth more than money; especially if your ass is on the line.

# 30

JOHN'S PLACE WAS EMPTY EXCEPT FOR ODELL SITTING IN HIS corner, eating a sandwich. He wouldn't even return my nod. It was hard to lose a friend like that, but things were so twisted that I couldn't really feel it, except as a pang in my lower gut.

As John served me whiskey I asked him, "You seen Jackson t'day?"

"No," John answered. "But he be here. Jackson need to be in a bar where they don't allow no fightin'."

"You gotta save his butt a lot?"

John shrugged. "Lotta people cain't stand the man. He smart but he stupid too."

I took the drink to the far end of his bar and waited.

John always had his share of drunks and a few businessmen plying their various trades. Every once in a while there'd be a woman doing business, but that was rare, as John didn't want trouble with the police.

Jackson Blue came through the door at about four-thirty.

"Hey, Easy," he squealed in his high, crackly voice.

"Jackson. Come on over here and have a seat."

He was wearing a loose and silvery sharkskin suit. His coal-black skin against the light but shadowy fabric made him look like the negative of a photograph of a white man.

"S'appenin', Ease?" Jackson greeted me like I was his best friend.

Once, five years earlier, I came close to being murdered by a hijacker named Frank Green. I was never sure if Jackson was the one who told Frank Green, now deceased, that I was on his trail. All I know is that one day I was talking to Jackson about it and that night Frank had a knife to my throat. It really didn't matter if it was Jackson, because he didn't have anything against me personally. He was just trading in the only real business he knew—information.

"It's bad, Jack, bad as it could be. You wanna drink?"

"Yeah."

"Bring Jackson his milk, John."

While John served the triple shot of scotch, Jackson smiled and said, "Whas the problem?"

"You know what happened at First African, right?"

"Yeah, yeah, sure. You know Rita dragged me there Sunday 'fore last. Said she'd keep me company on Saturday if I took her t'church."

This satisfied look came over Jackson's face and I knew that he was about to start bragging on the acts of love Rita had performed.

I interrupted his reverie, saying, "You hear anything 'bout them killin's?"

"How come?"

"Poinsettia got herself hung a while back and I found the body."

"Yeah, I heard," he said. Then a light went on in his yellowy eyes. "An' you fount the minister too. They think it was you?"

182

"Yeah, and the cops don't even know who the girl was. They'd like to say it was me."

"Shit," Jackson snorted. "Mothahfuckahs couldn't fines no clue if it was nailed to they ass."

"You know sumpin' 'bout it, Jackson?"

Jackson looked over his shoulder, at the door. That meant he knew something and he was wondering if he should tell it. He rubbed his chin and acted cagey for a half a minute or so.

Finally he said, "What you doin' at City College, man?"

"What?"

"You go there, right?"

"Yeah."

"So what you takin'?"

"Basic like, remedial courses. Gettin' some basic history an' English I missed in night school. I got a couple'a advanced classes too."

"Yeah? What kinda history?"

"European. From the Magna Carta on."

"War," he stated simply.

"What's that you say?"

"Whatever it is I read about Europe is war. Them white men is always fightin'. War'a the Roses, the Crew-sades, the Revolution, the Kaiser, Hitler, the com'unists. Shit! All they care 'bout, war an' money, money an' land."

He was right, of course. Jackson Blue was always right.

"You wanna go to school there?"

"Maybe you wanna take me t'class one night. Maybe I see."

"What about the church, Jackson?"

"You say the cops don't even know who that girl is?"

"Nope."

"Maybe I go t'school an' be a cop."

"You gotta be five-eight at least to be a cop, Jack."

"Shit, man. If I ain't a niggah I'm a midget. Shit. You wanna get me another one, Ease?"

He pointed a long ebony finger at his empty glass.

I signaled for John to bring another. After he'd moved away Jackson said, "Tania's her name. Tania Lee."

"Where she live?"

"I'ont know. I just got it from one'a the young deacon boys—Robert Williams."

"He didn't know where she from?"

"Uh-uh. She just always tellin' him t'be proud'a his skin and to worship Africa."

"Yeah?"

"Yeah." Jackson grinned. "You know I 'preciate a girl like a dark-skinned man but you ain't gonna find me in no Africa."

"Why not, Jackson? You 'fraid'a the jungle?"

"Hell no, man. Africa ain't got no mo' wild than America gots. But you know I cain't see how them Africans could take kindly t'no American Negro. We been away too long, man." Jackson shook his head. He almost looked sorry. "Too long."

Jackson could have lectured me on the cultural rift between the continents all night, but an idea came to me.

"You ever hear of a group called the African Migration, Blue?"

"Sure, ain't you ever seen it? Down on Avalon, near White Horse Bar and Grill."

I had seen the place. It used to be hardware store, but the owner died and the heirs sold it to a real estate broker who rented it out to storefront churches.

"I thought that was just another church."

"Naw, Easy. These is Marcus Garvey people. Back to Africa. You know, like W.E.B. Du Bois."

"Who?"

"Du Bois. He's a famous Negro, Easy. Almost a

hundred years old. He always writin' 'bout gettin' back t'Africa. You prob'ly ain't never heard'a him 'cause he's a com'unist. They don't teach ya 'bout com'unists."

"So how do you know, if they don't teach it?"

"Lib'ary got its do' open, man. Ain't nobody tellin' you not to go."

There aren't too many moments in your life when you really learn something. Jackson taught me something that night in John's, something I'd never forget.

But I didn't have time to discuss the political nature of information right then. I had to find out what was happening, and it was the African Migration that was my next stop.

"Thanks, Jackson. You gonna be 'round fo'a while?" I put a five-dollar bill on the counter; Jackson covered it with his long skinny hand. Then he tipped his drink at me.

"Sure, Ease, sure I be here. You prob'ly find 'em too. They got a meetin' there just about ev'ry night."

There was a meeting going on in the gutted hardware store that evening. About forty people were gathered around a platform toward the back of the room to listen to the speakers.

A big man stopped me at the front door.

"You comin' to the meetin'?" he asked. He was tall, six-four or more, and fat. His big outstretched hand looked like the stuffed hand of a giant brown doll.

"Yeah."

"We like a little donation," the big man said, unconsciously rubbing the tips of his fingers together.

". . . they don't want us and we don't want them," I heard the female speaker in the back of the large room say.

"How little?" I asked.

"One dollar for one gentleman," he smiled.

I gave him two Liberty half-dollars.

The people in the room were a serious sort on the whole. Most of the men wore glasses, and every other person had a book or papers under their arm. Nobody noticed me. I was just another brother looking for a way to hold my head up high.

Among the crowd I made out Melvin Pride. He was intent on the speaker and so didn't notice me. I moved behind a pillar, where I could watch him without being seen.

The speaker was talking about home, Africa. A place where everybody looked like the people in that room. A place where the kings and presidents were black. I was moved to hear her.

But not so moved that I didn't keep an eye on the deacon. Melvin kept looking around nervously and rubbing his hands.

After a while the crowd broke out into a kind of exultant applause. The woman speaker, who wore wraparound African robes, bowed her head in recognition of the adulation before giving up the podium to the man behind her. She was chubby and light brown and had the face of a precocious schoolgirl, serious but innocent. Melvin went up to her, whispering while the next speaker prepared to address the crowd.

What looked to be a wad of folded money changed hands.

The man on the platform spoke in glowing terms about a powerful Negro woman who had shown leadership beyond her years. I knew it had to be Melvin's friend, because she took out a moment from her transaction to make eye contact with the speaker.

Melvin had finished his business anyway, he headed for the exit.

". . . Sonja Achebe," the speaker said. The crowd applauded again and the young woman headed for a doorway at the back of the room.

\* \* \*

"Miss Achebe?"

"Yes?"

She smiled at me.

"Excuse me, ma'am, but my name is Easy, Easy Rawlins."

She frowned a bit as if the name meant something to her but she couldn't quite remember why.

"Yes, Brother Rawlins."

The mood of the Migration, like that of so many other black organizations, was basically religious.

"I need to talk to you 'bout Tania Lee."

She knew who I was then. She didn't say anything, just pointed at a doorway. We walked toward it as another speaker began to preach.

"What is it you wanted to know about Sister Lee?" she asked. We were in a large storeroom that was cut into tiny aisles by rows of slender, empty shelves. It was like a rat's maze, dimly lit by sparse forty-watt bulbs.

"I need to know who killed her, and why."

"She's dead?" Miss Achebe made a lame attempt at surprise.

"Com'on, lady, you know what happened. She's one'a you people." I was reaching but I thought I might be right.

"You tell the police that?"

I stuck out my bottom lip and shook my head. "No reason. Least not yet."

Miss Achebe didn't look like a little girl anymore. The lines of an older woman etched her face.

"What do you want with me?" she asked.

"Who killed your friend and my minister?"

"I don't know what you're talking about. I don't have anything to do with killings."

"I saw you with Melvin and I seen him with Tania and Reverend Towne. Somethin's goin' on wit' you and the church. I know they gave you at least thirty-six hundred dollars, honey, but you see I don't care about that. The police lookin' at me for murder an' I cain't be worried 'bout you-all's li'l thing."

"We didn't kill Towne."

"Why'm I gonna believe that?"

"I don't care what you believe, Mr. Rawlins. I didn't kill anyone—nobody I know killed anyone."

"Maybe not." I nodded at her. "But all I gotta do is whisper a word to the man and he might just wanna prove that you did."

She snorted in place of a laugh. "We live with danger here, Mr. Rawlins. The police and the FBI make weekly visits. They don't scare me and you don't either."

"I don't wanna scare ya, Miss Achebe. What you got here looks good to me, but I was in the wrong place at the wrong time an' I gotta have some answers."

"I can't help you. I know nothing."

"Didn't Melvin say anything?"

"Nothing." She shrugged and glanced over my shoulder.

"Okay. But I gotta know . . ." I was interrupted by a heavy hand on my shoulder.

I turned to look up into the face of the man who took my money at the door.

"Anything wrong?" he asked.

"Yes, Bexel," Sonja said. "Mr. Rawlins here thinks that we're somehow involved with the murder of Reverend Towne."

"He do?" You could see how it hurt the big man that I could think such a thing.

Sonja smiled. "He wants to tell the police that."

"Naw?" When Bexel balled his hands into fists the knuckles of his fingers did an impression of popping corn.

I guess that my fights with Willie and Agent Lawrence had made me a little cocky. I made like I was going to step away from the sergeant-at-arms and then I dropped my right shoulder to deliver an uppercut to his lower gut.

It was a perfectly executed blow that I followed with an overhand left just below Bexel's heart. I danced backward until I felt a row of shelves behind me. It wasn't far but I didn't expect my quarry to be in any shape to trap me.

Then I looked up into his placid, smiling face.

Bexel leaned forward and pushed me with his great padded paw. My hurtling body shattered the shelves behind and the shelves behind them. My lungs collapsed in my chest and I felt pain in places that I'd never felt before.

Still smiling, the big man grabbed me roughly by both shoulders and lifted me until our faces almost touched.

I kicked him. Hard. And, to give myself a little credit, his left eye winced for a split second. But then he let go of my shoulders and grabbed me by the head.

"Bexel!" Sonja Achebe shouted. "Release him!"

I hit the floor certain, at least for that moment, that these were not the killers. I was fool enough to go into their den and blame them for the crime of murder. They could have killed me. Should have done.

I was on the floor thinking about cooked spaghetti and wondering if I was bleeding when Sonja asked, "Are you all right, Mr. Rawlins?"

"No, I sure ain't that."

Bexel was still standing before me. I was looking at his bloated black brogans. They were the largest shoes I had ever seen. He grabbed me by my jacket and lifted me to my feet. That was the first time that night that I had the sensation of flight.

"You should go now," Sonja Achebe said. "We didn't do anything wrong, but I don't expect you to believe that. It doesn't matter what you think, however, because we are not afraid."

I looked at Bexel. He wasn't even breathing hard. I remember hoping that I had finally learned to be cautious. But somewhere in my heart I knew that I'd never learn.

"Sorry," I said.

I shook Sonja Achebe's hand. "I know you might not believe this, but I was moved by your speech. There's a lotta people need what you have to offer."

"Not you?" She smiled for the first time and became a young girl again.

"I got me a home already. It might be in enemy lands, but it's mine still and all."

I liked Sonja Achebe and what the Migration stood for. I didn't want to see them come to harm. I found myself hoping that they hadn't been involved in Towne's death. I found myself wishing the same thing about Chaim Wenzler. It seemed to me that I was on everybody's side but my own.

# 31

MELVIN PRIDE LIVED ON ALAFORD STREET. A QUIET BLOCK of one-family homes behind a row of well-kept lawns and trimmed bushes. There was a smell of smoke in the air. I wondered at that, because it was unusual for anyone to be burning trash at that time of night.

I had to knock for a full minute before Melvin came to the door.

"What you want, Easy?" he asked through the screen, as hushed and stony as the grim reaper.

"I wanna talk to you about Reverend Towne and Tania Lee and the African Migration."

"Who?"

"I saw you there tonight, Melvin. I know you were siphoning off money to them 'cause you were all officers. Thing is, I cain't see why you would do it. I mean, Towne's got religion and a social conscience. But you just care about the church, and Winona an' Jackie be happy with a mirror. But even if I knew why they would do it I can't figure why you'd wanna kill anybody."

Melvin looked mean, but actually he was paralyzed. I pulled open the screen door and stepped past him into the house.

"You talkin' crazy, Easy Rawlins." Melvin moved to the side, and I took a step back from him. We were dancing like wary boxers in the first round of a title fight.

"That's right. I'm talking murder, Melvin."

"Murder who? I got someone t'say where I was fo' when they was killed. The po-lice already questioned me."

"I bet that was Jackie, or one'a his girls."

When I said "Jackie," Melvin's cheek jumped.

Then I said, "Come on, Melvin! You know all you people was stealin' from the church." It was just a guess but it was a good one. There weren't many places where a man like Jackie Orr could lay his hands on a thousand dollars. "You was all takin' money. Towne for the Migration, Winona and you for Towne, and Jackie . . . well, Jackie just caught on to a good thing."

"You cain't prove I killed nobody. And you cain't prove I stole nuthin'."

"You right 'bout the stealin'. I cain't prove that, not wit' you burnin' the books out back I cain't."

Melvin gave me a twitchy smile.

"But it's murder I can burn you on."

"Hell no! I ain't killed nobody! Never!"

"Maybe not, but all I gotta do is tell the cops an' they will beat you till you confess. That's how the game is played, Melvin."

Melvin turned his head as if he wanted to look into the door behind him. That door probably led to a bedroom.

He licked his lips. "You think I killed Towne? That's a laugh."

"I ain't laughin', Melvin. What I wanna know is why. You workin' with Wenzler or what?"

The look on Melvin's face was either a perfect job of acting or he knew nothing.

"You the one most prob'ly killed Towne, Easy." His tone was so certain that my sweat glands turned cold.

"Me?"

"Yeah, you. We got the lowdown on you, Easy."

"You said that before, Melvin. What does that mean?"

"It means that somebody blabbed on you, man. They told."

"Who?"

"I ain't sayin'. But it ain't just one, and I ain't the onliest one who knows, so you better not be thinkin' nuthin' like you gonna get at me. I know and Jackie does and the white man know too."

There was a righteous tone to Melvin's voice. He actually thought that I was the killer.

It took me a couple of days to decide on what happened next.

Melvin pushed me backwards, yelling, "You got him but you hain't gonna get me!" My foot turned on the carpet. Melvin stepped over me and connected with a solid right against my jaw. I was already falling and so I twisted over trying to roll out of the way. I hit a chair though and fell with my head toward the ground. Then there was a dull thud against my left thigh and I realized that Melvin had kicked me and probably meant to stomp me into the floor. I let myself roll sideways and stuck my legs between Melvin's so that when he tried to kick me again he fell forward, and I slammed my fist into the side of his head.

That's when we fell together, wrestling. Melvin was biting and growling like a dog. His attack was ferocious but it was unplanned. I kept giving him rabbit punches to the back of the neck. I did that until he removed his teeth from my left shoulder. Then I got to my feet holding Melvin by the shirt. I was terribly angry, because his attack scared me and because my mouth was in tremendous pain. I hit Melvin with everything I had. He went backwards across the room and I expected him to go down into a cold heap, but instead he kept on going and ran from the room.

At first I thought the fight was over. I had put all of my anger into that one blow and my violence was sated. But then, in the same moment, I remembered Melvin looking toward that door earlier.

By the time I burst through the doorway Melvin was turning from the night table next to his bed. There was a coal-colored pistol in his hand.

And for the second time that night I took flight; right into Melvin Pride.

The force of our bodies hitting the wall broke through the plaster. The sensation was the stutter effect of stepping on ice and then having that ice give way to free-fall. Melvin grunted, so did I. A timber sighed. Gravel slithered down my cheek and the pistol barked mutely, packed between the girth of our two bodies.

I felt the bite of the shot and automatically pushed away from Melvin to block up the hole in my chest.

I was covered with blood. I knew from my experiences in the war that I would soon lose consciousness. Melvin would murder me. Everything was over.

Then I heard Melvin slump down and I gave a wide grin in spite of the terrible pain in my jaw. It was Melvin who had taken the bullet; I had just felt the concussion of the shot.

Melvin's face was contorted in pain. A dark patch was forming on his shirt.

He was sucking down air and groaning, but Melvin was still trying to lift the pistol to shoot me. I took the gun from his blood-streaked hand and threw it on the bed. The craggy man groaned in fear as I stood over him. My jaw hurt me so bad that I had no desire to quell his fear. I tore a pillowcase in half and shoved it under Melvin's bloody shirt until it was directly over the wound.

"Hold this tight," I said. I had to lift his other arm and show him what to do.

"Don't kill me, man," he whispered.

"Melvin, you gotta get a hold of yourself. If you don't start thinkin' straight you gonna go into shock an' die."

I held his hand down hard over the wound to cause a little pain for him to focus on and to show him what he should be doing. The pistol he had was a .25-caliber so the wound wasn't too bad.

"Please don't kill me, please don't kill me," Melvin chanted.

"I don't want you dead, Melvin. I ain't gonna kill you, even though I should after this shit."

"Please," Melvin said again.

I pocketed the pistol and went to the bathroom, where I washed the blood off my shoes and from the cuffs of my black pants. Then I took an overcoat from Melvin's closet and used it to cover the rest of me.

In the backyard the incinerator was smoking away at various official papers from First African. Melvin had been trying to erase the accounting trail of the theft he and the others had perpetrated against the church. I hosed down what was left.

Back inside I found that Melvin had crawled into the kitchen. He was holding himself erect at the kitchen counter. I figured that he was trying to get a weapon, so I helped him to a chair. Then I went to the phone on the kitchen table and dialed Jackie Orr. He answered on the seventh ring.

"Hello."

"Hey, Jackie, this is Easy. Easy Rawlins."

"Yeah?" he said warily.

"Melvin's been shot." There was silence on the other end of the line. "I didn't shoot him, man. It was an accident. Anyway he's got a bullet in his shoulder and he needs a doctor."

"You ain't gettin' me over there with that lie, Easy. I ain't no fool."

"What I want with you, man?"

"You want my money."

"You got a thousand dollars in yo' bottom drawer, right? If I didn't take that then I don't need no money you got."

"I just call the cops, man."

"You do an' I hope you ready fo'jail, Jackie, 'cause I got all the proof I need that you been takin' money out the church. But here, talk to Melvin."

I cradled the phone next to Melvin's ear and left them to whisper their fears to each other.

On the drive back to my house I almost passed out from the pain in my mouth. At home I changed clothes, downed a few mouthfuls of brandy, and got back in my car.

Jackson was still spending my five dollars on whiskey at John's bar.

"Ease!" he shouted as I was coming across the room. Odell looked up from his drink. I nodded at him and he made to leave.

So I turned toward Jackson.

"I need you to come with me, Jackson," I said as

fast as I could. The pain was unbearable. John stared at me, but when I didn't say anything he turned away.

"You know where I could get some painkillers?" I asked Jackson.

"Yeah."

I handed him my keys when we got out to the car. "You drive," I said. "I got a toothache."

"What's wrong, man?"

"Dude busted my tooth. He busted my fuckin' mouth!"

"Who?"

"Some guy wanted to rob me outside of the African Migration. I fixed him. Oh shit, it hurts."

"I got some pills at my place, man. Let's go get 'em."

"Oh," I answered. I guess he knew that meant yes.

Jackson had morphine tablets. He said all I needed was one, but I took four against the bright red hurt in my mouth. I was doubled over in pain.

"How long 'fore it kicks in, Jackson?"

"If you ain't et nuthin', 'bout a hour."

"An hour!"

"Yeah, man. But listen," he said. He had a fifth of Jim Beam by the neck. "We sit here and drink an' talk an' fo' long you will have fo'gotten you even had a tooth."

So we passed the bottle back and forth. Because he was drinking, Jackson loosened up to the point where he'd tell me anything. He told stories that many a man would have killed him for. He told me about armed robberies and knifings and adulteries. He named names and gave proofs. Jackson wasn't an evil man like Mouse, but he didn't care what happened as long as he could tell the tale.

"Jackson," I said after a while.

"Yeah, Ease?"

"What you think 'bout them Migration people?"

"They all right. You know it could get pretty lonely if you think 'bout how hard we got it 'round here. Some people just cain't get it outta they head."

"What?"

"All the stuff you cain't do, all the stuff you cain't have. An' all the things you see happen an' they ain't a damn thing you could do."

He passed the bottle to me.

"You ever feel like doin' sumpin'?" I asked the little cowardly genius.

"Pussy ain't too bad. Sometime I get drunk an' take a shit on a white man's doorstep. Big ole stinky crap!"

We laughed at that.

When everything was quiet again I asked, "What about these communists? What you think about them?"

"Well, Easy, that's easy," he said and laughed at how it sounded. "You know it's always the same ole shit. You got yo' people already got a hold on sumpin', like money. An' you got yo' people ain't got nuthin' but they want sumpin' in the worst way. So the banker and the corporation man gots it all, an' the workin' man ain't got shit. Now the workin' man have a union to say that it's the worker makes stuff so he should be gettin' the money. That's like com'unism. But the rich man don't like it so he gonna break the worker's back."

I was amazed at how simple Jackson made it sound.

"So," I said. "We're on the communist side."

"Naw, Easy."

"What you mean, no? I sure in hell ain't no banker."

"You ever hear 'bout the blacklist?" Jackson asked.

I had but I said, "Not really," in order to hear what Jackson had to say.

"It's a list that the rich people got. All kindsa names

on it. White people names. They movie stars and writers and scientists on that list. An' if they name on it they cain't work."

"Because they're communist?"

Jackson nodded. "They even got the guy invented the atomic bomb on that paper, Easy. Big ole important man like that."

"So? What you sayin'?"

"Yo' name ain't on that list, Easy. My name ain't neither. You know why?"

I shook my head.

"They don't need yo' name to know you black, Easy. All they gotta do is look at you an' they know that."

"So what, Jackson?" I didn't understand and I was so drunk and high that it made me almost in a rage.

"One day they gonna th'ow that list out, man. They gonna need some movie star or some new bomb an' they gonna th'ow that list away. Mosta these guys gonna have work again," he said, then he winked at me. "But you still gonna be a black niggah, Easy. An' niggah ain't got no union he could count on, an' niggah ain't got no politician gonna work fo' him. All he got is a do'step t'shit in and a black hand t'wipe his black ass."

# 32

I WOKE UP IN MY HOUSE, HUNG OVER AND IN PROFOUND pain. I got Jackson's bottle of morphine from my pants on the floor and took three pills. Then I went into the bathroom to wipe off the grime and smell of the night before.

Jackson's words stuck in my head like the pain of my tooth. I wasn't on either side. Not crazy Craxton and his lies and half-truths and not Wenzler's either, if indeed Wenzler even had a side.

I thought of going to a dentist. I was even looking in the phone book when the knocking came at my door.

It was Shirley Wenzler, and she was in worse shape than I was.

"Mr. Rawlins," she said, her lower lip trembling. "Mr. Rawlins, I came here because I didn't know. I mean, what else could I do?"

"What's wrong?" I asked.

"Come with me, Mr. Rawlins, please. It's Poppa, he's hurt."

I got my pants and my pullover sweater. She walked me to the car.

"Where to?"

"Santa Monica," she said.

I asked her if she had called a doctor and she answered, "No."

On the ride out she gave me more instructions, but that was it. I was nauseous and in pain, so I didn't push her. If Chaim needed a doctor I could figure that out when we got there.


It was a small house across the street from a park. The park was small too. Just one little grassy hill that rose up to the street on the other side. No trees or benches. Just a hill that was only fit for the two little children who rolled down it, pretending that they'd lost control.

I expected Shirley to have a key in her hand but she just pushed the door open and walked in. I limped behind her. The morphine dulled the hurt in my jaw, but then I could feel the tenderness of my left ankle and thigh.

The house was decorated in some cool, dull color, green or blue. The ceiling was so low that I remember ducking to go through the door from the living room to the bedroom.

The color there was red death.

Chaim was hunched over a chair. Most of the blood was right there under him. But there was also blood on the dresser and in the bathroom. Blood on the phone, in the dial. There were bloody handprints on the wall. He'd gone all the way around the room, propping himself up with his bloody hand.

Next to his body was a light green cushion, splattered and clotted with blood. He'd pressed the cushion to his chest, trying to staunch the bleeding, but he must have known that it wasn't going to work.

Shirley's eyes were wide and she wrung her hands. I pushed her back through the door. It was then I noticed the few drops of blood on the living-room carpet. I hadn't seen them before in the unlit room.

"He's dead," I told her. Even though she already knew it, she needed someone else to pronounce him gone.

There were two small-caliber bullet holes in the door. Maybe somebody had knocked and when Chaim asked who, they shot him through his own door.

"Let's get to the car," I said. I tried smudging any surface I'd touched, but there was no telling where a fingerprint might show up. I let my head hang down when we left the house and when we got in the car I sat so low that I could barely see over the dash. I didn't sit up straight until we were far from there.

We got to a small coffee shop in Venice Beach. A little place that had sandy floors and nets with seashells that hung from the ceiling. Our window looked out onto the shore. It was a cool morning, no one was out yet.

"When'd you find'im?"

"This morning. Poppa," she said and then she choked on a sob. "He wanted me to bring him something."

"What?"

"Money."

"How'd you know where to find me?"

"I called the church."

I had a coffee. I had to drink it carefully, because if I let the warm liquid on the wrong side I got a stabbing pain from my tooth.

"What did he need the money for?"

"He had to run, Easy. The government wanted him."

"Government?" I said as if I had never heard of the FBI.

"Poppa's a member of the Communist Party," she said, looking down into her knotted fists. "He got something, some papers, and the FBI has been hounding him. The last time they came by, last night, they said that they'd be back. Dad thought they'd take him, so he called me to bring him some money."

"Those FBI men at the house when I was there last week?" I asked just to see what she'd say.

"Yes."

"What is it he had?"

She looked reluctant to talk, so I said, "He's dead, Shirley. What we do now we gotta do for you."

"Some kind of plans. He got them from a guy at Champion Aircraft."

"What kind of plans?"

"Poppa didn't know but he thought that they were for weapons. He was sure that the government was making weapons to kill more people. Poppa hates the atomic bomb. He thinks that America will kill millions more due to imperialism. He says the plans are for a new bomber, maybe for atomic weapons."

The fact that she spoke of her father as if he were still alive bothered me, but I couldn't see setting her straight.

"What was he going to do with them?"

She shook her head, weeping.

"I don't know," she moaned. "I don't know."

"You gotta know."

"Why? Why is it important? He's dead."

"I didn't know him too long, but Chaim was my friend. I'd like to know that he wasn't a traitor."

"But he was, Mr. Rawlins. He believed that the kind of government we have only wants to make war. He wanted to take America's secret weapons plans and give them to a socialist newspaper, maybe in France, and to have everybody know about them. He wanted to make it so everybody was aware of the danger. He . . ." She began crying again.

Chaim was my friend and he was dead. Poinsettia was my tenant and she was dead too. One way or another both deaths were my fault. Even if it was only because of me not telling the truth or not having compassion when I could have.

She was shivering, so I put my hand out to cover hers.

The white cook came out from behind the counter and a few people turned all the way around in their chairs to watch.

Shirley didn't notice it.

She said, "He wanted to get out of the country, Easy."

"An' we gotta get outta here," I said.

When we got back to my house I asked her in. I don't know why. I was dirty and hurting and the last thing I wanted was to be entertaining some young woman, but I asked and she accepted, so we walked past the daylilies and the potatoes and strawberries up the dirt path to my house. And when I was fishing around in my pocket for the key she looked up at me and I stopped to look at her for a moment or two. Then I decided to kiss her. I leaned forward kind of quickly . . .

It wasn't the shot that bothered me.

It wasn't the hole torn in my front door or the car taking off down the street; nor was it the little yell or the look in Shirley Wenzler's eye, the look that could break a man's heart, that got to me. It wasn't bad luck or broken teeth or the remnants of a hangover or the whisper of a breeze that suggested death at the back of my neck. It wasn't political ideas that I didn't care about or understand that made me mad.

It was the idea that I suffered all of this because I wasn't, and hadn't been, my own man. I didn't even know who it was who was shooting at me in front of my own house! People hanging and shot dead for no real reason; that's what got me mad. Real mad. Something I could feel, like I felt the stirrings of an erection for Shirley when what I really wanted was a good night's sleep, a competent dentist, a peaceful death at the hands of a jealous husband or a racist cop.

Like most men, I wanted a war I could go down shooting in. Not this useless confusion of blood and innocence.

I stood there looking into Shirley's frightened face. She was shivering. I put my arms around her and said, "It's all right." Then I took her into my house without even looking after who it was that shot at us. I decided then that he was a dead man, whoever he was. I was going to start killing him at the soles of his feet. Whoever he was, he was going to remember me in hell.

"Do you think it was the government?" Shirley stammered as I helped her get the glass of whiskey to her lips.

"Prob'ly," I said, but I really didn't believe it. "They think you might get away wit' them papers."

"Oh, Easy!" She grabbed my arm. "What can we do?"

"You gots to run. Run hard."

"Where? Where can I go?"

"There's a hotel downtown called the Filbert. You go there and take a room. Call yourself Diane Bowers. I once had a girlfriend called that. Call me when you check in. I might not be here right when you call, but if I'm not I'll get to you under that same name, Diane Bowers."

She shuddered and pulled close to me.

"Let me stay for a while before I go. I'm too scared to drive."

And so we took off everything but our underclothes and my pistol. We lay in my bed holding each other until she stopped shivering and we both fell to sleep. I held her tightly, more for my own comfort than hers. I dreamt that there was a trapdoor next to my mother's deathbed. I fell a long way down a passage that was similar to a well. At the bottom was a long river, but I knew it was a sewer, and there were men, desperate white men, searching for me. Sometimes the men would change into crocodiles and search for me in the water, sometimes the crocodiles would change into men. I was pressing back against a rocky wall, hiding. My hand, every now and then, unconsciously pushed into the recess of the wall, and every time that happened the wall hurt. It was a terrible pain and I came half awake massaging the side of my jaw where Melvin had broken my tooth.

I winced in pain, almost coming awake when I saw Mofass laughing behind his desk and then asking me about how could the IRS let me off. I saw him bad-mouthing Poinsettia and refusing to help sign my papers over to him.

Dreams are wonderful things, because they're a different way of thinking. I came to, for just a moment, with a clear idea of the path I should take. I knew who killed Poinsettia and I knew why. Even in my dream I knew it; even in my dreams I was plotting revenge.

# 33

WE BEGAN KISSING IN OUR SLEEP. IT WAS PASSIONATE AND sloppy kissing while we were still unaware. When we came awake it was still dearly felt but neither of us wanted it to go anywhere. She got up and wandered around the room, maybe as her father had. I went up to her and kissed her again. I pressed her against the wall, she wrapped her legs around my hips and held on tight. . . .

Rather than sex it was a kind of a spasm, like vomiting or cramps. The sounds we made were the sounds boxers make when they take a blow to the body.

We didn't whisper about love. We didn't say anything until it was over.

Then all I said was that I'd call at the Filbert as soon as I could. I gave her EttaMae's number and told her to call if she couldn't get to me.

"Tell Etta what you need and tell her I said to call Mouse."

"Who?"

"A friend'a mines," I said.

"Oh, I remember." She smiled for the first time. "He's the man you said reminded you of Poppa."

"Yeah, that's right."

I didn't know what was going to happen with Shirley. All I could think about was vengeance, and, I thought, I knew how to go about getting it.

It was just getting dark outside and I saw Shirley to her car, pretending all the while that I was looking out for a bad guy. But I knew that shot was meant for me. And I knew who took that shot.

There was ice in my veins.

Primo's place was out in East Los Angeles, the Mexican neighborhood. He used to own a big house and rent out rooms to illegal aliens, but the board of health got down on him and condemned the place. So he put three hundred dollars down on a two-story house on Brooklyn Boulevard in Boyle Heights and tore out all the walls on the first floor. He and his wife, Flower, and all their eleven children lived on the upper level while Primo and Flower ran an informal luncheon café downstairs.

It was a dark room with bare, unfinished beams that were once hidden by walls. A few mismatched tables and chairs here and there. Flower was from Panama originally, but she knew her Mexican cooking well enough to make an egg-and-potato burrito and fried sausages to make you cry. Any Mexican day laborer within three miles came to Primo's for lunch. There was tequila and beer from the package store next door and smells so good that a Tijuana man might think he was back home with his family.

It was late when I got there, but I knew the family would be downstairs. Dinner with Primo started at about five and went on until the older children carried their sleeping brothers and sisters to bed.

"Easy! *Hola!*" Flower shouted when I stuck my head in the door. I never knocked at the family hour because there was too much noise for that type of pleasantry.

She crossed the large room and folded me in her soft embrace. Flower was bigger than EttaMae, and obviously a Negro, but we still considered her Mexican because she was from south of the border and cursed in Spanish when she got mad.

"Easy!" Primo said. He shook my hand and pounded my shoulder. "Get him a drink, somebody. Jesus! It's your godfather Ezekiel. Get him a bottle of beer."

Silent and shy, the little child jumped up, running the obstacle course of children, dogs, and furniture for the kitchen in back. Jesus Peña. Most of the Peña children were light-colored, honey, like their father, with big moonlike eyes. But Jesus was a duller hue with more Asiatic eyes. He wasn't their natural child. He was a boy I found eating raw flour from a five-pound bag. He'd been abused by an evil white man; a white man who had paid for his evil with a bullet in his heart. I brought Jesus to Primo and Flower. They kept him as long as I promised to take him back if anything ever happened to them. We'd drawn up the papers and Jesus was my godchild. I was proud of him, because he was smart and strong and he loved animals. The only thing wrong about Jesus was that he wouldn't talk. I never knew if he remembered anything about his past, because I couldn't get him to talk, and whenever I asked him about it he hugged me and kissed me, then he ran away.

"What's wrong, Easy?" Primo asked.

"Somethin' gotta be wrong fo'me to wanna see my friends and my godchild?"

"Something wrong if you got a jaw that big."

It must've swollen while I napped.

"Got in a fight," I said. "I won, though."

Flower frowned at me. She jabbed the side of my mouth with her finger, and I nearly fainted.

"That's infected," she said. "You gotta see somebody or it'll get bad."

"Soon as I take care of some business."

"That tooth going to take care of you," she said, making her eyes big and round. The children all laughed and mimicked her.

"Okay!" Primo shouted, then he yelled something in Spanish and waved his hands as if he were making a breeze to blow the children upstairs.

At first the children resisted, but then Primo started slapping them and shouting.

Flower got them up the stairs and turned to see Primo waving at her. "You too, woman. Easy's here to talk to me."

Flower laughed and stuck out her tongue, then she turned and stuck her butt at us. She ran up the stairs before Primo could grab something to throw.

I pulled out the little glass bottle I'd gotten from Jackson Blue. There were five or six tablets left.

"What you taking for that, Easy?"

"Morphine," I said.

Primo made like he was going to gag. "That's bad stuff, man, I seen it in the war, in the Pacific. They give the boys that till they got the monkey on the back."

The morphine was wearing off. I felt like there was a gorilla in my mouth.

"I got a serious problem, Primo. After I take care of that maybe I could see a dentist."

"Oh." He nodded. "What's that?"

"Somebody been on my ass, man. I'ma have t'satisfy myself who it is, an' then I'ma kill'im."

"Who?"

"I ain't gonna tell ya, Primo. If you don't know nuthin' then cain't nobody blame you fo'nuthin'."

I think that the lack of sleep, the pain, the morphine and liquor were all factors in my craziness then. I could tell that Primo thought I was less than rational, because he spoke softly and in short sentences. He didn't laugh or make jokes as he usually did.

"So what can I do for you?"

"Me and my girlfriend, EttaMae, might have to get away after it's done. I thought maybe you wanna take a vacation down in Mexico, back to that town in the badlands you always talk about."

Primo loved to talk about Anchou. It was a town in central Mexico that wasn't on any map; no one knew where it was but the people who came from there, or the rare few who were invited by one of the inhabitants. He once told me that the town was mobile; that if they knew trouble was coming they could pack up and move in just a couple of hours. But the Federales didn't want to mess with Anchou. An Anchou woman, Primo said, would bite off a Federal's prick and serve it to her man for a love potion.

"Why don't you just go down to Texas? They won't find you."

"Cain't. Government in this. They ain't thought they gone to work 'less they cross a state border."

Mr. Peña frowned at me for a while. He took a drink from his beer and then frowned at me some more.

I was massaging the hinge of my jaw.

"Take the pills, Easy," he said at last.

I took three, washing them down with the beer Jesus had brought. There were three left in the bottle.

"Take the rest of them," Primo urged.

"This is all I got left."

"I got more. Take them so it really stops hurting."

I downed the rest of the bottle, hoping that the aching would stop and I could sleep well enough to do what had to be done the next day.

"I've got five hundred dollars right here, man," I said. I pulled a folded envelope from my back pocket and handed it to him.

Money always made Primo laugh. The more he had the more he laughed. He counted the twenties and tens I'd squirreled away in my walls. Every bill made his grin wider, his eyes glassier.

Maybe it was the dope kicking in, but I got a flash of

fear that Primo was up to no good. Maybe he was in on all that bad luck I was having.

"You gonna help me, man?" I asked.

The fears must've shown in my voice, because Primo said, "Yes," very seriously. He handed me a clay jug from the side of his chair.

"Tequila?" I asked.

"Mescal."

I took a swig. I knew that it was potent liquor because I felt it even through the descending opiate haze.

Primo told me stories about Anchou.

"It's an old town," I remember him saying. "There was a chief there forty years ago who ran with Zapata before he was hung."

Every now and again he'd reach out to poke my jaw. If I told him it hurt he'd pass the jug over. But after a while there wasn't any pain.

Primo laughed too. After a while Flower came down and drank with us. She kept me company while Primo rummaged through some old boxes he kept in the corner of the large room.

"She's a mighty fine lady, Primo," I said when he came back. He had something like pruning shears in his hand.

"I found it," he said.

"Yeah," I continued. I heard him but I was too intent on my own purpose to heed. "I got a woman like'er down in one'a my buildin's. She got a strong arm like yo' woman here and she smell like sweet flowers too."

I fell forward in my chair, trying to kiss Mrs. Peña on the lips if I remember right. I landed on her and got about as close as her shoulder. Then the room started spinning. I found myself on my back, on the floor with Flower above my head. She was pinning my shoulders down with her considerable weight.

". . . my cousin was a dentist in Guadalajara many

210

'years ago. I kept his tools," I heard Primo say. My stomach was flopping around, and I would have followed it but for Mrs. Peña's grip.

"Open wide, Easy," Primo was saying. He held my nostrils closed with one hand as he held the deadly-looking shears in the other. But they weren't shears really, they were more like streamlined pliers with an extended, toothy clamp at the nose.

"This is the one," Primo said as he frowned.

That's when I started fighting. I couldn't yell because of that damned tool and I couldn't turn away because of Flower's hold. But I bucked. I humped and bucked under Primo like he was my first love. I fought him and bit until all the fight went out of me and I felt something far off in my mouth like boulders rolling around in there.

Jesus Peña was squatting down next to my head. He was staring intently into my face. When he saw that my eyes were open he smiled. I saw that he was missing a tooth, and I moved my own tongue toward the pain in my mouth; at least toward where the pain had been. What I found was a bitter-tasting gauze.

I sat up and spat the wad of cheesecloth to the floor. Jesus jumped back like a frightened kitten. The cloth was tooth-shaped and filled with tiny branches and leaves. It was also deeply stained with blood.

The blood reminded me of Poinsettia's feet and floor, of the hand marks on Chaim's walls. I lurched up off the cot. They had put me behind some boxes toward the back of the café. A few men were already there, eating buttered wheat tortillas and drinking beer for their breakfasts.

At least it's only morning, I remember thinking.

Flower was standing at the stove, off to my right. She was smiling in the steam that rose from a black kettle.

"Come over, Easy."

She handed me a bowl of broth topped with a skin

of tiny crackers. There was a poached egg toward the bottom of the bowl.

"Garlic soup," she smiled.

I sat on a stool next to her. The first swallow made me gag, but I kept on eating the stuff. I hadn't been eating very much and I thought I needed the strength.

The sun was coming through a little window in the back of the kitchen. Tiny motes of dust, like a school of minute silvery fish, floated in the ray. I thought of the Magnolia Street apartments and of Mofass, that shit-brown carp, pulling himself up the long stairs.

After a while my stomach settled down. My tooth socket barely ached.

"Here you are," Flower said. She was holding out a handful of tea bags. "If it hurts, bite down on one of these until it goes away."

I pocketed the bags and asked, "Where's Primo?"

"He went to see his brother in San Diego. They gonna come up here while we're down south."

So the plan was in action.

"Thanks for the dentist work, Flower. I guess I was a little outta my head what with the pain and the dope."

"We love you, Easy," was her reply.

It was all I could do to keep from crying.

# 34

WHEN I GOT HOME I TOOK A LONG SHOWER AND CALMED down. Murder was quieter in my heart. It was still there but softer, a little less insistent. I took a long time toweling off and dressing. I took time to appreciate the crisp lines of my walnut chairs and the spirally grain of the pine floor in the bedroom.

I put on a nice tan pair of slacks that an old girlfriend had bought me but I had only worn once, and a red Jamaican shirt that was hand-painted with designs of giant green palm leaves. I put on white nylon socks and basketlike woven black leather shoes. My .38 was the last item I chose. It hung unnoticed at the back of my pants, under the billowing red blouse.

Once I was dressed I went out into the yard to appreciate the garden. I sat, hidden from the street, in the cast-iron chair for half an hour watching a jay dance in the grass. He was proud and happy in moist grass that had gotten too tall in past weeks. He didn't have a natural enemy in sight, and that was all he needed to be happy.

I thought about the Mexican badlands. They sounded pretty good.

Roberta Jefferson, Mofass' sister, didn't live far from my house. She and her husband, George, had a small place. They both worked for the Los Angeles Board of Education. He was with the board's internal delivery service and she was a breakfast cook at Lincoln High School.

She was home when I got there, wearing a big yellow handkerchief around her round brown face. I took my time walking up to the door. She was inside ironing shirts, there was the smell of collard greens in the air. Dozens of iridescent green flies hovered around the screen door. Flies love the smell of cooked greens.

There was no need to knock.

"Hi, Easy," Roberta said. "How you doin'?"

"Fine, Ro, just fine."

I stood there in the doorway, taking my time, waiting.

"Come on in, baby, what brings you here?"

"Lookin' fo' Mofass is all."

"I ain't seen'im in two or three days. But you know sometimes a month go by an' he don't come round."

"Yeah," I said. I pulled up a high stool next to where she was ironing. "He left me a note to pull a refrigerator out of one'a his places, but he didn't say what apartment. You know I don't wanna be pullin' out no po' son's icebox. I might be takin' his last po'k chop."

We laughed nicely and then Roberta said, "Well, I ain't seen'im, Easy. He show up though. You know Billy-boy don't trust nobody an' he will make sure you did it right."

"That's what you call'im?"

Roberta laughed. "Yeah. Billy-boy Wharton. That's why he don't like seein' us, 'cause I ain't about t'let him fo'get his Christian name."

"Yeah," I said. "Yeah."

I asked her about her husband and children. They were fine. George Jr. had just gotten over a case of the chicken pox and little Mozelle had grown titties and said she wanted a baby to go with them. Normal things. Roberta said that the board was hiring and maybe it was time for me to get a regular job. I said I'd look into it.

"Your momma down Louisiana, ain't she, Ro?" I asked to finish off the questions about her family.

"She'll live there till she dies."

"How old is she now?"

"Close enough to seventy so she could kiss it, but she always say sixty-two. Not that she don't look young enough to lie 'bout it. My sister Regina tole me jus' yestiday that Momma got a new boyfriend down there."

"At seventy!" I was scandalized.

"I guess it ain't worn out yet."

"She must be in good health."

"Strong as a hog," Roberta answered.

We traded some more pleasantries and then I excused myself.

I rode down to the Magnolia Street apartments next. It was like walking into the past. Nothing had changed. I saw an aluminum gum wrapper that had been in the gutter across the street the last time I had been there. I was amazed to think that the apartments were still my property. Who had maintained my rights on them while I was gone these long days?

"Good morning, Mr. Rawlins," Mrs. Trajillo said.

"Morn'in, ma'am. How are you today?"

She smiled in answer and I walked up to her window. There was a portrait of Christ on the wall behind her. His chest was cut open, revealing a Valentine's heart crowned in thorns. He was staring at me, holding up two fingers as if to say, "Go slow, child, find your nemesis."

"Have the police been back?" I asked.

"Sealed off the apartment and asked us all questions about who did it."

"Did they know? Did they find the killer?"

"I don't think so, Mr. Rawlins, but they asked a lot about you and Mr. Mofass."

"Mofass was here that day?"

"I didn't see him, and I told that nice colored man that Mr. Mofass wouldn't crawl through a window."

Only just on his belly, like a snake, I thought.

"I told them everything I saw, Mr. Rawlins. There was only the people that live here and the postman with a special delivery and a white insurance salesman."

"What salesman was that?" I asked.

"Just some white man in an old suit. He said that it was life insurance he was selling." Mrs. Trajillo snorted. "Just trying to steal poor people's money." She didn't like white people too well.

"Did he try to sell any to you?"

215

"I wasn't interested, but he went up and down in here looking for somebody to rob."

I wasn't interested in an insurance man, though. "So that was it, huh?"

"I think so, Mr. Rawlins. That white policeman was checking the door around back. He said that it looked like it had been forced open not too long ago."

I thanked her and bid her goodbye. But I must have looked grim, because she said after me, "You take care now, Mr. Rawlins. You know it is nobody's fault when someone dies."

"No?"

"It is only God who takes life."

I kept the laughter inside of me, like a caged wolf.

I still felt dirty when I got home, so I took a long bath. I wanted to be clean, perfect. I put a chair beside the tub and laid my .38 on it. I left the door open and all the lights on. Shadows would be my alarm.

I called Dupree but Mouse was out, playing with LaMarque.

There was one chance that I had of staying in Los Angeles. That chance depended on some creative handling of the top-secret papers.

So I dressed in dark worker clothes, loaded a squirt gun with ammonia, wrapped a canvas tarp I used for painting, and bought three steaks from the corner store. Then I went to the car graveyard on Vernon and went around the back, because it was nighttime and the place was closed. I made it over the barbed-wire fence by laying the canvas tarp over it. I didn't have time for the regular business hours.

The yard was made up of wide alleys formed by stacks of automobiles. I had worked my way down three lanes before the dogs got my scent. I saw two of them, a boxerlike monster and a shepherd, round the aisle of cars. The first one was growling and running at me fast, his brother hot on his tail. I squirted them both directly on their snouts with my ammonia gun. A dog would rather gnaw off his tail than have a snout full of that poison.

The papers were right where Andre had said they'd be. They were bound in a leather notebook, the kind that zips up the side, behind the seat of an ancient Dodge pickup truck. I tucked them under my arm, thinking about how Chaim put those papers there. I hadn't really said goodbye to my friend.

By the time I reached the tarp-covered fence the dogs were on me again. The boxer/greyhound showed his teeth and snarled, but he was tentative for all that and hung back behind the three or four other dogs. I took out the squirt gun and splashed the first snapping dog—no breed would describe him—on the snout.

He couldn't get away from me fast enough. The other dogs were on their way soon after, and I got out of the whole thing with no more than a small cut I suffered opening the truck's door. I left the steaks on the ground near the fence. Those dogs couldn't bark after me, causing unwanted attention, if they had their mouths full of T-bone.

Before I knocked on the door I heard screaming. High-pitched yelling mixed with words like "no" and "no mo'."

I knocked. When Etta opened the door the yelling was still going on behind her. Mouse and LaMarque were wrestling on the couch. They were both yelling, but LaMarque was on top, playfully pounding the sides of Mouse's head. Mouse was bowing low, pretending to be in pain and screeching like his name-sake.

Etta put her hand to my chest, which I felt all the way down to my knees, and said, "Thank you, baby, Raymond done come back t'life fo' him."

"Etta, do you love me?" I whispered.

"Yes, Easy, I do," she whispered back.

I wanted to ask her to run with me, to go down to Mexico, but I'd wait until Mouse was somewhere else.

"Easy!" Mouse shouted from inside.

"Hi, Unca Easy," LaMarque said.

I wondered if LaMarque would come with Etta and me down to Mexico or would she leave him with her sister. He was still young enough to pick up a language if he had to.

"Hi, boys," I said. Then, "Raymond."

"Yeah, Ease?"

"I need yo' help on sumpin'."

LaMarque had looked away from us to a round table that they used for meals. Across it lay Mouse's long .41-caliber pistol. It looked obscene there, but I supposed it was safer than if Mouse wore it while they tussled.

"I'll make tea," Etta said. Raymond's artillery didn't seem to bother her. She just pushed it to one side and another as she wiped off the table.

"No, honey," I said. "Raymond an' me got business. We gots to go."

And so we left.

In the hall I said, "I need some help, Mouse."

"Who you want me to kill?" he asked, pulling out his pistol to prove his readiness.

"I just need you to come with me, Raymond. I gotta look into a couple'a things and I could use somebody at my back."

Raymond was smiling as he holstered his long gun.

We drove out to Mofass' office. I had the key, so it wouldn't be a case of burglary.

"What we lookin' fo', Ease?" Mouse asked me. He was working at his golden teeth with an ivory toothpick that he carried.

"Just sit'own, Raymond. I gotta search Mofass' files."

"You don't need me fo' that."

"Somebody tried t'shoot me out in front'a my house yesterday," I told him. "I was standin' out there with a friend and I just happened t'bend over or the lights woulda been out on my show."

"Oh," Mouse said simply. He felt for his pistol under his coat and sat back in Mofass' swivel chair. He put his feet up on the desk and smiled at me as I went through the filing cabinet.

In his files Mofass kept a book of all the properties he managed. There were twelve columns to the right of each address or unit, where he indicated, on a monthly basis, if the place was occupied or not. If the property was vacant for that month there was an $x$ marked in pencil.

There were about twenty unoccupied apartments, the longest vacancy being on Clinton Street. I listed them, but I really didn't think Mofass would try to hide in an apartment. People didn't like Mofass, and they were likely to blab his whereabouts if given the opportunity.

Mofass also managed a group of business properties and seven warehouses. All of them were rented. One warehouse was rented to Alameda Fruits and Vegetables Incorporated. Mofass had told me when they had gone out of business. The president, Anton Vitali, also owned the building. He'd cleared out the building but kept paying the rent, to himself, because he needed people to believe he was solvent as a real estate owner. Mofass was happy with that, because he still got his percentage and didn't have to lift a finger.

I gave Mouse all the addresses, telling him to check the warehouse first.

"You want me to kill'im, Ease?" Mouse asked as simply as if he were offering me a beer.

"Just hold him, Ray. I'll do what killin's gotta be done."

# 35

HE ANSWERED THE PHONE HIMSELF ON THE FIRST RING.
"Craxton!"

"Hello, Mr. Craxton."

"Well, well, Mr. Rawlins, I thought you might've
run out on me."

"No, sir. Where'm I gonna go?"

"No further than I can reach, that's for sure."

"I been kinda busy, gettin' news."

"What kind of news?"

"Chaim Wenzler is dead."

"What?"

"They shot him through his front door. Shot him
dead."

"How do you know about it?"

"Shirley Wenzler, Chaim's daughter, brought me
there. Seems like I'm the only one she trusts."

"Does she know who did it?"

"She thinks it was you."

"Horseshit!"

"Don't get me wrong, I ain't saying' no government
man gonna do somethin' like that. All I'm sayin' is
that she really thinks that the government did it."

"You got anything I can use?"

"I think he was in it with somebody down here.
Like you said, he was working with somebody colored. But I don't know who it is. Whoever it is,
though, they pegged me early on."

"How'd they do that, Easy?" Craxton asked.

"I don't know, but I think I know how to find out."

"Did you find anything in his house?"

"Like what?"

"Anything," he said evasively. "Anything I might be interested in."

"No sir. But then again I didn't spend any too long checkin' it out either. I don't like keepin' company with the dead."

"But you're working for me, Rawlins. If you can't get your hands dirty, then why should I help you?"

"Maybe if I knew what it was you were lookin' for I could nose around. But you ain't told me shit, man, Agent Craxton."

That cut our conversation for a moment. When he finally spoke again it was in forced calm and measured tones.

"What about the girl, Easy? Does she know why he was killed?"

"She don't know nuthin'. But I heard a thing or two down at First African."

"What things?"

"You got your secrets, Mr. Craxton, and I got mines. I'ma look this thing down until I find out who killed Wenzler. When I find out I'm'a tell you, all right?"

"No." I could almost hear him shaking his head. "That's not all right at all. You're working for me . . ."

I cut him off. "Uh-uh. You ain't payin' me an' you ain't done a damn thing fo'me neither. I will find your killer and I figure he will be the key to whatever it is you lookin' for. At that time you an' me will come to a deal."

"I'm the law, Mr. Rawlins. You can't bargain with the law."

"The fuck I cain't! Somebody put a bullet two inches from my head yesterday afternoon. This is my life we speakin' on, so either you take my deal or we call it quits."

For the most part I was blowing smoke. But I knew things that Craxton didn't know. I had the papers and I knew who Chaim and Poinsettia's killer was. One thing had nothing to do with the other, but when I was finished everything would be as neat as a buck private's bunk bed.

I had Craxton over a barrel. He finally said, "When will you have something for me?"

"Six o'clock tomorrow. I got some irons in the fire right now. By six tomorrow I should know everything. If not then, then the day after."

"Six tomorrow?"

"That's the time."

"All right. I'll expect a call then." He was trying to sound like he was still in charge.

"One more thing," I blurted out before he could hang up.

"What?"

"You gotta make sure the police don't mess wit' me before then."

"You got it."

"Thanks."

In the darkness of my house I spun plans. None of them seemed real. Mofass was all I had. He was the only one who connected everything. He had been up to something with Poinsettia, and I was the one who told him about the taxes and First African. He was the only one I could suspect. If I was guessing right he told Jackie and Melvin about me nosing around First African. So he was really to blame for Reverend Towne and Tania Lee, or maybe he killed them too. And Mofass was the only one with a reason. He wanted my money. He knew that the government would take my property and that he could buy it before it ever went to auction. He knew how to make payoffs. That's why he didn't want to sign, because he wanted it all.

I was going to kill Mofass, mainly because he had killed my tenant and I felt that I owed her something. But also because he had killed Chaim and I had come to like that man. He had destroyed my life, and I felt I owed him something for that.

All the things I'd told Craxton were half-truths and lies for him to follow down while I was on my way to Mexico.

Mexico. EttaMae and I and maybe even LaMarque. It was like a dream. It was better than what I had, at least that's what I told myself.

I sat waiting for a call. No radio and no television. I turned a single light on in the bedroom and then went to the living room to sit in shadows. I had been reading a book on the history of Rome, but I didn't have any heart for it that night. The history of Rome didn't move me the way it usually did. I didn't care about the Visigoths and the Ostrogoths sacking the Empire; I didn't even care about the Vandals, how they were so terrible that the Romans made a word out of their name.

I didn't even believe in history, really. Real was what was happening to me right then. Real was a toothache and a man you trusted who did you dirt. Real was an empty stomach or a woman saying yes, or a woman saying no. Real was what you could feel. History was like TV for me, it wasn't the great wave of mankind moving through an ocean of minutes and hours. It wasn't mankind getting better either; I had seen enough murder in Europe to know that the Nazis were even worse than the barbarians at Rome's gate. And even if I was in Rome they would have called me a barbarian; it was no different that day in Watts.

Chaim wanted to make it better for me and my

people. Chaim was a good man; better than a lot of people in Washington, and a lot of black people I knew. But he was dead. He was history, as they say, and I was holding my gun in the dark; being real.

# 36

I WAS JOLTED AWAKE BY MOUSE'S CALL.

"Got'im, man," he said. There was pride in his voice. The kind of pride a man has when he's paid off a bank note or brought a paycheck home to his wife.

"Where is he?"

"Right here in front'a me. You know, this boy sure is ugly."

I heard Mofass' gruff voice in the background, but I couldn't make out what he said.

"Shut up, fool!" Mouse shouted in my ear. "We don't need to hear from you."

"Where are you, Raymond?"

"On Alameda, at that warehouse you said. I come in a window an' fount his stuff. You know all I hadda do was wait an' he come grubbin' up the slide."

The entrance to the building was in the alley off the main street. Two tall doors held together through the handles with a chain and padlock. When I rattled the door a window opened above and Mouse stuck his head out.

"Hey, Easy. Go on down the alley a little ways and they's a chute for loadin'. It's open."

It was a two-foot-square aluminum slat, reinforced by a wooden frame, that lifted away from the wall. It opened on a metal slide, leading up into the building. That slide was slick from all the merchandise they dropped down into delivery trucks.

When I made it up to the second floor I dusted off and released the safety on my pistol. There were aisles formed by huge stacks of cardboard boxes and wooden crates. There was some light, but the long rows melted into darkness, giving the place the feeling of great depth. I could have been in Solomon's mines.

"Over here, Easy," Mouse called.

I followed the sound of his voice until I came to a little square kiosk. From inside that office the light came. Thick and yellow electric light, and cigarette smoke. There was a large gray metal desk with a thick green blotter. Mofass was behind the desk, sweating and looking generally undignified. Mouse was leaning against a wall, smiling at me.

"Here he is, Easy. I put a apple in his mouth if you want it."

"What's the idea, Mr. Rawlins?" Mofass started up. "Why you got this man to kidnap me? What I do to you?"

I simply lifted the pistol and pointed it at his head. Mouse flashed his friendliest smile at no one in particular. Mofass' jaw started to quiver because of the spasm going through his neck and shoulders.

"You got this wrong, Mr. Rawlins. You pointin' that peacemaker at the wrong man."

"Go on, Easy, kill'im," Mouse whispered.

That's what saved Mofass' life. Mouse didn't even know why I had that man there, he didn't care either. All he knew was that killing satisfied some nerve he had somewhere. I was growing the same nerve, and I didn't like that idea at all.

"What you mean, wrong man?" I asked.

Instead of answering, Mofass broke wind.

Then he said, "It's that tax man, Easy, it's Lawrence."

"What?" I hadn't thought anything he could say would surprise me. "Com'on, man. You could do better than that."

"You don't lie to no loaded gun at your head, Mr. Rawlins. It was Lawrence sure as I'm sitting here."

The smell of Mofass' flatulence filled the room. Mouse was waving his hand under his nose.

"You better come up with somethin' better than that, Mofass. This is your life right here in my hand."

I moved the muzzle of the gun closer to Mofass' sweaty brow. He opened his eyes a little wider.

"It's the truth, Mr. Rawlins. He pulled me down on a tax charge ovah a year ago."

Mouse kicked a chair around so that he could sit on it. Mofass leaped up out of his seat.

"Sit down," I said. "An' go on."

"Yeah." A smile appeared on Mofass' lips and vanished just as fast. "I ain't paid no tax, not ever. I filed it but I always lied like I didn't make nuthin'. Lawrence caught on, though. He had me by the nuts."

"Uh-huh, yeah, I know what you mean."

"He told me that he was goin' t'court wit' what he had. So I ast'im could we talk it over, over a drink." Mofass smiled again. "You see, Mr. Rawlins, if he let me buy him a drink then I knowed I could buy him. I got to a phone an' called Poinsettia. She hadn't paid no rent even way back then. She told me she'd be nice t'me if I let'er slide, but you know I don't play it like that."

For no reason Mouse grabbed Mofass by his wrist, roughly, and then let him go. The surprise made the fat man yelp like a dog.

"It's the t-t-truth, man. I called'er an' told'er that if she was nice to my friend I'd let her slip by the summer."

"So you put 'em together?"

"Yeah. Lawrence couldn't hold his liquor worth a

damn. An' you know when Poinsettia got there, an' started strokin' 'im, he was drinkin' it like water an' swaggerin' in his chair. I took 'em down to a hotel that night."

"So?"

"What could I do?" Mofass hunched his sloped shoulders. "He had me run her out to'im much as three times a week. They always be drinkin'. Sometimes I didn't even take 'em nowhere but they just do it in the car."

"While you drivin', man?" Mouse asked.

"Yeah!"

"Shit! Thas some white boy you got there, Easy."

"I don't believe a word of this shit," I said. "I seen Agent Lawrence, he straight as a pin."

Mofass put his hands up to placate me. Mouse, as usual, smiled at the sign of surrender.

"You ain't seen 'im when he gets to drinkin', Mr. Rawlins. He get crazy-like. An' you know Poinsettia be gettin' him so high on love. Then sometimes he'd get mean an' beat her till she stayed inside fo'a week."

I remembered seeing Poinsettia in sunglasses on cloudy days.

"All right, Mofass. You got a story here but I still don't see what it gotta do wit' me."

"'Bout six months ago they was shackin' up in a house I was brokerin' down on Clark. Lawrence got drunk an' th'ew Miss Jackson down the stairs. She was hurt pretty bad an' we hadda take her to a doctor I know."

"She didn't have no accident?"

Mofass shook his head, swallowed to wet his throat, and continued. "At first he was guilty an' wanted t'pay fo'her. Thas when he set up Rufus Johnson."

"I know him. He's one'a the men on that list in yo' desk."

"Yeah, a colored man. Live in Venice Beach. Lawrence set him up for tax fraud, and then I snuck in and tole Mr. Johnson that I could free him up fo' some cash."

"An' you split the money?" I asked.

"Lawrence took most of it, I swear."

"An' now he's after me."

"We worked that job on five other people. Never nobody I knew. An' he was okay for a while but then he got like he needed money fo' him. He started complainin' 'bout how Poinsettia an' his own wife an' child were anchors on his neck. He started on me about findin' one rich Negro an' then he could leave for good."

"An' you give'im me?"

Mofass' eyes filled with tears but he didn't say a word.

"How did he think he could get my money?"

"We was gonna get you t'sign yo' property ovah t'me an' then we'd play like he got the tax law on me, but really we'd sell off the property and he'd get the money on the sly. He was gonna take it all. He knowed how black people don't hardly ever fight with the law."

"But if that's true, why didn't you let me sign my money over when I asked?"

"You ain't no fool, I should know that, right? I figured that if I jumped at yo' idea you'd know sumpin' was up. So I told Lawrence t' sweat ya. Make you scared and you'd beg me t'take what you got. Then when I had tax troubles later on an' the IRS took my money you'd know what it was like an' jus' be happy it wasn't you."

"But you lyin', man. Even if this tax shit is true, why would he kill anybody?"

"Why'd I kill'em, man?" he yelled.

Mouse, holding up a solitary finger, said, "Keep cool, brother." Then he slapped Mofass across his face with the pistol.

Mofass' head whipped around hard and his big body followed it down to the floor. He got up holding his bloody cheek with both hands.

"What you hit me fo'?" he screamed like a child.

Mouse held his finger up again, and Mofass was silent.

"Answer me, Mofass," I warned.

"I don't know. All I know is that he called me to his house right after that FBI man cut you loose. He told me he wanted to know ev'rything you did. So I tole'im 'bout you workin' fo' the church. You know how you said you was keepin' tabs on Towne?"

"An' how come you didn't come t'me wit' none'a this?"

"He had me by my balls, Mr. Rawlins. I was a tax evader an' I helped him rob them people. An' you know he was crazy too.

"He tole me that if the FBI got hold of his files on you they would know what we were up to. That's why he had me go to Jackie and Melvin. He went t'Towne hisself."

"An' killed him?"

"I don't know. All I know is that he went there and that Towne is dead."

I went on, "But you didn't say nuthin' when people started gettin' killed, did you, Mofass?" The muscles in my arm twitched, and I shifted the pistol so as not to shoot him before I knew it all.

"At first I didn't know. I mean, why would I think that he gonna kill Poinsettia? An' by the time Towne got it I was scared about me."

"Why'd Poinsettia get killed? What she have to do with this?"

"He offered her money, money so that she would call the po-lice an' blame you for beatin' her."

Mofass lifted his hands in a gesture of helplessness. The side of his face was swelling around the deep red welt on his cheek.

"You know how that girl was. She said sumpin' to'im. Like how she gonna go to you if he don't pay her some more. She blamed him fo' her bein' sick an' she wanted to be taken care of."

"Man, that don't make no sense. Why he want her to blame me fo' hittin' her in the first place?"

"If you was in jail the FBI would have to find somebody else and then he could still get your money and save his ass."

Mofass began to weep.

"And you were going to let me give it to 'im, huh?"

"What was you gonna do fo' that FBI, man? Ain't that what he had you doin'? He said he'd save yo' money if you do somebody else dirt, ain't that right? How come you any different than me?"

Mofass hurt me with that.

"Let's get it over, Ease," Mouse said. He waved his pistol in the general direction of Mofass. I wouldn't have believed such a fat man could cower in his chair.

"No, man."

"I thought you wanted this boy's blood?" Mouse sounded indignant. "He fucked wit' you, right?"

"Yeah, he did do that."

"Then le's kill the mothahfuckah."

"That's all right. I got a better idea."

Mofass let another fart go.

"Like what?" Mouse asked.

"I want you to give me Lawrence's address, Mofass."

"You got it."

"And I want his home phone number too."

"Yes, sir, Mr. Rawlins, I got it right here," he said, tapping his temple.

"Don't mistake me, Mofass," I warned. "This ain't no merry-go-round here. You go fast right to the grave if you make a bad step. My man Raymond here is death, yo' death if you do sumpin' wrong."

"You don't have to warn me on that account," Mofass said in his business voice. "But can I ask you what it is you plan to do?"

"Same as you'd get if you play this wrong."

After he'd written the information I told him, "Go home, Mofass. Go somewhere. It will all be over by this time tomorrow."

After Mofass fled, Mouse said, "We shoulda killed'im."

"No reason," I answered.

"He tried to cheat you, man. Tried to steal yo' money."

"Yeah, he did. But you know we wasn't never friends. Uh-uh, Mofass an' me was in business. Businessmen steal just to keep in practice fo'they legal work."

I was glad the big man had left. He was so gaseous that he'd smelled up the whole office.

"Thank you, Raymond," I said. We shook hands.

"You my friend, Easy, you ain't gotta thank me. Shit! You the one set my head straight about LaMarque. You my best friend, man."

As I drove for home I thought about how I intended to take Mouse's wife and son and disappear in the Mexican hills. I couldn't kill Mofass, because I was no better than he was. Once I got home I dialed the number Mofass had given me.

"Hello?" a timid woman's voice said.

"May I speak to Reggie Lawrence, please?" I asked.

"Who is this?" she asked. There was fear in her voice; fear so great that it shook me.

But still I told her who I was and she went to fetch my nemesis.

"Rawlins?"

"I want twenty-five hundred dollars," I said. "Don't gimme no shit, 'cause I know you got it. I want it in tens and twenties and I want it tomorrow evening."

"What the hell . . ." he started.

But I cut him off. "Listen, man, I ain't got no time fo' yo' shit. I know what you been doin' an' I could prove it too. Mofass spilled his guts, an' I know you cain't afford no close look. So drop this shit an' bring me the money or they gonna turn yo' office into a jail cell."

"If this is some trick to get out of your taxes . . ." he said. He was trying to sound like he was still the boss, but I could hear the sweat on his tongue.

"Griffith Park, Reggie. Down below the observatory just inside the woods. Eight P.M. An army man will know how to be on time."

I told him how to get there, and before he could say another word, I hung up on him.

And you know that felt sweet.

# 37

AT ABOUT SEVEN A.M. I was parked down the street from 1135 ½ Stanley Street. It was a block or so north of Olympic Boulevard, and a solidly white neighborhood, but I took the chance that the police wouldn't see me. I had most of the plans wrapped up in an envelope, his name lightly taped in the center, next to me in the front seat. I wore black gloves, a porter's cap, and a uniform from a hotel Dupree once worked for in Houston.

At eight-fifteen Lawrence walked out his front door. I scooted down, squinted, and jammed my tongue into the socket Primo and Flower had created in my jaw. He went to his car and drove off, leaving his wife and child at home.

I waited another half an hour so she wouldn't be suspicious, and then I knocked at the door. There was crying in the background. It got louder when the door opened.

Mrs. Lawrence was small and redheaded, though there was lots of gray in the red. She seemed to be young, but her head hung forward as though it were weighed down. She had to lift her head and screw up her eyes to look at me. The stitched scar coming down the left side of her mouth was jagged, the flesh around her right eye puffy and discolored. There was bright red blood in the white of her eye.

"Can I help you?" she asked.

"Delivery, ma'am," I said in the crisp tone I used to address officers in WWII.

"Delivery for whom?"

"I got it here for a Reginald A. Lawrence," I said. "It's from a law firm in Washington."

She tried to smile, but the child started hollering. She turned away and then back to me, quickly. She put her hand out and said, "I'm his wife, I'll take it."

"I don't know . . ." I stalled.

"Hurry, please, my baby's sick."

"Well . . . okay, but I still need one ninety-five for the COD."

"Hold on," she sighed on an exasperated note. She went back into the house, running in the direction of the crying.

I slipped in the front door, taking out a sheet of government secrets that I'd folded into eighths. The door opened into a little entrance hall that was designed to make the house seem larger. There was a coat rack and lacquered ornamental desk in the hall. I opened the drawer to the desk and shoved the little slip of evidence under a pile of maps.

I moved into the living room, where the lady was

233

fretting over a folding bed. The bed wasn't big, but the child in it was so slight that you could have gotten four or five children his width to lie there. He was almost as long as the bed, but his arms and legs were so skinny that they could have belonged to an infant. His wrists were torn and scabrous; his naked chest was covered with sharp, blue-green bruises. One of his eyes drifted around and the other fastened onto me as he moaned.

"Ma'am?" I said.

"Yes?" She didn't even turn to me, just cried as she wilted next to the child, who was weeping softly now that his mother was near.

I helped her to her feet.

"What happened to him?" I asked.

"Polio," she replied.

Who knows? Maybe she believed it.

She shot a quick glance at the child and stood up.

"He needs me," she said. "I have to be here. He needs me, he needs me."

I folded my arms around her, thinking of how her husband tried to shoot me the last time I'd held a woman. I helped her to a chair.

I removed Lawrence's name from the envelope and put the evidence in her lap.

"This ain't nuthin' important," I whispered. "Just give it to him when you got the chance."

I was at Griffith Park by seven P.M. I stopped my car on a fire trail below the observatory and hiked up through the trees behind the great domed building. It was a long hike, but I thought that it was worth the extra insurance to have a vantage point before the government man showed. There was a rustling of branches in the trees behind me as I made my way, but that didn't worry me.

It was almost eight-fifteen before Lawrence showed. He walked right down the grassy hill behind the lower wall and walked almost to the line of trees. He stretched out his left arm and snapped his wrist to his face to look at his watch. He was still gawky and awkward, but there was a new kind of aggressiveness in his gait. He strutted like a rooster, cocking his head from side to side as if he were spoiling for a fight.

"Evenin', Reggie," I called out from behind a scraggly pine. I walked out of the trees to meet him with both hands in my pockets.

He made a gesture toward his breast, but I brought my right hand out to show him the little pistol I held, then I shoved it back in my jacket pocket.

He gave me a lopsided smile and hunched his shoulders. His big, bruising hands hung peacefully at his side.

"You got the money?" I asked.

He leaned forward slightly, indicating a brown paper parcel he held in his jacket.

"But if I give you this money, what guarantee do I have that you'll let me be?" he asked.

"I know you a killer, man. I'ma run wit' this here money. Run someplace you cain't find me."

He smiled at me, and we both froze in time. I could see that he didn't plan to move until I said something else, so I asked, "Why, man?"

He jumped slightly from a tremor running through his body.

"Hey! Fuck you!" he said, twisting his neck from side to side. I could smell the gin.

"Uh-uh, really. I gotta know, man. Why you do all this shit?" I asked. I knew he was crazy, but I just wanted to have some reason.

There was a fever in Agent Lawrence's eyes.

"Niggers and Jews," he said. It was a toss-up whether or not he was talking to me.

"Like your wife an' child?"

He looked me in the eye then. But he was quiet.

"I mean, why Towne? Why Poinsettia?"

"I told the nigger minister about you. You know what he did?"

Lawrence brought his fists to his shoulders, so I said, "Cool it, man."

"Yeah." Lawrence sputtered a laugh. "He threw me out. But I went back there. Yes sir, I did."

He giggled again. I took the pistol from my pocket.

"And the bitch lived like a pig." Agent Lawrence was breathing hard. "Filthy. And she acted like I could, could ever be like that . . . All you had to do was pay. All you had to do was follow the program. I didn't want to kill them. But it was my ass out there on the line."

"Chaim Wenzler wasn't nuthin' to you, man."

"He was something to the FBI. If he was out of the way then they wouldn't need you."

"But then you tried t'kill me!"

Lawrence giggled again, and bit his thumb.

Twilight was falling. Actually it felt as if the darkness was rising out of the trees. It was time for me to collect my money and leave.

"Okay," I said. I had my hand on the pistol like another time. "Gimme the money."

I'd planned to act nervous when I took his money; but I didn't need to act.

"I thought you might be a nigger with nuts," he said, suddenly somber.

I felt my gorge rise, but I didn't give in. The night was coming on faster, soon we'd just be shadows.

"You don't really think that I'm going to let you get away with blackmailing me, do you?"

"Do somethin' stupid an' you'll see what kinda nuts I got."

Suddenly he made his decision. He took the package from the recess of his jacket and handed it to me.

I said, "Nice to do business with ya. You could go now."

The moment I touched the envelope he lunged forward and shouldered me in the chest, hard. Because we were on a hill I had the feeling of flight again, but this time I landed on my backside, my hands shooting out behind.

I tried to bring my gun around but couldn't. Lawrence ran down and kicked my shoulder. He grinned at me as he yanked awkwardly at the pistol in his pocket.

"Don't do it, man!" I shouted in warning. But he had the pistol out.

He said the word, nigger, and then he flew backwards about six feet. When he was in the air I heard the cannonlike pistol shot from down among the trees. I was running before the echoes were through shouting my name.

As fast as I ran, Mouse was already in the car by the time I got there.

He smiled at me and said, "You a damn fool, Easy Rawlins. We shoulda kilt that man the minute he showed his ugly face."

"I had to know, Raymond. I had to know for me."

We were driving down away from the observatory, through the forestlike park.

"You like some stupid cowboy, Easy. You wanna yell 'Draw!' 'fore you fire. That kinda shit gets ya killed."

He was right, of course, but that way I convinced myself that I wasn't a murderer. I gave him a chance to walk away from it—at least until I'd told the police about him.

"Was he the one?" Mouse asked. He really didn't care.

"He did the killin's."

"What you gonna do now?"

"Pray nobody saw us an' tell the FBI man that Lawrence forced me to tell about the work I was doin'. That he stole the papers from Wenzler. That he turned into a spy for profit. And I'll prove it by sayin' he was into tax cases fo' profit."

While I talked I counted out a five-hundred-dollar pile for Mouse.

I didn't intend to keep anything. I gave to the families of the dead people, including Shirley Wenzler. I figured that Lawrence should at least pay dollars for the havoc he'd caused. I even donated a thousand dollars to the African Migration. Sonja Achebe has sent me postcards from Nigeria for over thirty years.

Mouse stuck out his lower lip. "Not too bad. Not too bad."

I lit a couple of cigarettes while he drove. There were no sirens or any special activities on the road. I handed a cigarette to Mouse and breathed deep.

"Where you goin' now?" He asked after five or six miles of driving. We were on Adams Boulevard and all the police cars ignored our progress.

"I tole LaMarque I'd come by and take him for hot dogs."

And then I'd take him to Mexico, I thought.

# 38

BUT THERE WAS NO REASON TO RUN ANYMORE. THERE wasn't a killing they could pin on me. When they found Lawrence and uncovered his crimes they hushed up the whole thing. His pistol was matched for Reverend Towne, Tania Lee, and Chaim Wenzler. I gave them a list of hotels that Mofass had driven Lawrence and Poinsettia to. They found his fingerprints in her apartment. Mrs. Trajillo recognized the photograph of the annoying insurance man.

I was ashamed of what I'd done to Mouse and what I planned to do. Mofass shamed me because we were just alike. I made like I was friends with people and then I planned to do them dirt.

I was at the Filbert Hotel that night. I knocked at the door and was admitted by Shirley. She was dressed in a simple pink shift that came down to her knee. She smiled shyly at me. I was surprised to remember that we had been lovers.

"Hi," she said and then ducked her head.

The room was just large enough for two single beds and a chair and dresser.

"I was afraid that you might be the government men," she said. "I was sure that they'd kill you and then come to get me."

"No," I said. "They know who did it now. The man that killed your father, that is. It wasn't the government at all. Just a man who wanted to make some fast money. He thought he could take those plans and sell 'em."

"Who was it?"

"Nobody. Nobody you'd know."

I sat on one of the beds and Shirley settled beside me. I could feel her weight.

"It's okay now. You don't have to worry. I don't think the government wants to mess with you."

She didn't respond. I knew she wanted me to hold her, but I didn't. I'd already gotten her father killed, already destroyed her world.

After a long while I asked, "What are you going to do now?"

"I don't know. Go home, I guess. But are you sure it's true?"

"Yeah, this guy was involved with First African. He was kind of crazy. He hated communists and black people and things like that."

"He killed Reverend Towne?"

"Yeah."

"Have they caught him?"

"Not yet."

"What's his name?"

"I didn't get that. But whoever he was he thought I knew somethin'. That's why he shot at me in front of the house. He wasn't tryin' t'kill you at all."

I saw the relief in her face and then the guilt she felt for being glad that I was the target. I touched her hand.

"You can go home now, Shirley. It's all right."

She trusted me. I might as well have been the one to shoot her poor father through the door, but she didn't know that. And I wasn't going to tell her.

Primo trusted me too. I told him that the bad man was dead but that I didn't need to leave anymore.

"I already spent half the money, Easy," he said, acting a little cagey. "And I got my brother up here to take care of the place."

"That's okay, man. You an' Flower have a good time down there."

"Okay," Primo said. He was laughing, so I figured that he had my five hundred dollars in his pocket. "But you know Jesus will be too sad if he knows you ain't coming, Easy. That boy loves you. I think you should take him until we get back."

"What?"

"He's your boy, Easy. He loves you. Take him and if you want I'll take him back when we come."

"How long?"

"Three months, maybe four."

So I said goodbye to Primo and Flower and I got Jesus in the bargain.

They were gone for three years. By then Jesus was my son.

Craxton was just as happy as Primo. They had found Lawrence facedown beside the observatory. He called me to his office, one floor above Lawrence's room on Sixth Street.

"You say that Lawrence was in it with Wenzler? How can that be when he could only know Wenzler through you?"

"He tried to bribe me, Mr. Craxton. He put the squeeze on Mofass and then when you got involved he tried to get me in trouble."

"How did you find out about it?"

"Mofass finally broke down and told me."

Craxton nodded.

"I told him that I was going against a white guy doin' charities for the church. I didn't know that he was crazy."

"What about the girl, your tenant?"

"He knew about my buildin' and he wanted to squeeze me for a payoff, so he killed her I guess to put me in jail. If I was in jail I couldn't work for you."

"But if you were in jail for murder, how could he get your money?"

"I don't think he meant to kill her, really. I think he only wanted to hurt her. That's why her face was so bruised up. When she died he tried to make it look like suicide."

That last little bit of thinking was a little too sophisticated for what Craxton thought a Negro could come up with. He looked at me suspiciously but didn't say anything. Craxton didn't want to rock the boat. He had a dead communist and a man dealing in espionage. He had the evidence I planted at Lawrence's house and two bodies. I imagined that he'd get a promotion out of it.

"And where is Shirley Wenzler?" he asked.

"She's home, Mr. Craxton, and you know she don't have nuthin' t'do with this. She didn't have anything to do with what her father was doing."

"You like her, huh, Easy?"

"She's clean, man."

Craxton chuckled. He was on top of the world.

"But let me ask you somethin'," I said.

"Yes, Easy?"

"Why didn't you tell me about them papers Wenzler had?"

"Because you weren't supposed to know. Nobody was. It was a secret project that Champion had scrapped. Lindquist was supposed to have destroyed the copies he had. I was supposed to make sure that he had done that. We both slipped up."

"You mean they weren't even anything you were gonna use?"

"It would still have looked bad if they showed up in Russia."

"Look bad?"

I didn't tell anybody about Jackie Orr and Melvin Pride, or about Winona. I sent a letter to Odell, though; I didn't want to burn my brothers and sisters but I didn't want them to continue stealing from the church either. I left the African Migration out of it completely.

"I don't know, Mr. Rawlins, I don't know. It's all real neat, but who killed Lawrence?"

"I don't know," I said. "I wasn't there."

Craxton was true to his word and I took two years to pay off the money that the IRS said I owed. He also took the heat off of Shirley Wenzler and gave me his private number where I could get to him anytime.

Andre Lavender and Juanita got back into circulation. He never stood trial because Craxton never brought up his name. The FBI man wanted smooth sailing over a sea of death and silence.

Everything was fine.

The night after I spoke to Craxton I went to see Etta. I opened the door with my key. The apartment was dark, but I expected that. The door to LaMarque's room was open. I looked in to see him smiling in the arms of a giant teddy bear that I was sure came from Mouse.

"That's it, Etta," I heard him say. His voice came right through the wall, as if he were whispering in my ear. "Oh yeah, yeah. You know I missed that."

Then a loud smacking sound and then, "I love you, Daddy."

"You say what?" Raymond Alexander asked his wife, his woman.

"I love you, Daddy. I *need* you."

"You need this?"

And she made a sound that I cannot duplicate. It was deep and guttural and so charged with pleasure that I got dizzy and lowered myself to the floor.

The sounds Etta made got louder and even more passionate. She never made those sounds because of me; no woman ever had.

Mouse is crazy, I thought, just crazy!

But I wished for his insanity.

Etta did too.

# 39

THE BOY AND I WENT TO MOFASS' OFFICE A FEW DAYS later.

Jesus went through the door first and pulled out the chair for me to sit in front of my employee.

Mofass was staring at a plate of eggs and ham, with hash browns on the side. He'd probably been doing that for a quarter of an hour.

"Mo'nin', Mr. Rawlins." He had a leery look in his eye. Any man who survived a death threat from Raymond Alexander was leery.

"Mofass. What's goin' on?"

"They took me down to the federal detention center fo'a couple'a days there."

I opened my eyes as if I was surprised.

"Yeah, they did," he continued. "But I guess I gotta thank you fo'not pressin' no charge at the IRS."

"Part'a the deal the FBI guy made. I don't cause no trouble and they let me pay off my back taxes, on the quiet side."

"Well, I guess I should thank you anyway. That was a tight spot we was all in. You coulda taken it out on me."

"Should have too," I said.

Mofass glared.

"Jesus," I said. I fished a quarter out of my shirt pocket and flipped it to him. "Go get us some candy at that store we saw."

He gave me a mute grin and ran for the door.

I waited for the sound of his steps down the stairs to fade before talking again.

"That's right, Mofass, I shoulda let Raymond waste your ass. I should have but I couldn't, 'cause you my own personal hell. But it don't matter. You see, I lost sumpin' since that day we talked about that letter. I lost a lot. I got a good friend who hates me now 'cause he think I got his minister killed. An' I cain't go to him 'cause it was my fault, really. An' I lost my woman because I wasn't good enough. There's a lotta people dead 'cause'a me. And I turnt Poinsettia out. You told me to do it, but it's on my head, 'cause . . ."

He interrupted me. "I don't see what all this gotta do with me. If you want my keys to the places, I got 'em here."

"I made a good friend, Mofass, but yo' friend cut 'im down. Didn't even look in his face. Shot him through the door."

"What you want from me, Mr. Rawlins?"

"I ain't got no friends, man. All I got is Jackson Blue, who'd give me up fo'a bottle'a wine, and Mouse; you know him. And a Mexican boy who cain't speak English hardly an' if he did he cain't talk no ways."

Sweat had appeared on Mofass' brow. I must've sounded pretty crazy.

"I want you to keep on workin' fo' me, William. I want you to be my friend."

Mofass put the cigar between his fat lips and puffed smoke. I don't think he knew how big his eyes were.

"Sure," he said. "You my best customer, Mr. Rawlins."

"Yeah, man. Yeah."

We sat there staring at each other until Jesus came back. He brought three tubes of chocolates disks, Flicks they were called. The three of us ate the chocolate in silence.

Jesus was the only one smiling.

POCKET BOOKS
PROUDLY PRESENTS

# *A LITTLE YELLOW DOG*

## Walter Mosley

Coming Soon
in Paperback
from Pocket Books

The following is a preview of
*A Little Yellow Dog . . .*

# Chapter 1

*W*hen I got to work that Monday morning I knew something was wrong. Mrs. Idabell Turner's car was parked in the external lot and there was a light on in her half of bungalow C.

It was six-thirty. The teachers at Sojourner Truth Junior High school never came in that early. Even the janitors who worked under me didn't show up until seven-fifteen. I was the supervising senior head custodian. It was up to me to see that everything worked right. That's why I was almost always the first one on the scene.

But not that morning.

It was November and the sky hadn't quite given up night yet. I approached the bungalow feeling a hint of dread. Images of bodies I'd stumbled upon in my street life came back to me. But I dismissed them. I was a workingman, versed in floor waxes and bleach—not blood. The only weapon I carried was a pocket knife, and it only pierced flesh when I cut the corns from my baby toe.

I knocked but nobody answered. I tried my key but

the door was bolted from the inside. Then that damned dog started barking.

"Who is it?" a woman's voice called.

"It's Mr. Rawlins, Mrs. Turner. Is everything okay?"

Instead of answering she fumbled around with the bolt and then pulled the door open. The little yellow dog was yapping, standing on its spindly back legs as if he were going to attack me. But he wasn't going to do a thing. He was hiding behind her blue woolen skirt, making sure that I couldn't get at him.

"Oh, Mr. Rawlins," Mrs. Turner said in that breathy voice she had.

The adolescent boys of Sojourner Truth took her class just to hear that voice, and to see her figure— Mrs. Turner had curves that even a suit of armor couldn't hide. The male teachers at school, and the boys' vice principal, made it a point to pay their respects at her lunch table in the teachers' cafeteria each day. They didn't say much about her around me, though, because Mrs. Turner was one of the few Negro teachers at the primarily Negro school.

The white men had some dim awareness that it would have been insulting for me if I had to hear lewd comments about her.

I appreciated their reserve, but I understood what they weren't saying. Mrs. Idabell Turner was a knock-out for any man—from Cro-Magnon to Jim Crow.

"That your dog?" I asked.

"Pharaoh," she said to the dog. "Quiet now. This is Mr. Rawlins. He's a friend."

When he heard my name the dog snarled and bared his teeth.

"You know dogs aren't allowed on the property, Mrs. Turner," I said. "I'm supposed—"

"Stop that, Pharaoh," Idabell Turner whined at the dog. She bent down and let him jump into her arms. "Shhh, quiet now."

She stood up, caressing her little protector. He was the size, but not the pedigree, of a Chihuahua. He settled his behind down onto the breast of her caramel-colored cashmere sweater and growled out curses in dog.

"Quiet," Mrs. Turner said. "I'm sorry, Mr. Rawlins. I wouldn't have brought him here, but I didn't have any choice. I didn't."

I could tell by the red rims of her eyelids that she'd been crying.

"Well, maybe you could leave him out in the car," I suggested.

Pharaoh growled again.

He was a smart dog.

"Oh no, I couldn't do that. I'd be worried about him suffocating out there."

"You could crack the window."

"He's so small I'd be afraid that he'd wiggle out. You know he spends all day at home trying to find me. He loves me, Mr. Rawlins."

"I don't know what to say, Mrs.—"

"Call me Idabell," she said.

Call me fool.

Mrs. Turner had big brown eyes with fabulously long lashes. Her skin was like rich milk chocolate—dark, satiny, and smooth.

That snarling mutt started looking cute to me. I thought that it wasn't such a problem to have your dog with you. It wasn't really any kind of health threat. I reached out to make friends with him.

He tested my scent—and then bit my hand.

"Ow!"

"That's it!" Idabell shouted as if she were talking to a wayward child. "Come on!"

She took the dwarf mongrel and shoved him into the storage room that connected C2 to C1. As soon as she closed the door, Pharaoh was scratching to get back in.

"I'm sorry," she said.

"Me too. But you know that dog has got to go." I held out my hand to her. The skin was broken but it wasn't bad. "Has he had his rabies shot?"

"Oh yes, yes. Please, Mr. Rawlins." She took me by my injured hand. "Let me help."

We went to the desk at the front of the class. I sat down on the edge of her blotter while she opened the top drawer and came out with a standard teacher's first-aid box.

"You know, dog bites are comparatively pretty clean," she said. She had a bottle of iodine, a cotton ball, and a flesh-colored bandage—flesh-colored, that is, if you had pink flesh. When she dabbed the iodine on my cut I winced, but it wasn't because of the sting. That woman smelled good; clean and fresh, and sweet like the deep forest is sweet.

"It's not bad, Mr. Rawlins. And Pharaoh didn't mean it. He's just upset. He knows that Holland wants to kill him."

"Kill him? Somebody wants to kill your dog?"

"My husband." She nodded and was mostly successful in holding back the tears. "I've been, been away for a few days. When I got back home last night, Holly went out, but when he came back he was going to . . . kill Pharaoh."

Mrs. Turner gripped my baby finger.

It's amazing how a man can feel sex anywhere on his body.

"He wants to kill your dog?" I asked in a lame attempt to use my mind, to avoid what my body was thinking.

"I waited till he was gone and then I drove here." Mrs. Turner wept quietly.

My hand decided, all by itself, to comfort her shoulder.

"Why's he so mad?" I shouldn't have asked, but my blood was moving faster than my mind.

"I don't know," she said sadly. "He made me do something, and I did it, but afterwards he was still mad." She put her shoulder against mine while I brought my other hand to rest on her side.

The thirty desks in her classroom all faced us attentively.

"Pharaoh's a smart dog," she whispered in my ear. "He knew what Holly said. He was scared."

Pharaoh whimpered out a sad note from his storage room.

Idabell leaned back against my arm and looked up. We might have been slow dancing—if there had been music and a band.

"I don't know what to do," she said. "I can't ever go back there. I can't. He's going to be in trouble and I'll be in it with him. But Pharaoh's innocent. He hasn't done anything wrong."

As she talked she leaned closer. With me sitting on the desk we were near to the same height. Our faces were almost touching.

I didn't know what she was talking about and I didn't want to know.

I'd been on good behavior for more than two years.

I was out of the streets and had my job with the Los Angeles Board of Education. I took care of my kids, cashed my paychecks, stayed away from liquor.

I steered clear of the wrong women too.

Maybe I'd been a little too good. I felt an urge in that classroom, but I wasn't going to make the move.

That's when Idabell Turner kissed me.

Two years of up early and off to work dissolved like a sugar cube under the tap.

"Oh," she whispered as my lips pressed her neck. "Yes."

The tears were all gone. She looked me in the eye and worked her tongue slowly around with mine.

A deep grunt went off in my chest like an underwater explosion. It just came out of me. Her eyes opened wide as she realized how much I was moved. I stood and lifted her up on the desk. She spread her legs and pushed her chest out at me.

She said, "They'll be coming soon," and then gave me three fast kisses that said this was just the beginning.

My pants were down before I could stop myself. As I leaned forward she let out a single syllable that said, "Here I am, I've been waitin' for you, Ezekiel Porterhouse Rawlins. Take my arms, my legs, my breasts. Take everything," and I answered in the same language.

"They'll be coming soon," she said as her tongue pressed my left nipple through thin cotton. "Oh, go slow."

The clock on the wall behind her said that it was seven-oh-two. I'd come to the door at six forty-nine. Less than a quarter of an hour and I was deeply in the throes of passion.

I wanted to thank God—or his least favorite angel.

"They'll be coming soon," she said, the phonograph of her mind on a skip. "Oh, go slow."

The desks all sat at attention. Pharaoh whimpered from his cell.

"Too much," she hissed. I didn't know what she meant.

When the desk started rocking I didn't care who might walk into the room. I would have gladly given up my two years of accrued pension and my two weeks a year vacation for the few moments of ecstasy that teased and tickled about five inches below my navel.

"Mr. Rawlins!" she cried. I lifted her from the desk, not to perform some silly acrobatics but because I needed to hold her tight to my heart. I needed to let her know that this was what I'd wanted and needed for two years without knowing it.

It all came out in a groan that was so loud and long that later on, when I was alone, I got embarrassed remembering it.

I stood there holding her aloft with my eyes closed. The cool air of the room played against the back of my thighs and I felt like laughing.

I felt like sobbing too. What was wrong with me? Standing there half naked in a classroom on a weekday morning. Idabell had her arms around my neck. I didn't even feel her weight. If we were at my house I would have carried her to the bed and started over again.

"Put me down," she whispered.

I squeezed her.

"Please," she said, echoing the word in my own mind.

I put her back on the desk. We looked at each other for what seemed like a long time—slight tremors going through our bodies now and then. I couldn't bear to pull away. She had a kind of stunned look on her face.

When I leaned over to kiss her forehead I experienced a feeling that I'd known many times in my life. It was that feeling of elation before I embarked on some kind of risky venture. In the old days it was about the police and criminals and the streets of Watts and South Central L.A.

But not this time. Not again. I swallowed hard and gritted my teeth with enough force to crack stone. I'd slipped but I would not fall.

Mrs. Turner was shoving her panties into a white patent-leather purse while I zipped my pants. She smiled and went to open the door for Pharaoh.

The dog skulked in with his tail between his legs and his behind dragging on the floor. I felt somehow triumphant over that little rat dog, like I had taken his woman and made him watch it. It was an ugly feeling but, I told myself, he was just a dog.

Mrs. Turner picked Pharaoh up and held him while looking into my eyes.

I didn't want to get involved in her problems, but I could do something for her. "Maybe I can keep the dog in the hopper room in my office," I said.

"Oh," came the breathy voice. "That would be so kind. It's only until this evening. I'm going to my girlfriend's tonight. He won't be any bother. I promise."

She handed Pharaoh to me. He was trembling. At first I thought he was scared from the new environment and a strange pair of hands. But when I looked in his eyes I saw definite canine hatred. He was shaking with rage.

Mrs. Turner scratched the dog's ear and said, "Go on now, honey. Mr. Rawlins'll take care of you."

I took a step away from her and she smiled.

"I don't even know your first name," she said.

"Easy," I said. "Call me Easy."

# Chapter 2

*H*i, Easy," EttaMae Harris greeted me in our common Texan drawl. She was an old friend who I was almost always happy to see—but not then. Etta worked with me, and the business I had just gotten through was nowhere near my job description.

She was standing outside of bungalow C. Behind her sprawled the nearly empty asphalt yard. The pavement gave off a yellowish glow in the dawn light. There were already two girls playing tetherball and a small group of boys sitting on the ninth-grade lunch court. Beyond them, at the southern end of the school yard, sat the fenced-off gardens. Up on a high grassy hill, behind me, stood the old brick buildings that housed the administration offices, library, and most of the classrooms of the school.

"Hey, Etta. How you doin'?"

She didn't answer me, just turned her gaze down toward the shivering dog in my arms.

"It's Mrs. Turner's dog. They fumigated her house and she had to bring him in with her," I said, happy that my old-time lying reflex was still intact. "I'ma put him back in the hopper room in the main office."

"Uh-huh," she said. "Yeah."

We walked across the playground, past the nine classroom bungalows, to the larger tan structure that was the maintenance building; a building that the custodians and workmen called the main office.

"Nice day," I said.

"Uh-huh," Etta replied.

She rolled back the steel-encased fire door and I followed her in. It was a large room with a long rectangular table down the middle. The cluttered table was strewn with newspapers and magazines that the janitors, carpenters, and electricians read on their union-guaranteed coffee breaks. The walls were lined with shelves that held various cleaning materials.

In the back corner stood a large ash desk where I sat every afternoon administering the laborers who kept the school running.

Behind the desk was a door that led to my personal hopper room.

I unlocked the door to the deep storage closet and tossed Pharaoh in among the steel shelves. He yelped when he hit the chilly cement floor and I felt a coldhearted satisfaction.

"I thought you couldn't have no animals not in a cage around here, Easy?" Etta asked.

"It's just a special thing, Etta. Dog'll be gone tonight."

"Uh-huh," she said for the third time.

"What's wrong wit' you?" I asked.

"All I can say is that you could take a niggah out the street but you sure cain't pull him outta his skin."

"What the hell is that s'posed t'mean?" My language got closer to the street as I got angrier.

"What you doin' moanin' an' groanin' up in that woman's classroom?"

"What you doin' sneakin' at the door?" I asked back.

If we were men it might have come to blows. But EttaMae was nobody I wanted to fight. She was a large woman with powerful arms and I'd been in love with her, off and on, for my entire adult life.

Before she could reply, the fire door slid open and Jorge Peña walked in.

Peña was a red-colored Mexican-American who was loose-limbed, chubby, and fast with a grin. He had a deadly handsome mustache and dark eyes that laughed silently and often.

"Mr. Rawlins, Miss Harris," Peña greeted us. "How are you?"

"Jorge," Etta said, pronouncing the name in English fashion.

"Hey, Peña." I waved and went to sit down at the head of the table. I lit up the best-tasting cigarette that I'd had in a month and remembered, with a slight shock, what had happened down in bungalow C2.

Over the next fifteen minutes my whole day staff reported in. First came Garland Burns, my daytime senior custodian, a hale vegetarian from Georgia who was the only black Christian Scientist I knew. Helen Plates dragged in moaning about how tired she was. Helen was an obese blond Negro from Iowa who claimed her good health was due to the fact that she ate a whole pie every day of her life. Archie "Ace" Muldoon was right on time; he was the first white man who was ever properly in my employ. And finally, last as usual, Simona Eng appeared. She was an Italian-Chinese girl who was working her way through night school.

They were my work gang, my union brothers, my friends.

I had spent most of my adult years of hanging on by a shoestring among gangsters and gamblers, prostitutes and killers. But I never liked it. I always wanted a well-ordered working life. The Board of Education didn't pay much in the way of salary but my kids had medical insurance and I was living a life that I could be proud of.

After some coffee and laughs I gave out the special jobs from reports and requests left on my desk.

Everybody set out on their daily tasks and the special jobs I gave. The cue for them to leave was me standing up; that meant it was time to go to work.

One of the notes was a request for me to appear in the office of the principal, Hiram T. Newgate. I took the long tier of granite stairs up past the large hill of grass to the older campus. By afternoon any one of us could have taken those steps at a run, but the first time was always hard.

Idabell was coming out of the side door of the administration building when I got there.

"Hi, Easy," she said.

"Mrs. Turner," I said with emphasis.

"Easy."

"What?"

"I've got to go see about something."

"What's that?"

"Nothing important, I just have to leave the campus for a while."

"You wanna get your dog?" I asked.

"No. No, I'll be back a little later," she said. "Easy?"

"Yeah?"

"What if Holly came down here to the school and tried to pull me right out of my classroom?"

"Don't worry about that," I said. A few kind words that I meant to keep her from fretting. But Mrs. Turner heard salvation in my voice.

"Oh, thank you," she warbled.

She reached out for me but I pushed her hands down and looked around to make sure that no one saw.

"I'm sorry," she said. "It's just that I haven't met such a good man in a long time." She stood there for a moment, a kiss offered on her lips. When she saw that I wasn't going to collect right then she smiled and went slowly past.

As I watched her descend the stairs I remembered reading the words "A good man is hard to find." With somebody like Idabell Turner looking for him I could see why.

Look for
*A Little Yellow Dog*
Wherever Paperback Books Are Sold
Coming mid-June
from Pocket Books